Matt yanked up the armrest between them and turned in his seat.

"Talk to me, Rachel," he said. "Like you used to."

"Can we just go?"

Her ragged breath filled the otherwise silent cab. She needed comfort, and that was all he was offering when he hooked an arm around her shoulders and pulled her body across the seat.

"It'll be okay. You and Chastity will have each other to lean on."

She tilted her head up. Worry clouded her brown eyes. "What if I fail her? What do I know about being a mother? Or teenagers? I had all these fantasies about how great we'd get along, but... it's not going too well."

"You need to be her parent not her friend. You'll find your feet. We survivors always do." Hope-filled eyes met his. And held. His pulse thumped in his ears and his groin. He should push Rachel away, but he couldn't. Why did she affect him like no other woman?

Only one way to find out.

He pulled her closer. Her lips parted on a gasp a split second before he covered them. Then it happened. That shooting star sensation he hadn't experienced since Rachel had kissed him fourteen years ago...

Dear Reader,

What would you do if you had a chance for a "do-over" on the biggest regret from your past? Would you be willing to give up the good parts of your present life to erase that one bad decision?

Rachel and Matt's story is the fruit from my writer's brain which grew that idea. It led to more questions, such as how could something wrong also be right, and is it ever okay to tell a lie? Writers (especially me!) can spend hours debating issues like this.

Second Chance Mom is one of those stories that's been slugging it out in my brain for a while. I only wish I'd had more pages! I feel as if I've only scraped the surface of Rachel, Matt and Chastity's story. It will be interesting to hear what you think.

Emilie Rose

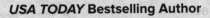

USA TODAY Bestselling Author

EMILIE ROSE

Second Chance Mom

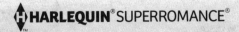

Recycling programs
for this product may
not exist in your area.

ISBN-13: 978-0-373-60953-6

Second Chance Mom

Printed in U.S.A.

USA TODAY bestselling author and two-time RITA® Award finalist **Emilie Rose** lives in North Carolina with her own romance hero. Writing is her third career. She's managed a medical office and a home day care—neither offered half as much satisfaction as plotting happy endings. Her hobbies include gardening, fishing, cooking and traveling to find her next book setting. Visit her website, emilierose.com, or email her at EmilieRoseAuthor@aol.com.

Books by Emilie Rose

HARLEQUIN SUPERROMANCE

A Better Man
The Secrets of Her Past
Starting with June

HARLEQUIN DESIRE

Her Tycoon to Tame
The Price of Honor
The Ties that Bind

SILHOUETTE DESIRE

Pregnant on the Upper East Side
Bargained Into Her Boss's Bed
More Than a Millionaire
Bedding the Secret Heiress
His High-Stakes Holiday Seduction
Executive's Pregnancy Ultimatum
Wedding His Takeover Target

Other titles by this author available in ebook format.

To my readers: without you,
I could not have lived my dream for 36 books.

CHAPTER ONE

RACHEL BISHOP RETRACED the path to the detention officer's classroom that she'd taken dozens of times nearly fifteen years ago. Her anxiety level increased with each step, even though she wasn't the one in trouble. This time.

She'd faced down inner-city thugs, armed militants and deadly diseases: none of which had terrified her as much as the huge responsibility waiting inside room 127.

A second chance at parenthood. Was she up to it?

She had to be. Moments ago she'd signed papers accepting full custody of Chastity. She'd failed the child once before. She couldn't—*wouldn't*—this time.

Her knees locked in front of the closed classroom door. She blotted clammy palms on her pants and endeavored to subdue her rampant nerves. It said a lot about the conforming citizens of Johnstonville that their combination middle and high school only needed one room for the troublemakers. The school had changed little since she'd left.

Would prune-faced Miss Gentry still be sitting behind the desk wearing her perpetual scowl?

Time to find out. Rachel pushed the door. It yielded with a sucking whoosh. Through the six-inch gap Rachel saw the old maid wasn't in the front of the room. Instead, Matt Johnston, the last person she wanted or expected to see, occupied the teacher's chair. Rachel froze, her automatic fight-or-flight response engaging. Every instinct screamed run. But she couldn't.

She had loved Matt with all the passion her seventeen-year-old heart could contain, then she'd wronged him unforgivably. She wasn't ready— would *never* be ready—to face him.

In seconds, her adrenaline-sharpened focus registered that his hair was darker than the sun-bleached blond she'd run her fingers through. But then his mesmerizing, make-her-forget-her-own-name blue eyes swung her way, and her stomach dropped as if she'd flown into an air pocket.

A roar filled her ears, and dizziness swamped her. She wanted to blame her reaction on jet lag, but her racing pulse said otherwise. It was fear. Not of Matt. But of everything he embodied. He represented her greatest failure. One that had nearly destroyed her. Afraid she'd fold into a heap on the floor, she gripped the door frame tighter and forced air into her constricted chest.

"May I help you?"

His familiar deep voice sent a fresh wave of

panic through her. The hairs on the back of her neck prickled to attention. Matt didn't know. He couldn't. *Her secret was safe.* Hope had been the only one who'd known the truth, and her sister would never have told anyone—doing so would have damaged her saintly reputation.

Matt's politely curious expression turned into annoyance when Rachel didn't respond. He rose and crossed the room, blocking her entry by gripping the door in one big, familiar hand—one that had touched her intimately and taught her so much about pleasure. His defensive position displayed the added breadth of the chest and shoulders on which she'd once relished resting her cheek. That combined with the golden late-day stubble on his square chin magnified his masculinity and made him far more handsome than the twenty-one-year-old college boy he'd been back then.

But his crisply pressed shirt and pants told her one facet of his personality hadn't changed. Matt had always been a little too polished and perfect. His neatness had challenged her, and she'd loved mussing his thick, perfectly combed hair and yanking his shirttail from his pants to run her hands over his muscles.

Her fingertips tingled. She fisted her hands and shoved them into her pants pockets to keep them out of trouble. Matt hadn't been the man for her then. He wasn't now—never could be. She should have left him alone all those years ago. But she'd been too self-destructive to be smart.

That was then. She'd learned a lot of painful lessons since.

"May I help you?" he repeated in a firmer tone.

"Hello, Matt." Her voice came out as little more than a whisper. Before she could clear her throat and try again, his eyes narrowed. Then he recoiled in recognition. That stung.

"Rachel?" His gaze flashed over her like wildfire, igniting dormant cells like a match to a dry savanna. When his eyes returned to hers she saw his surprise and understood it.

He might look the same—only better—but she bore little resemblance to the mischief-making teen she'd been. Her loose cotton shirt and wrinkled khakis were a far cry from the formfitting clothing she'd once worn to entice him, and these days she adorned her face with nothing more than sunscreen.

She touched a hand to her hair. Most of it was still in the haphazard knot she'd twisted it into before beginning her exhausting trek, but bits and pieces had escaped. After four different airports and three time zones, she probably looked a mess. A touch of her old vanity made her wish she'd spruced up before entering the building.

"Yeah. Long time no see." Her feigned nonchalance sounded believable. To her anyway. She leaned to look past him and into the classroom

where the office secretary had said Rachel's dau—
niece was supposed to be, but the solid block that
was Matt obscured her view. She heard a buzz of
whispers. Was Chastity's one of them? Excitement
fizzed through Rachel's veins.

Distrust flickered in Matt's eyes. Could she
blame him? No. She'd earned it.

"We'll talk outside." He turned to the class. "Get
back to work on those essays." He moved forward,
forcing Rachel to retreat, then he closed the door
between them and the students.

His scowl could scare small children. "It's about
time you showed up."

"I came as soon as I could."

"Hope's funeral was weeks ago." Anger and
condemnation tinged his quiet words and flattened those sexy lips.

Irritation washed over her. Instead of asking
why she'd missed her only sibling's funeral, Matt
seemed to be passing judgment on her like everyone else in this unforgiving town had always
done. No one had ever bothered to ask why Rachel had rebelled. They'd only condemned her for
it. At one time Matt had been the exception, but
now he seemed to have boarded the censure train
with everyone else.

Reining in her temper, she glanced down the
hall and fought for calm. The eerie silence of a
school after hours surrounded them. The corri-

dor seemed private and intimate. Fertile ground for trouble.

She met Matt's disapproving gaze but decided not to waste her breath with explanations. "I'm here now. Is Chastity in there?"

"Yes. She's striking out at everyone who tries to help with her grief and stirring up all kinds of trouble. Her schoolwork and behavior have suffered."

"And the answer to her pain is to send her to detention?"

Matt's lips curled downward. "The staff has been as helpful and patient as possible, but she cussed out a substitute teacher. That left us with no options except detention or expulsion."

"Who'd she curse at? And what unfeeling sonofabitch would punish a grieving kid?"

His frown deepened grooves beside his mouth—grooves he hadn't had when she'd kissed every inch of his face. "Me. I cut her some slack, but I can't allow her to undermine my authority with my students." His eyes narrowed. "Acting out to get attention is something you should understand all too well. It's no surprise you'd make excuses for her. Or that you'd show up here days late."

Guilt over her past behavior heated her chest, neck and cheeks, yet chilled her at the same time. She hugged her middle. Only Matt had understood that her rebellion had been a cry for her parents' attention, but they'd been too busy saving the world to help one confused teenager. Rachel would have given anything to have them pay half as much attention to her as they had to strangers. Instead, they'd dumped her on her older sister. But Hope had been no substitute for her mother or her father.

Rachel squashed the memories. "I was in a flood-ravaged village in a third world country with minimal communication and access to the outside. I didn't get the message about Hope until six days after her…passing. I came as soon as I could."

She didn't bother telling him that she'd had to wait for a rare supply flight because the country-side surrounding them had been controlled by rebels, and crossing by land was too dangerous. He wouldn't want to hear it. Wouldn't care.

Matt folded his arms across his impressive chest and narrowed his eyes. "Really."

His skepticism sobered her. Matt had known her when deceiving people had been her MO.

"I was working, Matt." She hated defending herself. There hadn't been a need to do so since she'd left this narrow-minded town. Her dedication and the quality of her work spoke for itself. "I faxed Hope's lawyer my power of attorney, so she wouldn't have to lie in the morgue until I could get here."

She'd seen too many morgues. The idea of her sister lying in one had been unbearable.

Matt's expression hardened. "How considerate

of you. Chastity needed you sooner. She's struggling and afraid."

That made two of them. "I'm here for her now. I'll take her back home with me, and we'll...we'll get through this together."

She had no idea how she'd fit a teenager into her life. She always threw herself into her work, exhausting herself each day so she could sleep at night. Suppressing one's needs was a common fault in her profession, and she was as guilty of it as most. Maybe more so since she had a past she wished she could forget.

A gaggle of chattering cheerleaders rounded the corner. They snapped to attention when they spotted Matt, then eyed him as they sashayed past, but he seemed blind to their flirtatious smiles.

Rachel watched them, her heart heavy with the unjustness of life. That old song was right. The good were the only ones who died young. When Rachel had irritated her parents to the point they could barely stand the sight of her, Hope had generously offered Rachel a home so she could attend normal American school for her senior year. Rachel had jumped at the chance to escape the vagabond life of near poverty in which she'd lived in the mission villages. Hope had bailed Rachel out of countless disasters, culminating in relocating to anonymous Atlanta to help Rachel hide the shameful consequences of a teenage pregnancy. Hope had taken her kindness even further by adopting

Rachel's daughter when Rachel had voiced her fears of relinquishing her baby girl to strangers.

And then there were their missionary parents who'd devoted their lives to bringing goodness and religion to the world. They'd died for their cause in some dirty village because they lacked basic medical care. If it hadn't been for Hope, Rachel would have died with them.

Of all the good people in her family, only she, the bad seed, lived on, and she was hardly qualified to raise an impressionable teen. But from the moment she'd looked into the eyes of her newborn baby girl she'd sworn to do whatever was best for the child—no matter the personal costs. And the cost had been living with the knowledge that she hadn't been good enough for her own daughter.

The girls in their flipping short skirts disappeared around the corner, and Rachel's gaze returned to Matt, only to find him observing her with frowning intensity. He rubbed a finger across his upper lip, drawing her attention to his mouth and flooding her with memories that did crazy things to her equilibrium. She jerked her gaze back to his. Remembering his kisses, how he'd listened and how special he'd made her feel, would get her nowhere good.

"Chastity's had enough disruption in her life. There's only five weeks left before summer break. Let her finish out the school year here. She just lost her mother. Yanking her away from her friends, home and support network would be too traumatic. Or did you even consider her welfare?"

The unjustness of his question hit Rachel like a hard slap. Rachel had always, *always* put Chastity's well-being first. But the thought of staying in judgmental Johnstonville and having to prove to these people that she wasn't the selfish brat she'd once been was unthinkable.

But the biggest risk in staying was having Matt uncover the truth or having Chastity tainted by her birth mother's reputation if others discovered her secret. Both possibilities flat-out terrified her. The longer she lingered here, the greater the probability of discovery and disaster.

Sweat trickled down her spine. "We can't stay."

"It's better for Chastity to come to terms with her mother's death here in familiar surroundings. Give her a chance to find her feet and say her goodbyes."

"Matt, I have to get back to my job."

"What about Chastity? As much as you hated your childhood, are you going to subject her to the same nomadic lifestyle by hauling her all over the globe and back to…wherever you were?"

Never. "That was a one-time assignment. I live and work in Atlanta. She's always loved it there."

"Who'll watch her when you're at work? She's too old for day care. Are you going to leave her home alone when she's emotionally vulnerable? That's a recipe for disaster."

Rachel's stomach sank. She worked two to three twenty-four hour shifts per week, then volunteered at the local clinic or picked up an eight-hour shift at the hospital on her days off. She was rarely at home. But leaving a teen home alone definitely wasn't an option—especially not in her neighborhood. What would she do with Chastity? Rachel had chosen to live in the inner city and help those who didn't get even basic medical care. Her volunteer work within the community bought her protection, but she couldn't guarantee it would extend to Chastity. Her apartment was no place for a young girl. She'd never willingly expose Chastity to the seamier side of life that she experienced daily or send her to the tough school near the apartment. As much as Rachel hated to leave her neighbors, she'd have to move.

"I haven't hammered out all the details."

"You need a plan before you pack her up and move."

True. Instantly becoming a mother to the child she'd given birth to thirteen years ago terrified her—probably more now than it had then when she'd been less equipped but naively eager to try. Back then Hope had convinced her that a baby needed a parent who was stable and reliable. Rachel hadn't been either.

Could she be now?

Yes, damn it. Yes. She didn't know how, but she would be.

"Cut me some slack. I just lost my sister. I haven't had time to think. By the time I've packed up Hope's house and put it on the market, I'll have a plan for Chastity."

Her thoughts reeled over the long to-do list. Dealing with Hope's estate was only the tip of the iceberg, according to the lawyer she'd met with before coming to school.

Matt's concern for Chastity's welfare sounded genuine, even though he had no idea the girl shared his DNA. That only confirmed what Hope had said all those years ago—that Matt was too good for Rachel. Back then he'd been a star quarterback with a future in the NFL after college. Rachel had been self-destructive and in trouble more often than not. She and a baby would have held him back.

Staring into his disapproving face, she truly believed she'd done the right thing when she'd severed the connection between the all-American boy and the black sheep of the Bishop family. No matter how many second thoughts she'd had, neither Matt nor Chastity had deserved being tied to the self-centered twit she'd been back then. Corrupting a truly good person, as her parents had reminded her often, was a sin. Yet no matter how hard Rachel worked to make amends for her mistakes, she could never change the fact that she'd robbed Matt and his wonderful family of the opportunity to know his child.

Did he have others? She surreptitiously glanced at his left hand. No ring. But that didn't mean anything. And neither did the relief coursing through her. His marital status meant nothing to her. *Nothing.*

"Does Chastity have any family on her father's side? We wanted to notify them but couldn't find a name or number in Hope's paperwork."

Matt's question jerked her back to the present with heart-thumping alarm. Her otherwise virtuous sister had lied to cover Rachel's mistake, and Rachel didn't know all the details of the story Hope had concocted. Best to say as little as possible.

"No."

"You're all she has?"

"Yes. My parents died before Chastity was born." Losing them and relinquishing her baby in the same year had seemed just punishment for her misdeeds. She was alone in the world now, except for the daughter she couldn't rightfully claim. Grief blossomed, but she crushed the bud.

"I'm sorry about your folks."

She'd been a total disappointment to them. "Thanks."

The door whooshed open a sliver and a dark-haired girl's overly made-up face appeared in the gap. Recognition hit Rachel with the force of a tsunami. Shock followed. Chastity had grown up. The round-faced child Rachel had known was gone, replaced by a young woman with heavily painted brown eyes and overly teased hair.

"Aunt Rachel?"

Chastity's sullen face resembled the one Rachel had seen in her own mirror when she'd been a student here. The haunted look in the girl's eyes tore at Rachel's heart. Empathy and love swelled within her. Her mouth dried. Nodding, she devoured the sight of the lanky teenager squeezing past Matt.

"Hello, Chastity." She opened her arms.

Chastity hesitated, and it felt as if an elephant settled on Rachel's chest. She bit her lip to stymie the sob building inside her. Then the girl launched forward. The impact of her body against Rachel's nearly knocked her over. Rachel hugged her. It felt so good to hold her again. It had been so long. Five years too long. She squeezed tighter, never wanted to let go. She inhaled a shaky breath and choked on heavy perfume. That brought a smile to her lips. She and Chastity had so much in common.

It had been the hugs Rachel had missed the most since Hope had ended their visits. The unconditional love had been a close second. Chastity had actually loved *her* when it had seemed no one else did. Happy tears burned paths down her cheeks. She rocked gently and stroked Chastity's tangled hair.

Chastity jerked away abruptly, swiping her eyes and smearing blue mascara across her cheekbones. She sniffed and tried to look cool, as if she hadn't nearly broken Rachel's ribs or soaked her shirt. "Glad you came."

"Me, too." Rachel had to force the words past her constricted throat.

"I didn't think you would. I would've been okay if you hadn't." Chastity's voice wobbled, and her chin tipped up in false bravado. She wore an expression that said the world had done her dirty, and she was fully prepared for it to do so again.

Rachel had been that same defensive girl. She dabbed her own cheeks and hoped Matt didn't notice. "Fat chance of me not coming, kiddo. I'm sorry it took so long to get here. I was out in the wild with unreliable generators and intermittent electricity, radios instead of phones, and no internet."

Chastity shuddered dramatically. "That's roughing it."

Then Rachel realized she now stood eye to eye with the child—one who'd developed hollows in her cheeks and curves in her breasts. The gap-toothed eight-year-old she remembered was on the brink of womanhood.

"Chastity, you've grown a foot."

Chastity grinned. "Yep." Then she leaned forward. "Thanks for the bras," she whispered. "Mom said I was too young for one." She glanced over her shoulder as if to make sure Matt hadn't overheard.

"You're welcome." Those emails had kept Rachel going, and being allowed to order and ship occasional gifts to Chastity had helped her feel connected.

"Can we go now?" Chastity pleaded.

Matt shook his head. "Your aunt will have to sign you out, and I'd like to talk to you both about what put you in detention in the first place."

"Aw, c'mon, Coach Johnston. I know what I did and I'm sorry. Stuff has been shit—tough lately. I've had church ladies praying over me nearly every minute and somebody in my grill worrying about every little thing 'til I'm about to crawl outta my skin. I just want to be left alone."

Matt's expression softened slightly. "Taking your frustrations out on others is never the answer."

Chastity rolled her eyes. "I know. 'God loves a gracious and forgiving person.'"

Chastity's chanted words plunged Rachel into the past. That phrase had been yanked out every time Rachel had strayed from the narrow path of her upbringing—which had been pretty frequently. She'd come to hate the verse. Apparently Hope had carried on their parents' tradition. That was a practice Rachel intended to break. Guilt and a sense of failure were not good leverage.

She shook off the restrictive feeling and gave Chastity a wink and a squeeze. "How do I spring this delinquent, Ma—Mr.—Coach Johnston?"

Matt's brows lowered at her levity. "In here."

He reentered room 127. Chastity grabbed Rachel's hand and dragged her along. "Hey, everybody. This is my aunt Rachel. She's a Life Flight helicopter nurse in Atlanta. When she's not flying to nasty wrecks and stuff she travels all over the world with medical teams to rat-infested villages trying to save people from floods, Ebola, tsunamis and other noxious stuff."

Matt's head snapped around. The bubbles of pleasure Rachel was experiencing over the fact that Chastity sounded proud of her popped under Matt's scrutiny.

"Is that right?" His inspection made her feel like bacteria under a microscope. He leaned his hip against his desk, crossing his long legs in front of him. His thigh muscles rippled with the movement, distracting Rachel. Matt still had an athletic body.

"Yes. I...um...volunteer my vacation time to work with a traveling medical team."

"Perhaps you'd like to share some of your experiences with us. Tell us why you chose to go into nursing. If I remember correctly, that wasn't your plan when you were their age."

Rachel snorted. "I wanted to be a rock star back then. The fact that I sing like a scalded cat might have something to do with my change of heart." Truth was, she'd wanted to do something that would make people—specifically, her parents—sit up and take notice of Rachel Bishop.

Smiling faces looked expectantly at her. Being the center of attention—something she'd once sought with nearly religious fervor—caused her skin to flush and her ears to burn. "Some other time."

"I'll hold you to that, Ms.—is it still Bishop?" Rachel nodded. "Career day is the last Thursday of school. I'll add you to the docket."

Standing in front of a gym filled with bored kids didn't appeal to her. It sounded downright horrifying. She was hardly a sterling example to hold up to anyone, and next month she and Chastity would be back in Atlanta anyway.

"It'd be really cool to have someone interesting for a change, Aunt Rachel. We usually suffer through a bunch of boring old farts—"

"Chastity!" Rachel and Matt reprimanded simultaneously.

Chastity grimaced. "Well, who wants to grow up and be a mortician anyway?"

Several kids muttered agreement.

Rachel felt cornered but at the same time compelled to respond. "Somebody has to do it and do it correctly. Otherwise disease and vermin become a problem. I've witnessed that more than once overseas and even in our own country after natural disasters—" She caught Matt's raised eyebrows in her peripheral vision. "Well, anyway. Another time. I'll, uh…see about next month. Where do I sign Chastity out?"

Matt scooped up a pen and a sheet of paper. Their fingers touched when she took them from him, and a spark shot up her arm. Static electricity. That's all it was. All she'd allow it to be. But the fact that he'd startled proved he'd felt it, too. Not something she wanted to contemplate.

He turned to Chastity. "Did you finish your essay?"

"It's right there on your desk, Coach."

"Then you can go. Rachel? We'll talk later."

She stiffened. His tone sounded like a threat.

"See you around," Rachel said, hoping she wouldn't, and steered Chastity toward the door.

If she saw Matt first, she'd avoid him, and if she didn't see him again before she got out of Johnstonville, that would be fine with her, too.

HELL-RAISING RACHEL, a nurse? Hard to believe.

Matt tried to make sense of the past ten minutes, but the woman with the baggy clothes, falling-down hair and pale, makeup-free face bore little resemblance to the sexual fantasy creature from his memory.

The Rachel he remembered had been a red-lipped, hip-swinging, irreverent femme fatale bent on having a good time. She'd charged into his life and blitzed him off his feet like a defensive linebacker. He'd been raised by parents who lived by structure, rules and a very strict moral code. His dedication to sports and learning had only reinforced his disciplined attitude. He'd had no idea how to handle her. But he'd tried.

To Rachel, rules had been hurdles to circumvent. She'd find ten different ways to do the same old thing while he'd chosen proved methods. Her adventurous nature had captured his attention, but what had sucked him under like swirling white water had been the vulnerability she'd fought so hard to hide. He'd tried to save her from herself and ended up losing—a lot.

From the moment she'd kissed him under the mistletoe at a church party during Christmas break his junior year of college—a hot openmouthed kiss in the fellowship hall of all places—he'd been hooked on her brand of excitement. He'd held on for the ride of his life and loved every minute of it.

Her disappearance without explanation and her refusal to answer his letters had stunned, hurt and confused him, as if he'd hit a submerged river boulder when he'd thought the stream clear and deep. Until Hope had enlightened him years later, he'd wondered what he'd done to drive Rachel away. Hope had told him that Rachel had been bored in Johnstonville, and he'd been a diversion, nothing more.

A pencil dropped, forcing his focus back to the students shifting restlessly in their seats while they wrote, but it didn't stay there long. This mature Rachel, with squared shoulders and deliberate movements, spoke of a confidence she hadn't possessed as a teen. Her looser clothes flowed over her body in a way that hinted at the womanly shape they concealed. He found her natural beauty ten times more attractive than the attention-grabbing outfits that had once done a number on his hormones. Back then she'd been testing her womanly wiles, and he'd felt like a sixteen-year-old with a Ferrari. But he was older and wiser now. There would be no rekindling of his romance with Rachel. The fact that she was a flight nurse revealed she was still an adrenaline junkie. She'd just found a profitable way to exploit her need for thrills.

Matt pinched the bridge of his nose. He was losing his mind. He'd been born in Johnstonville and intended to die here. He had a long-standing family legacy of community service to fulfill— one he could not blow for a woman. He had the house with the white picket fence and a dog. All he needed to make his life perfect was a nice, church-going wife who could accept him as he was and give him children.

The woman who'd blown into his life like a hurricane was not a likely candidate. Life with Rachel would never be predictable or uncompli-cated. Life with her sister, Hope, on the other hand, might have been.

CHAPTER TWO

RACHEL FELT AT least three sets of curious eyes watching her from the school office window as she put the car in gear. The sensation resembled a spider climbing her spine. She could almost hear the condemning whispers.

She's a bad seed, that one.

How could someone like Hope be related to someone like her?

Her dear parents must have been so ashamed.

"Cool. A Mustang." Chastity pushed knobs and twisted buttons. The radio blasted loud enough to rattle Rachel's teeth. "I love red cars," the teen shouted over the noise.

Rachel lowered the volume, earning a pout from Chastity. "Don't get excited. It's a rental."

"What do you usually drive?"

"I don't own a car, so I take public transit. I ride the MARTA or the bus."

"The bus? You ride a stinking bus?"

"Public transportation is very good in Atlanta." And a car in her neighborhood might get stripped or stolen.

"You'll need a car here, and Mom's…" Chastity's hair flew as she quickly averted her face to stare out the window, blinking fast. "It's toast."

The broken words squeezed Rachel's heart. Hope's car had been totaled, the police officer had said. He'd offered to text pictures, but Rachel had declined.

"I have this one for now."

"So we'll shop for one? A red one?"

Rachel's heart sank. "Probably not, sweetie."

"But how will we get around?" Worry tightened Chastity's features.

"We'll use the bus and MARTA."

"You're going back to Atlanta? But…where will I live?"

Rachel reached across the console and covered a knotted fist. "You'll live with me."

"Your apartment only has one bedroom, and your neighborhood stinks. Mom said it wasn't even safe for us to visit." Chastity pulled away to dig a lipstick out of her pocket. She flipped down the visor mirror and slathered on a bold red color that would look good on her in about twenty years.

"We'll find a bigger place near good schools. Maybe even a house with a yard big enough to have a garden."

"Mom has—had a garden."

"I know."

"I hated working in it. Bugs. Sweat. Weeds."

Rachel didn't point out that Chastity had often

bragged in her emails about her section of the garden. "Okay. No garden. But I've never found tomatoes as good as your mom's anywhere in the world. I was hoping you'd tell me her secret."

Silence reigned, then Chastity blurted, "I don't want to move."

Rachel's heart clenched with empathy. How many times had *she* said that? "Change is difficult, but together we'll find the perfect place."

"My friends are here."

"I know. But you'll make new friends, and we'll visit your old ones." Maybe. That would be risky.

"Does Atlanta have good shopping?"

"Second only to New York."

"Good, 'cause you need an intervention. You're a fashion 'don't.'"

Ouch. "I'm dressed for the heat and the ethics where I was working—*and* for traveling."

"Yeah, well…you look like a bag lady."

"Thanks, so much. I love you, too, kid."

"Will I get to buy cool clothes?"

"Sure."

"You'll let me pick out the house?"

"I'll let you help."

For nearly a mile, silence echoed in the car. "Could I be called Chaz there instead of Chastity? I catch a lot of grief over my name. Mom might as well have named me Perpetual Virgin or something equally lame."

"You can be Chaz if you want. Or even Faith."

"God, no. My middle name's as bad as my first. Chastity Faith. I mean, *seriously*, who does that to a kid?"

"Faith is my middle name."

"And you don't use it, either. Can I get a dog? Mom always said no, but pets are important for teaching responsibility."

Rachel laughed. The kid was playing all the cards. "We'll discuss it when we figure out where we'll live."

"Moving might be okay. I'll think about it."

Chastity didn't have a choice, but Rachel didn't push the point as she turned into Hope's neighborhood.

Chastity stroked the dashboard. "Can I drive the rest of the way home?"

Rachel did a double take. "You're thirteen."

"Jess Weaver drives her mom's car sometimes."

"You're not Jess Weaver." Rachel wanted to slap a hand over her mouth. How many times had her parents or Hope given her that patronizing kind of answer? She'd always sworn she'd never say that to a kid of her own. But she hadn't planned to have any children—any more children, that is.

Logic might work better than argument. "Driving at your age is illegal. If you get caught, you can't get your license when you turn sixteen."

"That would suck."

"We'll find some go-carts somewhere."

"Go-carts are for babies."

This wasn't getting them anywhere. "So…Matt Johnston is the detention officer? I didn't know he'd moved back to Johnstonville."

She wasn't shamelessly milking information out of a kid. Okay, she was, but curiosity was killing her, and she needed to change the subject.

"He's the athletic director and the varsity football coach, too. His team's state champion. Sometimes he substitute teaches or does detention when there's no ball practice."

Matt had dreamed of playing professional football after college. What had happened to his plans? Rachel had always expected to see his handsome face on a cereal box or something. He'd been a gifted athlete, smart and driven. Not smart enough to avoid her, but still…the last place she'd expected to find him living was Johnstonville. He'd known exactly what he'd wanted out of life and had a plan to achieve his goals. She'd envied that.

She tamped down the thought. "You had him as a substitute?"

"Yeah. In English. I hate English." Chastity directed her response to the nonjudgmental window.

As Rachel drove through the streets dappled by the sun peeking through an oak canopy, her thoughts circled back to those brief weeks with him fourteen years ago. Matt had been perfect in a way she could never be—like Hope. And Rachel had deliberately set out to lead Johnstonville's golden boy astray. She'd tempted and teased him into taking a walk on the wild side, all in a bid to tarnish his halo. But she hadn't expected him to be understanding, supportive and encouraging. She definitely hadn't anticipated falling in love with him. Needing him. Wanting forever with him. Or conceiving his child. She'd never cared for any-one with that intensity before or since. She hadn't let herself.

"He was dating mom."

Chastity's words hit Rachel's solar plexus like a fist. Her foot went slack on the gas pedal. She struggled to regain her breath and balance. "Re-ally?"

"They were gonna get married."

Another hit. Bile burned her throat. She debated pulling off the road and hitting the ditch to empty her stomach. She reminded herself Matt wasn't hers. She'd dumped him and walked away. But the image of him making love to her sister was more than her over-traveled nerves could handle. A sour taste filled her mouth. "Your mom was older than Matt."

"Only by a few years."

"She, um, never mentioned being…engaged."

"They hadn't announced it, but I heard them talking a couple times after they thought I was asleep." Chastity fussed with the cheap beads on her wrist. "Coach would have been a pretty cool dad."

Yes. He would have. Rachel couldn't get a sound out.

"He's a babe—for an old guy. And probably good in bed since he was a jock and all. They get a lot of practice. Girls always throw themselves at jocks."

But some jocks tried to save themselves for marriage.

Rachel battled to conceal the chaotic tangle of shock, guilt and denial thundering through her. As nonchalantly as she could, she looked at her niece/daughter and caught the calculating gleam in Chastity's dark eyes and realized the kid was trying to shock her. Since Rachel couldn't think of anything to say, she kept her mouth shut. But she wanted to scream.

Hope had taken her daughter. Did she have to take the only man Rachel had ever loved, too? Not that Matt had ever really been Rachel's. He'd have eventually realized Rachel was unlovable and dumped her. But for a short time she'd found someone who'd believed in her. Accepted her.

Chastity buffed her nails against her jeans. "I don't think he and Mom were doing it, though. He never spent the night. Anyway, Mom wasn't the type to get all hot and bothered, you know? She was like a prissy control freak."

An apt description. Rachel exhaled the breath she'd been holding. She was not relieved. Really, she wasn't. "Their private relationship was none of your business, Chastity. Or mine. And stop trying to shock me by talking trash."

"Aw, come on, don't you ever look at a guy and wonder what he looks like naked or what he'd be like in bed?"

Only Matt. Her other relationships had been more...cerebral. "Matt's old enough to be your father."

"Eeew, *I* don't want to sleep with *him*."

"You're too young to sleep with anybody."

Chastity fluffed her hair. "Oh, please. Do you think girls my age aren't doing it?"

"I know they are. But are you ready to be a mother?"

"No freaking way." Utter revulsion coated the words. "But there are condoms and birth control pills. I have friends using them."

"No birth control is fail proof. Trust me. When I volunteer at the clinic I see more pregnant thirteen-year-olds than you'd believe. Let's not forget the sexually transmitted diseases. Keep your panties on and don't be in such a rush to grow up. And don't turn sex into something as cheap and easy as picking up a pack of gum at the corner store. Making love should be...special. Meaningful."

With Matt it had been both, despite her initial intentions.

"Yeah, yeah." Chastity poked a wad of gum through her red lips. "You're more like Mom than I thought."

Rachel's heart pounded, and her hands were sweat-slick on the steering wheel. She'd had dreamy visions of the mother-daughter chats she would have shared with Chastity if she hadn't given her up. How she would have handled difficult conversations like this one so much better than her own mother had. But Rachel hadn't expected that day to be today. She wasn't ready. And she wasn't nearly as eloquent as she thought she'd be. In fact, she had no clue what to say that wouldn't sound like her mother's preaching. Or Hope's.

"Chastity, a lot of people claim to know all the facts about sex and end up in trouble anyway because there's so much misinformation out there. You can ask me anything. Anything at all. Anytime. Okay?"

Chastity rolled her eyes. "Right."

Disappointed by the lackluster response, Rachel steered the Mustang onto Hope's quiet street. "I mean it. No judgment. Okay?"

"Whatever."

Rachel hadn't been to Hope's house since her sister had packed them up just weeks after Rachel had discovered her pregnancy. As she drove down the street, the senior citizens working in their perfectly tended yards looked up from their spring flower beds to stare. Curtains twitched.

Nosy neighbors had been the bane of Rachel's stay in Johnstonville. The phone lines had probably started humming with the news that Rachel

Bishop was back the moment she identified herself at the lawyer's office. The good citizens would wait with baited breath for Rachel's next scandalous move. She'd disappoint them this time, though. She didn't create havoc anymore. She brought order. And she definitely wouldn't be corrupting any more golden boys.

As soon as they pulled in the driveway Chastity jumped out and sprinted toward the house. Rachel exhaled slowly. How was she going to become Chastity's mother? She'd never measure up to Hope's perfection. But she had to try. Chastity was her daughter, and she wouldn't fail her this time.

Rachel grabbed her duffel bag from the back seat and followed the teen up the flower-lined walkway. By the time she reached the shady porch Chastity had retrieved the key from beneath a flower pot full of blooms and unlocked the door. In the corner of the yard Hope's tiny vegetable garden was already green with the promise of summer fruits and vegetables.

"Matt said you've been staying with friends until I could get here?"

"His sister, Pam. I'll have to go and get my stuff."

Chastity had been staying with her aunt and didn't even know it. Rachel sealed the thought in a vault with other taboo memories.

"In that case, the house will probably be musty

and dusty and—" Chastity shoved the door open, and a waft of lemon polish–scented air cut off Rachel's words. Not one dust mote had settled on the hardwood floors or danced in the sunbeams streaming through the sparkling clean windows. Goose bumps lifted Rachel's skin. She almost expected Hope—the impeccable homemaker—to stroll from the kitchen at any moment with her apron on and her blond hair perfectly styled.

Chastity flounced down the hall, leaving Rachel frozen in the foyer. Maybe it was all a cruel joke. Maybe Hope wasn't gone. Rachel's gaze landed on an old family photograph hanging on the wall. Hope, their mother and grandmother were all blonde. Rachel, her father and Grandfather Bishop had darker coloring…like Chastity's.

A tap on the open door behind her brought Rachel around. Alice Wilkins, the worst busybody on the planet and Hope's next-door neighbor, stood outside. Small and birdlike, Alice had made a career out of chirping to Hope every time Rachel had sneaked out. She'd been friends with Rachel's great aunt who'd originally owned the house and left it to Hope.

"Martha called from the school to tell me you and Chastity were on your way home. There's nothing in the refrigerator, so I brought a casserole for your dinner and a salad. I grew the lettuce myself, and the dressing is my secret recipe."

The thoughtful gesture was unexpected. Rachel

didn't know how to handle it, but then she stiffened her spine. No doubt Hope's neighbors thought Rachel the Rebel incapable of feeding a child. But Rachel swallowed her pride, set down her bag, took the dishes and forced a smile. "Thank you."

"The church women's group and I have been keeping an eye on the place and straightening up a little since our dear Hope passed. She will be sorely missed."

That explained the spotless house. "Yes."

Alice showed no sign of leaving. The polite thing to do would be to invite her in, but Rachel couldn't imagine Alice wanting to chat with the girl who'd rearranged her flower beds until the purple and yellow pansies spelled something vulgar.

"Chastity tells me you're a nurse now."

"I am."

"She talks about you all the time. Wants to grow up to be just like her aunt Rachel and see the world. Of course, it used to break her mother's heart to hear Chastity say she wanted to move away like you did. But Hope was quite pleased with the way *you* turned out after she convinced you to finish school and get a responsible job."

Stunned speechless, Rachel merely stared. Hope hadn't said anything, and one word of praise from her sister would have been more welcome than a winning lottery ticket. The only thing Rachel had known for sure was that she'd disappointed Hope and their parents on a regular basis.

Miss Wilkins pointed to the casserole. "Bake it at three-fifty for thirty minutes. Call if you need anything. I can pop over anytime. I left my number on the pad by the phone."

"Thanks, again." For more than the food. Rachel shut the door behind her. After all the effort Rachel had expended to make the woman miserable, she couldn't fathom why she was being nice...unless she was fishing for information.

"Who was that?" Chastity had changed into jeans and a T-shirt and pulled her hair up into a ponytail on top of her head. Even though she still wore the heavy makeup, she looked more like a thirteen-year-old now than the thirty-year-old she'd been impersonating earlier.

"Miss Wilkins."

Chastity grimaced. "Whatever she says, I didn't do it. I've been at school all day."

Rachel laughed. "I used to say those same words. She brought dinner."

"Nah, she was checking up on us. Dinner is an excuse. What is it?" She peered under the foil. "Mmm, her chicken casserole. The old bat makes the best chicken casserole on the planet...even if she does make a career out of spying on me and making my life miserable."

Grabbing the dish, Chastity headed for the kitchen. Rachel followed with the salad. A smile tugged her lips at yet another familiar refrain. She'd hated the neighbors who seemed determined to mind her business and offer unsolicited advice. It seemed she and her daughter had more in common than genetics. Rachel shoved the bowl into the empty and sparkling clean refrigerator.

"You can sleep in the guest room. I'll help you unpack." Chastity reached for the duffel bag Rachel had dropped on the floor.

"Thanks, but I'll do it. I need to do my dirty laundry anyway."

"This bag feels empty. Where's the rest of your stuff?"

"I left most of it with the village women."

"Why?"

How could she explain the horror of watching children sift through the dump for clothing, food and supplies? "Because they don't have much, and there are no Walmart stores over there."

A moment of silence passed. "I guess you could borrow some of Mom's clothes. You're taller, but otherwise about the same size."

Stepping into her sister's shoes or clothing wasn't something she'd wanted to do if she could avoid it. "I'll wash what I have."

The phone rang, and Chastity bolted to answer it. While she chatted, Rachel headed to the laundry room. She dumped her soiled clothes in the washer and turned it on. While the tub filled, she opened the cabinet where Hope had kept the detergent.

The box was empty. She searched every other cabinet and realized they were out. She turned off the machine, but it was too late. Her clothes were saturated.

Carrying her bag she headed toward her old room. The first room she passed was Chastity's. It was decorated in ballerina pink with matching quilts on the twin beds and airy tulle bed skirts. It was every bit as adorable as the pictures Hope had sent.

Hope's room was next. Her sister had redecorated the space in creamy white since Rachel's time here. A pure room for the pure sister? Hope had been the unreachable ideal that Rachel's parents had expected her to model. But now Hope was gone. Loss swelled in Rachel's chest and tightened her throat. She swallowed, trying to ease the grip of grief. She and her sister had never been close. Even without their personality differences, the ten-year age gap had been too wide to bridge—and now it never would be.

And then an insidious, sickening thought slithered through her. Had Hope shared that bed with Matt? Had she been trying to give Chastity the father she deserved? The one to which she was entitled? Hope had always believed in family sticking together.

Rachel's trapezius muscles knotted. Rolling her shoulders to ease the tension, she continued toward her old room. The same floorboards creaked, but then she stopped in surprise on the threshold. Other than the furniture and the picture of her parents that she'd taken with her old camera, all traces of her stay here had been erased. The soothing sky-blue curtains, bedding and painted walls had been changed to deep plum with touches of lavender and lime.

This room had been her prison and simultaneously her sanctuary from the town in which she did not fit. She forced her feet forward and dropped her bag on the bed.

"What're you doing in my room?"

Rachel jerked around. "This used to be my room."

"It's mine now." Defensive. Territorial. "The guest room is that sissy pink one down the hall."

Only then did Rachel notice the nail polish and makeup in a plastic bin on the dresser. "Gotcha."

She backtracked to the ballerina bedroom, but she couldn't help wondering if her things were gone because her sister had redecorated the room for Chastity or was it something more? Had Hope been trying to eradicate Rachel from Chastity's life? She'd stopped Rachel's visits five years ago, reducing contact to emails and brief phone calls.

How badly had her sister wanted her gone?

MATT TOLD HIMSELF he was simply taking a shortcut home from the Cub Scout meeting. But he knew differently.

It was late. His knee ached. He should be in bed getting much-needed sleep. Why was he making an unscheduled detour by Hope's house? Because Rachel had looked ready to bolt earlier today. He wanted to see if she'd packed up her niece and taken off. Would she selfishly put her wants above Chastity's?

Turning onto Hope's street, he slowed his pickup. He was surprised to see a car in the driveway, even more surprised to see a lamp burning in the den. A shadow crossed in front of the window. He braked involuntarily. Rachel's? Had to be.

There wasn't anything to do in Johnstonville after ten, and Hope had refused to install cable TV. What was Rachel doing up at this time of night? Packing to hit the road at dawn?

The only reason he was out this late was because he'd had to clean up the volcano experiment he and the boys hadn't quite pulled off as planned at the meeting. His mind had been on other things, and he'd measured incorrectly. The volcano had erupted with too much enthusiasm, spreading its fake lava all over the church basement. He'd sent the dripping kids and their fathers home and gotten out the mop. His mistake. His duty to clean it up.

Against his better judgment, he turned into Hope's driveway. His headlights passed across the front of the house. A moment later Rachel's face appeared in the window. Too late to wise up and go home now. He cut the engine. When he climbed out of his truck, she dropped the curtain. He tapped quietly on the door and waited. Silent seconds passed. Did she plan to ignore him? He was about to knock again when the porch light came on. His mouth dried. The door eased open a crack.

Her chocolate-brown eyes looked red-rimmed in the light, but Rachel had always been too tough to cry. Tangled dark hair tumbled over her shoulders. He couldn't halt the memory of how it had felt when she'd dragged it across his chest and stomach when they'd made love. Not a thought he needed right now.

"What do you want, Matt?"

Her lack of welcome quenched the flickering ember of desire. "I saw your light. Is everything okay?"

She lowered her lids and rubbed her temple. She looked fragile. Fragile? Rachel? Impossible. Rachel was cast-iron tough. Hell on wheels. But the shadows beneath her eyes and hollows in her cheeks were impossible to miss.

"Jet lag. Can't sleep."

"May I come in?"

Her eyebrows shot up. "Are you sure you want to do that? By breakfast it'll be all over town that you were with Rachel the Rebel at midnight."

She was right, but he was a big boy now. And apparently not a smart one. "I'll risk it."

She stepped back, putting a finger to her lips, and the memory of her doing the same when they'd snuck out of this same house over a decade ago tackled him.

"Chastity's asleep."

Her whisper brought back a flood of emotions he didn't need. Following her inside, he rubbed the back of his neck. It felt strange to be in Hope's house without Hope. Stranger still to be here with Rachel. She wore the same clothes as earlier, only she'd untucked her baggy shirt. His mind immediately went to the last time they'd been alone together in the dark. Naked. Only then, he'd been the one to mess up her hair. God, he'd loved tangling his fingers in the silky strands and holding her close. Involuntarily, desire rekindled. He tried to snuff it out and failed miserably.

Focus. "Have you decided to let Chastity finish out the school year here?"

Rachel's brow dipped, and she shook her head. "I can't."

"Bad decision." He didn't want her to go. For Chastity's sake.

"Excuse me?"

Matt moved carefully as he approached her. The last thing he wanted was for his knee to buckle and dump him on the floor at her feet. All the kneeling from mopping and cleaning had strained the muscles. He needed his brace, but it was at home. Where he should be.

"Chastity doesn't need another change right now. She'll graduate from middle school in a few weeks and would be transitioning to high school for fall. Summer is the logical time to move her."

Rachel jammed her fingers into her hair and paced toward the sofa. "I understand what you're saying, Matt. I even agree with you to a point, but my job is very important to me. It would be difficult to get more time off."

"Try. For Chastity's sake."

She faced him, looking torn, exhausted and a little…scared? His protective instincts kicked in, but he dismissed them.

"You don't know what you're asking."

The fact that they continued to whisper like kids sneaking around only increased the southerly direction of his blood flow. Damn it, he was getting a boner. It irritated him that she still got to him.

"I'm asking you to put someone else's needs ahead of your own for once."

He couldn't decipher the look she gave him, but tangled in all the other emotions chasing across her face, he thought he caught a flash of pain.

"Fine. I'll call my supervisor in the morning and see if she can spare me a little longer. But don't get your hopes up."

"Good." He searched her face. This wasn't the sassy Rachel he remembered. This version looked as if she needed a hug. But he flattened the impulse to deliver one. He knew better. He came from a family of huggers, but holding Rachel definitely wouldn't be like comforting his sister. Rachel was the only woman who'd ever made him lose control, and that wasn't a trail he wanted to travel again. His relationship with her and her subsequent rejection had taken him to a moral low that he couldn't forget.

They stared at each other, the silence stretching awkwardly. Questions charged through his head like the punt return team. A part of him wanted to ask why she'd dumped him, to hear the reasons from her lips instead of conjecture from townsfolk or Hope's account. But Rachel's reasons didn't matter—water under the bridge and all that.

She'd left him when he'd been at the top of his game—so she definitely wouldn't want anything to do with him now that his glory days were over. And he was okay with that. He'd come to terms with disappointing his dad and the citizens of Johnstonville. He'd rebuilt his life and made it a decent one. He loved his job.

She licked her lips, folded her arms across her chest and shifted on her feet. How did she manage to look vulnerable when he knew she was anything but?

Despite his attempt to reason with himself, the old attraction pulled at him. He wanted to kiss her—but only to see if she still packed the same punch or if his inexperience had been what made their chemistry so explosive. He was pretty sure it was the latter—no woman since Rachel had affected him as strongly. And there'd been a few too many—all in an effort to exorcise her memory. Those meaningless encounters had gone against every principle his parents had taught him, and he wasn't proud of his behavior.

But one experimental kiss would answer so many questions. Did she taste the same? Feel the same? She'd always had the softest skin. All over. But especially her breasts. His heart slammed his rib cage as he erased the gap between them and lifted a hand to trace her cheekbone.

Rachel's eyes went wide. Her breath hitched, and she abruptly dodged sideways. "Matt, go home."

He should. But he didn't want to and couldn't pry his gaze from her flushed face and wide pupils. His lungs filled with her scent, something earthier and more exotic than he remembered.

"Please. Leave." Her soft, breathless voice said one thing, but the way she visually gobbled him up said something else entirely. Her head-to-toe examination halted at his mouth. Her lips parted, and hunger gripped him anew. He leaned closer. A second before their lips would have touched she ducked and spun away, this time putting the coffee table between them.

Her mixed signals confused him.

Her breasts rose and fell. "There won't be any

of that this time. So if that's why you're trying to get me to stay—"

"It's not." He shoved his hands into his pockets and struggled with his misplaced disappointment. What in the hell had he been thinking? Rachel was right. Getting entangled again was a bad idea. She was counting the seconds until she could leave town, and he had a duty to Johnstonville.

"I'm sorry about Hope." The words sounded empty, but he needed a minute to regroup after that kind of fumble.

"I'll bet you are," she snapped, then faced him, looking contrite. "I apologize. That was uncalled-for."

She straightened a picture frame on the side table. It was one of him, Chastity and Hope taken at a Memorial Day picnic about eleven years back. He'd been home visiting his folks and had run into Hope. He'd asked her about Rachel, and he'd learned more than he ever wanted to about how easily she'd forgotten him.

"Chastity told me you and Hope were engaged."

Matt startled in surprise. "Where'd she get that idea?"

"She overheard you talking."

"We discussed marriage." Twice. They were both lonely, and neither of them was getting any younger. They'd shared the same values, the same love of their quiet little town, attended the same church, and each of them wanted a large family.

And time for that was passing them by. "We decided against it."

Hope had known about his past and hadn't minded that his future wasn't as bright as it once had been. Coach of the Year was probably the best he'd ever be. A marriage between them had seemed like a good match on paper, but talking about it was as far as they'd gotten. They hadn't even told anyone they were considering it. Part of it was that he'd wanted the fireworks he'd experienced with Rachel, and the few times he and Hope had kissed, they hadn't generated any. Then Hope had died. He was sorry. But he was also a little relieved that he wouldn't have to disappoint her.

Rachel's expectant expression demanded more of an explanation. "Turning forty hit her hard. She thought she was…missing out on life."

Rachel nodded. "Hope is—was—the kind of woman you deserve."

Before he could respond Chastity shuffled into the room. "Hey, Coach. What're you doing here?"

Good thing she hadn't walked in a minute earlier. "I was on my way home and saw the light on. I stopped by to see if everything was okay."

He looked at Hope's daughter, noting that she actually looked like a girl her age should for a change. No war paint, no spandex, no surly attitude. If she'd dress like this for school, she might have more friends than just his niece.

Chastity glanced from one of them to the other, as if gauging the truth. "I'm thirsty."

Rachel reached out to tuck a strand of Chastity's dark rumpled hair behind her ear, and for a moment Chastity leaned into the embrace and rested her forehead against Rachel's. The strands of their hair mingled, and it struck Matt how much they resembled each other.

He glanced at the photo of the Bishop family. Hope had always attributed Chastity's coloring to the dominant genes from her father and grandfather's side of the family. Hope had been fair, blonde and petite like her mother.

When Chastity twisted away, Matt thought he saw regret flash across Rachel's face. "It'll have to be water, kiddo. Our cupboards are bare. And we used the last tea bags with dinner. I'll go to the store in the morning."

Chastity's expression turned sour. "Dogs drink water."

She flounced off toward her room. Matt heard Rachel sigh and felt the need to make her feel better. "She's been giving Hope a hard time for the past year or so," he explained. "Hope blamed it on puberty. The bad behavior has escalated since Hope's death."

Rachel frowned up at him. "Did Hope spend a lot of time with her?"

"Hope spent all her time with Chastity when she wasn't working or at a church function."

"And there are always a lot of those." Bitterness tainted her voice.

He had a sneaking suspicion where this was going. Rachel's parents had devoted the majority of their time to their missions and little to their daughters. Hope hadn't minded. She'd eagerly joined in her parents' cause until she'd gone to college to get her accounting degree. Rachel had been a different story. She'd insisted the lands her parents visited didn't need good ol' American religion when they'd been getting by for hundreds of years with the native variety.

"Hope was a great mom, Rachel. Ask anyone."

Rachel glanced at the photo, her expression sad. "I'm sure she was. She excelled at everything she did."

That didn't sound like a compliment. "Rachel—"

"Matt, it's late and I want to go to bed."

His lower unit throbbed at the image of Rachel in bed. A bed was one place they'd never been together. He inhaled, but it was shaky.

Cheeks flushed, she crossed to the front door and opened it. "I appreciate your concern, but we're fine. Or will be after I make a grocery run."

He wrote his name and cellular number on the pad beside the phone. "Call me if you need anything. Good night."

It was a neighborly gesture, one he'd make to anyone, he told himself as he heard the lock click behind him. The past was over. And no amount of wishing things had been different would change their situation. He was okay with that.

CHAPTER THREE

A PEPPERING OF knocks roused Rachel from a dead sleep.

"Breakfast! Come and get it," Chastity called through the closed bedroom door.

Groggily, Rachel shoved her hair off her face. She'd tossed and turned most of the night, finally crashing around three in the morning. Matt's visit had rattled her. She'd been pretty sure he'd intended to kiss her. And that could not happen.

She dragged herself from the bed and shuffled toward the kitchen. She'd kiss a frog for a cup of coffee right now. But Matt, not a frog, stood in the den holding a paper bag and a tray containing four tall cups from Johnstonville's only fast-food restaurant.

Rachel stumbled to a halt, going instantly from bleary-eyed to alert. She hadn't brushed her hair or her teeth. She was wearing one of Chastity's oversize Mickey Mouse sleep shirts. It hit midthigh, and she hadn't shaved her legs in… Ugh. Weeks. She probably looked even worse than she felt in her jet-lagged, coffee and razor-deprived state.

Matt's sober gaze raked her from head to toe, confirming she looked like his worst nightmare. He, on the other hand, personified perfection. His jaw gleamed from a recent shave. His hair had been combed, and his eyes were bright. A white polo shirt molded to his muscles in a way guaranteed to give a woman an adrenaline rush.

Chastity stood beside him, also fully dressed with her too-heavy makeup on and her hair teased. It was too late to retreat. Rachel checked her watch. It was only six thirty. Early birds. Both of them.

"Matt brought breakfast." Chastity grabbed the paper sack and a clear cup of orange juice from the tray and headed toward the kitchen.

"Good morning." Matt's voice rumbled over Rachel like an approaching thunderstorm. His amused tone did nothing to bolster her confidence.

Her skin prickled uncomfortably. She took a deep breath and tried to finger comb her hair into something less tangled than a mop. There was nothing she could do about the rest of her. "G'morning. Thanks for bringing breakfast."

He nodded and offered the paper tray. "Coffee, juice or both?"

She might as well make the best of the situation. "Coffee. Please."

"There's cream and sugar in the bag with the biscuits."

"Um…thanks." Rachel shifted on her bare feet

and dug her toes into the floor. She debated excusing herself to grab a bathrobe. But the only one available had belonged to her sister. Had Matt seen Hope in that robe…or taken it off her?

A coil of something unpleasant started deep inside her. She blamed it on hunger. "Don't you, um…have to get to work, or something?"

"I have a few minutes. I wanted to see if you needed anything."

"We need everything, but I'll hit the grocery store after I shower. Uh…thanks again."

"Sure. I guess I can just take my breakfast to go."

Realization dawned. Embarrassment scorched her cheeks. "Oh. You're eating here?"

"Well, only if you don't mind. Then I can give Chastity a ride to school to save Pam the trip."

She mentally smacked her forehead. She hadn't even thought about how Chastity got to school. "She doesn't take the bus?"

"Hope wouldn't let her. Pam or my mom carpool the kids."

Hope had *insisted* Rachel ride the bus. "That's nice of you, Matt. You guys head to the kitchen. I'll join you as soon as I dress."

Her clothes—except for yesterday's outfit— were all wet in the washer. Her underwear and bra were drying in the bathroom after the hand wash she'd given them last night. She'd have to borrow something of Hope's after all.

Reluctantly, Rachel entered Hope's pristine room. She kept her eyes off the bed that her sister might have shared with Matt and dug through the dresser drawers until she found something she couldn't picture her sister wearing. Sure enough, the trendy blue jogging suit still had the tags attached. Rachel slipped it on and zipped the jacket, hoping the fabric was thick enough to conceal her lack of undergarments. It felt incredibly soft against her bare skin.

She detoured to brush her teeth and hair. One look at her pallor and the purple circles ringing her eyes, and she grimaced. The blue fabric did nothing to help her complexion, but the shade would have matched Hope's eyes perfectly.

Unable to delay any longer, she removed the tags, then returned to the kitchen. Matt and Chastity sat at the table with their heads bent in identical angles over separate sections of the newspaper. The similarities between them stopped her in her tracks. Chastity had inherited her father's mouth and chin. How could Matt not see that? Had anyone else in Johnstonville noticed? It seemed too obvious to miss.

Chastity looked up first. "You made the paper. Your homecoming has been officially announced in the community everybody-wants-to-know-your-business section."

Matt glanced up, then did a double take. His

gaze raked her from head to toe. His Adam's apple bobbed, and his lips compressed. Ever conscious of her lack of underwear and borrowed clothing, Rachel slid into a chair.

Chastity jumped to her feet, pitched her trash into the receptacle, and then headed down the hall.

"Where are you going?" Rachel called in alarm over her chaperone leaving.

"To brush my teeth."

Rachel didn't want to be alone with Matt. He cleared his throat and studied his coffee, trying not to look uncomfortable when he obviously was.

"What?" Rachel asked, a tad defensively.

Matt cupped the back of his neck, then met her gaze. "I bought that sweat suit for Hope last Christmas. We were going to start working out together."

She suddenly felt every inch of the fabric abrading her skin as if it were burlap. Picturing Matt and Hope together bothered her. A lot. She planted her palms on the table and rose. "I don't have any clean clothes. I had to borrow something."

He covered her hand. "Rachel, it's all right. I doubt she ever wore it anyway."

The heat of his flesh on hers stirred memories best left undisturbed. Her pulse hitched. She sat back down and grabbed the coffee. Her parents had never been much for physical displays of affection. She'd forgotten how much of a "toucher" Matt was. "I didn't know—"

"It was stupid to give it to her. She hated exercise."

"I know. I'm the one who was always working up a sweat."

His deep blue gaze caught hers. "I remember."

She hadn't meant the comment sexually, but judging by the way his pupils expanded, that was clearly the way he'd interpreted it. Warmth pulsed through her.

Fourteen years ago, they'd spent their time together jogging, rock climbing and canoeing—all pursuits that led them to isolated places where not even the winter chill had kept them from getting naked and sweaty together. They'd planned to try a lot more outdoor activities when he returned home for spring break. But that had never happened.

Matt stood, breaking the spell, and gathered his trash. She thought she saw him wince.

"Are you okay?"

"I'm fine, but Chastity and I have to go if we want to be on time. Tardy bell's at seven fifteen."

Rachel took a mental step back, suddenly overpowered by Matt's presence, the memories and regret. "Thanks for…all this."

"That's what neighbors are for. We look out for our own. Chastity, let's go," he called out. "I'll be in the truck."

The front door closed behind him, and Chastity thundered out with a "See ya" thrown over her shoulder.

"Wait. Do you need lunch money or anything?"

She stopped. "Yeah."

Rachel dug in her purse, handed Chastity some cash, then watched the pair drive away. Looking out for one's own, Matt called it. He had no idea.

Then the emptiness of Hope's house enveloped her. This had never been Rachel's home, but it had been as close to one as she'd ever gotten. And she had to let it go.

JOHNSTONVILLE HAD GROWN, but there was still only one grocery store, and her shopping excursion was every bit as uncomfortable as she'd expected. Fellow customers studied her as if she were a new strain of bacteria in the petri dish.

A few women spoke to her, but mostly they watched in silence through narrowed eyes. It was almost as if they expected her to strip naked and dash through the aisles or, at the very least, open packages and start eating before she paid for the goods. The latter she'd done back in the day. The former she hadn't, although she'd been tempted— just to see if the manager's bad toupee would fall off when he chased her out of the store.

"Why, Rachel Bishop, I do declare."

Rachel identified the sacchariney sweet Southern drawl and cringed. Debra Sue Jensen, one of the girls who'd done their best to make Rachel's

time here miserable. The nasty rumors Debra Sue
and her besties had thrived on had only increased
once Rachel had caught Matt's attention. Wishing
she could ignore her and walk away, Rachel instead pasted on a polite smile and turned to face
the debutante witch of Johnstonville High.

"Hello, Debra Sue."

"What a surprise to see you back in town."
She sneered at Rachel's wrinkled clothing as if
she knew it had come off the laundry room floor.
"That's a new look for you. Isn't it?"

Rachel bit her tongue on a waspy comeback.
She'd decided to wear her own dirty clothes rather
than an outfit Matt had bought for her sister. But
she couldn't help feeling at a distinct disadvantage next to the Barbie doll perfection of her old
nemesis.

"And you haven't changed a bit." Debra Sue
was still a bitch who dressed like the beauty con-
testant she'd once been. How many other women
donned four-inch heels and a designer outfit to
buy a loaf of bread?

"I hear you're Chastity's guardian now? But
then I guess Hope didn't really have a choice,
what with your parents gone and no man of her
own. But for that poor child to be thrust upon a
stranger—"

Anger sparked like flint. "I'm not a stranger.
I'm her aunt."

"I'm sure Hope thought she was doing what was best for Chastity to leave her with family, but—"

"She was. I couldn't love Chastity more if she were mine, and I'll always do my best for her. Hope knew that."

A stenciled eyebrow rose. "Let's hope your best is good enough. It never used to be." With that parting salvo, Debra Sue hiked her nose in the air, pivoted on her fancy heels and stalked off, leaving Rachel with a stranglehold on her temper and her shopping cart.

People like Debra made lingering in Johnstonville impossible. If that gossipmonger even suspected the truth, she'd spread her tales far and wide, not caring that Chastity could be hurt in the process.

Rachel would have to pack the essentials and hustle Chastity back to Atlanta by the end of the week. Sometime this summer they'd come back, finish packing and put the house on the market. Chastity might hate it in the short run, but in the long run it was better than the truth getting out and imploding her world. If that happened, Chastity would lose her mother all over again, and she would hate Rachel.

DETERMINED TO USE the empty house to her advantage, Rachel dug out her phone and dialed her supervisor.

"Hey, Rachel, which time zone are you in?"

"Same one as you, Marcia. I'm in North Carolina. My sister…passed away."

"So that's why the hospital called looking for you. I'm sorry, Rachel. What happened?"

"A car accident. Single vehicle versus tree. Speed and alcohol were not factors." She relayed the words the police officer had told her in a matter-of-fact tone and recognized what she was doing—distancing herself from the horrific event. She did a lot of that in her line of work.

"Is there anything I can do?"

Nervousness churned Rachel's stomach. "Actually, I need your help finding an apartment or a house to rent by Friday. Any chance you know of one in an area with good schools?"

"Schools?"

"I gained custody of my…niece."

"Wow. How old is she?"

"Chastity's thirteen going on thirty. Do you think the school your kids go to would take her?"

"Hmm. It is a rotten time to transfer a kid with final exams just weeks away, but given your situation and a few letters of recommendation from the staff here who have kids already enrolled, they probably would. I'll ask around about housing, and I'll text you the school's contact info."

"That would be great."

"If the private school can't help you, then the public schools in my area are pretty good. You're still coming back Monday, right?"

"That's the plan. Thanks, Marcia. I'll be in touch." Rachel disconnected. Getting out of Johnstonville ASAP was critical. But she dreaded Matt's and Chastity's reactions to her plan.

"WHAT ARE YOU DOING?" Chastity asked from the doorway, her wide eyes fixed on the dozen cardboard boxes Rachel had picked up at the hardware store on the way back from the grocer's.

Rachel's heart skipped a beat. She hadn't heard a car drive up. Was Matt here? She glanced out and saw a minivan pulling away from the curb. "I'm getting ready to pack. Want to help?"

"No."

Rachel sat back on her haunches and sighed. "Chastity, I need your input on what you want to take with you right now. We'll have to come back this summer for the rest."

"You said we could stay here." She thrust out her bloodred bottom lip.

"No. I said I'd think about staying temporarily. And I did. But it won't work." Rachel rose and crossed the room. She reached out to smooth Chastity's over-teased hair, but the teen shied away. "My boss needs me to get back to work."

"You can be a nurse in Johnstonville."

"There are no helicopter crews here. I love the job I have and my team."

"I'll stay here."

"That's not an option. I thought you were excited about house-hunting and shopping. You'll make new friends. The schools are really good in Atlanta and—"

"I like Johnstonville. I like *my* school."

"Of course you do. They're familiar and comfortable, but there are new and exciting adventures around the corner."

"I don't want adventures."

Rachel's frustration spiked. Her hands were tied. "We can't stay here. I know transitions are hard, but we'll make it work. You've always loved Atlanta."

"If I move now I'll be the new kid. I won't know anyone. Don't you remember how much you hated it when your parents moved you to new schools all the time? You're turning into them."

Rachel flinched at the direct hit. "You'll only move once."

"Then I'll have to start a new high school in the fall. That's two new schools in only a few months."

True. Rachel sighed. "Chas—"

"I want to graduate middle school here with my friends. Can't you wait until school's out? Then I won't be the only new kid when I start high school."

"I can't get five more weeks off work. I've already been gone almost four."

"Have you even tried?"

Rachel hesitated. "There's a shortage of Life Flight nurses because of the additional training and certifications required. I can't leave my team in the lurch. It's not fair to them."

"It's not fair to me to make me move now. We have a lot to do here. If we stay this summer we can take our time and do it right. And we won't have to come back."

She applauded Chastity's mature logic, but she couldn't risk staying. "We're leaving for Atlanta Friday morning. We can visit the schools that afternoon and start house-hunting on Saturday."

"You can't make me go. I'll stay with the Weavers. They said I was welcome. They're my real family. They've been here for me through everything. You haven't been around for five years. And you're only here now 'cuz Mom's dead, and you don't have a choice." Chastity whirled and raced outside. The screen door slammed behind her.

Rachel started after her, then stopped. Chastity needed time to calm down. Weighed down by guilt, she slumped into a kitchen chair. Every word Chastity had screamed had touched an exposed nerve. Rachel was nothing like her parents. Other than her working vacations abroad she was stable, established and involved in the same community year after year.

She knew what it was like to be torn away from friends and dumped into a situation where you were the odd one out. Her parents' missionary work had meant moving from one assignment to the next whenever the call came. Rachel's happiness had never been a consideration.

Hope's offer to let Rachel spend her senior year in the same place and attend the same *American* high school had been a blessing. But Rachel had sabotaged herself when she'd discovered her pregnancy in early February. Rather than face the scandal in Johnstonville, Hope had packed them up and moved to Atlanta. In the impersonal metropolis, Rachel had finished her last semester of school the way she'd done every previous year—among strangers. Then she'd given birth to her baby girl.

Throughout Rachel's pregnancy Hope had pointed out repeatedly that having a baby out of wedlock was the one sin their parents would never forgive and had urged Rachel not to tell them. Then her preachy sister had shocked and humbled her by offering to claim Rachel's baby and raise it as her own. At the time, adoption had seemed like the best solution. At least she'd get to see her baby grow up.

With her parents living overseas, there had been little chance of them uncovering the truth. And then when they'd died right before Chastity's birth, Rachel had taken the coward's way out and let Hope clean up her mistake. She'd never ceased to regret it.

And now her weakness then was coming back to haunt her.

Protecting Chastity and giving her time to graduate in Johnstonville were mutually exclusive goals. She'd talk to Chastity, and they'd work it out. The teen would come around. She had to.

FIGHTING PANIC, RACHEL took another lap around the den, then paused by the phone and stared at the number written on the pad. Matt's number. She didn't want to call him. But Chastity had been gone five hours, and driving around town had turned up no sign of her.

Matt was the only one who could help her. It shamed her that he knew more about her own daughter than she did. Heart thumping with dread, she reached for the phone.

Headlights hit the front window, and her pulse lurched. Would it be the police with Chastity or news of her? Specters of Rachel's past—all the times she'd put Hope through hell—danced in her head. She raced to the door and yanked it open. Chastity, scowling ferociously, stormed past her. Relief and anger, along with a mess of other emotions, tumbled through Rachel.

"Let her go," Matt said from the steps, adding to Rachel's turmoil. "I've already given her an earful about running off."

Torn between going after her daughter and following Matt's advice, she asked, "Where has she been?"

"Hiding out with Jessica. My sister called me. Chastity claims you're leaving for Atlanta Friday."

"I have a job and bills to pay. I have to get back."

"You don't own a car. You live in the slums. What kind of bills could you possibly have?"

Apparently Chastity had given him an earful, too. "I pay utilities like everyone else. I also have student loans and a retirement plan that are directly withdrawn from my account monthly. Not that it's any of your business."

"You can take four weeks off to go globe-trotting and care for strangers, but you can't take five weeks for your own niece? What'll it take to convince you to put her needs ahead of yours? That's what parenting is about."

He didn't know what he was asking and didn't understand that she *was* putting Chastity's welfare first. And she couldn't tell him the truth because it would destroy so many lives—his included.

"I'm out of vacation time."

"Then use your sick days or take a leave of absence. She'll only run away if you drag her to Atlanta. Pam heard her plotting with Jess. Are you willing to risk that?"

At the shelter, Rachel often worked with young girls who'd been living on the streets. Some were runaways. Some had been forced into prostitution via drugs. The churning in her stomach told her Matt was right. She would have to choose the lesser evil.

Against her better judgment she would have to stay in Johnstonville until she could convince Chastity that moving would be a good thing.

She hoped she didn't live to regret it.

CHAPTER FOUR

RACHEL ROLLED OUT of bed before sunup. Tension knotted her neck muscles, and her skull felt tight—the precursor of a migraine if she didn't intervene.

Committing to five more weeks in Johnstonville seemed like taking the first step on a very slippery slope. It meant risking her secret getting out. It meant seeing Matt. Her stomach swooped.

She had an hour before she had to wake up Chastity. That gave her plenty of time for a run to shake off the sense of doom hanging over her.

Her tank with the built-in bra and shorts with the sewn-in panty were the norm by Atlanta standards, yet who knew what was acceptable here? But she'd left her sweatpants with the village women, and she refused to wear Hope's clothes again. Her shorts and tank top would have to do.

She yanked her hair into a ponytail and peeked in on Chastity. Her heart tugged. Chastity looked so innocent with her cheeks flushed and hair spread across the pillow. But she had Rachel's short fuse—a lesson learned last night.

In the kitchen, Rachel scratched out a note and

stuck it to the refrigerator before stepping outside to work the kinks from her limbs. Staying in Johnstonville was akin to sweating the incubation period after exposure to a dreaded disease. She would hope for a good prognosis, knowing full well that any hour a full-blown disaster could strike.

She finished her warm-up, then headed down Hope's driveway. If it weren't for Chastity, Rachel would donate everything her sister had owned, put the house up for sale and be gone by noon.

She couldn't let the teen control her with threats of running away. But how could she tell whether Chastity was bluffing or serious? She and Chastity definitely had a few bugs to work out of their relationship.

Rachel's soles slapped the asphalt as she tried to outrun her fears. The burn in her chest pulled her head out of the what-ifs. She stepped onto the grassy shoulder of the road, propped her palms on her knees and struggled to catch her breath. Scanning her surroundings beneath the pinkening sky, she realized she had no idea where she was. None of the landmarks were familiar. How far had she run? She hadn't a clue, but she knew her pace had been too fast. How many turns had she taken? Two rights and a left? Or the opposite?

Great. She was lost. And she'd left her cell phone at home. She didn't want Chastity to leave for school without seeing her—especially not after last night's debacle.

The sound of fast footfalls caught her attention. Optimistically, she glanced up. Maybe the fellow jogger could give her directions. Then she recognized the runner—Matt—and groaned. He kept catching her at her worst. Not that she cared what she looked like since she wasn't trying to impress anyone—especially him. But at least she'd shaved her legs.

He, on the other hand, looked fit and fabulous, of course. He reached her side. Blue eyes scorched over her, kicking her pulse rate back into the danger zone. "Good morning, Rachel. You okay?"

"'Morning. I'm fine. Just working in some exercise."

He wore a tank and track pants. The damp fabric clung to an abundance of taut, tanned, muscled flesh and revealed impressive biceps. Golden chest hair showed above his neckline. The memory of how ticklish he'd been when she used to tease the silky strands beneath his arms and raked her nails over his rib cage blindsided her. Trying to banish the mental images of his bronzed body, she bent to stretch her tightening hamstrings.

"I'm glad I ran into you. My parents would like you and Chastity to come over after church Sunday."

Rachel jerked upright, her gaze hitting his in surprise and dismay. How could she look Matt's parents in the eye knowing she'd denied them their grandchild? "I don't think—"

"Mom insists. Besides, Chastity always enjoys our cookouts. Pam's and Jake's herds will be there."

Rachel vaguely remembered Matt's siblings. "Pam and Jake have kids?"

"Pam has three. Jake has two. They'd appreciate the company to even the numbers for volleyball and touch football."

Chastity had cousins. Cousins she could never claim. Guilt landed another punch in Rachel's solar plexus. "I'll check with Chastity."

"It's just lunch, Rachel. She already eats half her meals with Pam's daughter, Jessica."

Ahh, Jessica from last night. "Is this the same Jess who drives her mom's car?"

"Only on the family farm. Can I tell Mom you'll be there? Or do I need to send her over to invite you?"

She didn't want that. "Yeah…we'll be there."

"One o'clock." Matt looked as if he were waiting for her to move on.

She shifted in her shoes, reluctant to reveal her stupidity. She hated it even more when his gaze meandered over her sweat-soaked body again, making her feel as naked as she'd been the day she'd realized she loved him. "I'm, ah…not sure where I am. Could you give me directions?"

She gave him points for not laughing. "This is Barnhill's Dairy Road. It's been paved since you lived here, and neighborhoods have replaced pastures. But you've been down this road before. It leads to the creek."

Where they'd often made out in his truck. Her cheeks burned. "Gotcha."

"Go to the end of the street. Take the next two lefts. That'll get you back to Hope's."

"Thanks."

"You sure you're okay?"

"Yes."

"You have water?" He offered his bottle.

She didn't. "I'm good, *Coach*."

"Rachel—" he warned.

She couldn't let her pride wipe her out. "Maybe a sip."

He unscrewed the cap and handed the plastic to her. She drank, fully aware that his lips had been exactly where hers were now. It didn't help that he focused on her mouth. She gulped, then handed it back. He took the bottle and drank from it. Sharing seemed…intimate. But they'd shared so much more.

She cleared her throat. "Thanks. See ya."

"You're welcome." He nodded, then took off.

Rachel allowed herself a selfish moment to admire his backside and the strength of his long legs, then she yanked herself up by the hormones. It didn't matter if Matt still had the best body on three continents. She wasn't interested in resuming their relationship. And even if she were, she couldn't chance it.

MATT GRITTED HIS teeth against the pain and continued putting one foot in front of the other. If he could fake it thirty more yards, he'd be out of Rachel's sight.

He finally reached the corner, then checked over his shoulder to confirm the coast was clear and collapsed against the first big oak tree. What in the hell had possessed him to sprint and catch up with her? He shouldn't have been running without the knee brace. But when Rachel had raced past his window as if she was running for her life, he'd dropped his free weights, grabbed his water bottle and hauled butt after her.

A high-pitched yap alerted him that he wasn't alone. Mrs. Hines and her twin yippy dogs were coming his way. The sympathy in her smile and pity in her eyes wrenched his gut. *Pity*, for crissakes. He could handle anything but that.

"'Morning, Matthew. Where's Buddy?"

He'd left so fast he'd forgotten his dog. "At home basking in the sun."

"Knee bothering you today?"

He cursed his weakness and his need to conceal his limitations from people. Forcing a smile, he answered, "No. I'm good, thanks. You're up early."

"My babies wanted their walk. Are you sure you're okay? That was a mighty fierce scowl on your face."

"I'm fine. But thanks for your concern."

"My arthritis acts up when a storm front moves

in. Maybe your injury does, too. I can call your mother if you need a ride home. I'm sure she's already up and in her garden."

That was the last thing he wanted. Mom would kick into overprotective mode, and she'd lecture all the way home. "The exercise is good for me."

"If you're sure."

"I am. Anyway, I have to set an example for my players. Have a good day, Mrs. Hines. I better head home if I'm going to make it to school on time."

She patted his biceps. "You're still our star, Matthew. Don't you ever forget that."

Humiliation scalded his neck. "Yes, ma'am."

He waved and walked away fighting every step not to limp.

"Your house is the other way, son."

He winced. "I'm going around the block, then cutting through the cemetery." Otherwise he might run into Rachel again. He didn't want her to see him like this. At least she'd dumped him before he'd crashed and burned on the field. The play had tangled up in his head that fateful day. Dyslexia was like that. Twisting things.

Usually, he could compensate, but sometimes when he was stressed, tired or distracted, things mixed up, and that day he'd thought he'd spotted Rachel in the stands. He'd been sacked, his knee destroyed, and just that quickly, his promising career had ended. Washed up at twenty-three. He'd returned to college for an advanced degree because he couldn't bear going home a failure. When he had come back, the pity in the townsfolks' eyes had burned him like acid. But he'd channeled his discomfort into being the best damned coach and athletic director he could be, and his team had made the championship again this year. He'd given the good citizens of Johnstonville another reason to be proud of him.

On the walk home the image of Rachel distracted him. Her body had matured well. Her legs were as sleek as he remembered, but she'd added lean muscles, and her breasts were larger. Not even a top that flattened them could hide her pebbled nipples.

His knee and crotch screamed for attention. He needed a cold shower and the ice pack he kept waiting in the freezer. Damn, he hated weakness. Almost as much as he hated realizing he wasn't over Rachel Bishop.

RACHEL PALMED HER PHONE, knowing she was about to make her boss and the rest of her team very unhappy. She hoped Marcia wouldn't fire her. She loved and needed her job, even if she hadn't yet figured out who'd watch Chastity during her shifts.

Marcia answered on the first ring. "Hey, Rachel. Home yet?"

She took a deep breath, as if preparing to dive from a high cliff. "No. I'm going to need more time off."

Silence. "How much more time?"

"Five weeks. Chastity isn't taking to the idea of changing schools. She wants to finish here… to make the transition easier." Empty air greeted her words. Rachel's pulse pounded her eardrums.

"You're putting us in a tough spot."

"I know, and I'm sorry. It isn't fair to ask others to pick up my slack. But this is important." Marcia was a mother with children close to Chastity's age. Maybe she'd have answers. "Chastity's threatening to run away if I force the move. I know it's a power play, but she's only thirteen, and I can't watch her 24/7 and make sure she doesn't follow through with her threat. Marcia, I don't know what to do."

A heavy sigh filled Rachel's ear. "You'll learn. She's at a difficult age. I'm there with my daughter, too. Chastity's a smart kid to hit you with the one thing you can't control. Let me think…" Marcia paused for just a few seconds. "Gaining custody is like an adoption. And I believe you can apply for family medical leave over the internet. That'll keep your health insurance intact and free me up to hire a temp until you return."

Relief flooded Rachel. She didn't have a computer, but she'd find one, even if it meant hanging out in the public library. "Thank you for understanding. I'll do it ASAP. And again, I apologize."

"Do what's best for your niece. We'll muddle through until you get back."

"I'm going to need another favor when we get

there… I'll need help finding someone to watch her during my shifts."

"I'll line up some possibilities."

"You're a lifesaver, Marcia."

Weak-kneed, Rachel sank into a chair. She'd be stuck in Matt's hometown for five more weeks. But not one day more.

CHASTITY'S HUMMING PROVED her excitement over the upcoming picnic. Rachel only wished she could share the enthusiasm. "You promise you won't give me grief in five weeks' time?"

"I promised like three times already. You don't have to keep asking."

Rachel *had* asked several times, but she was extremely nervous about the potential fallout if things went sour.

The Johnstons' house came into view. The white home with its black shutters and wraparound porch, decorated with hanging baskets overflowing with blossoms, represented every fantasy Rachel had ever had of a happy, normal home. She couldn't recall her parents ever having a permanent residence. When they'd lived in the States they'd been dependent on the church to provide temporary accommodations, because they were always waiting for the next mission, the next cause. They'd literally owned nothing except for their clothes and necessities.

Her stomach tensed and her hands tightened on

the steering wheel. The Johnstons had always represented the perfect family—the kind she'd wished she had—and she dreaded looking them in the eye, knowing how she'd wronged them.

It always came back to the mistakes she'd made. No matter how many good things she'd done since that traumatic turning point in her life, she felt as if she'd always be the screwup who'd tainted everyone and everything in her path. She'd disappointed her parents, made her saintly sister lie and hadn't been good enough to raise her own daughter.

She parked the car. Chastity launched from the vehicle and raced around the side of the house, leaving Rachel alone with her doubts. She forced herself to get out of the car and ordered her feet forward. They hesitantly complied. Then Matt came around the corner. Her heart crashed into her rib cage, and her courage fled.

With the sun glinting off his golden hair and the sky-blue color of his polo shirt accentuating his eyes, Matt looked every inch the all-American male, the hometown hero. Her mouth dried and her pulse raced. Apparently the old saying was true. A girl never forgot her first love.

"Glad you made it."

Rachel forced a smile, pretending she was happy to be there. She tugged at the suddenly tight neck of her T-shirt and smoothed a hand over her shorts to wipe her sweat-dampened palms, then used the excuse of stuffing her key and wallet into her pockets to avoid his outstretched hand. "Chastity was as thrilled as you predicted."

"You could have joined us at church."

"We were packing." She hadn't set foot in a church since the day she'd given birth. That day she'd stopped by the hospital chapel to beg forgiveness for her selfish ways and vowed to put others first from that moment forward if God would look out for her daughter. He'd upheld his end of the deal, and she had hers.

"Come on back." He held open the gate to a white picket fence. She sidled through the gap, being careful not to touch him. He represented everything she couldn't have and didn't deserve. No point in torturing herself. The gate snapped shut behind them, startling her with the finality of that clang.

A dozen people occupied the backyard, giving Rachel a serious case of stage fright. Chastity and a blond-haired girl sat poolside, dangling their feet in the water and leaning close to whisper. A couple of men, beers in hand, guarded the grill, and several giggling, squealing children played in a water sprinkler on the lawn.

Chastity fit right in here. But Rachel had denied her the opportunity to be part of this rambunctious, happy family. Would they have accepted "Rachel the Rebel's daughter"?

A woman with the same golden hair as Matt's, albeit glinting with silver strands in the sunlight, came toward them. Rachel identified Matt's mother even though they'd never met. Carol Johnston had passed on her chiseled lips and determined chin to her son and granddaughter. How could they not see the resemblance? The knot of guilt tightened in Rachel's belly.

"Rachel, welcome. I'm Carol, and I've been looking forward to meeting Chastity's idol." She grasped Rachel's hand and patted the back of it.

Thrown by the comment, Rachel blinked. "Her idol?"

"Chastity talks about you nonstop. Practically every conversation is peppered with 'Aunt Rachel this and Aunt Rachel that.' You are her hero."

Rachel's joy was quickly doused by the knowledge that Hope must have hated that as much as Rachel had hated living in her saintly sister's shadow.

Rachel stuffed her fists into her pockets as soon as Carol released her. "I guess it's just her age. My job and travel probably sound exotic."

"Or it could be she sees you're out there making a difference in the world. It's harder to do that here in Johnstonville."

Matt frowned. "How do you know all this?"

Carol shrugged. "Chastity and Jessica are practically inseparable. When they talk, I listen like a good nana. It's the only way to know what they're plotting. And from the stories Chastity tells, you're far braver than I am, Rachel."

Chastity got to spend time with her grandmother even if she didn't know it. Had Hope arranged that on purpose? "I'm sure Chastity enjoys her time here and that Hope appreciated your help."

Carol's smile fell. "We'll certainly miss Hope. I'm not sure what the Church Women's Auxiliary will do without her. She was a powerhouse of ideas and energy."

Carol embraced her. Rachel froze in surprise. Hugs hadn't been a part of her life. She wasn't sure how to respond. Before she could figure it out, Carol withdrew. "I need to make sure the men aren't charring our lunch. Matt will get you something to drink and introduce you to everyone. You might remember Pam. She graduated a couple of years ahead of you. And Jake was a year behind you."

Rachel dreaded the introductions. Did Matt's siblings remember the rumors? Debra Sue and her cronies had told anyone who'd listen that Rachel had slept with half the males in the senior class.

A slender blonde with pixie-cut hair met Rachel and Matt halfway across the lawn. "I'm Pam. We're so glad you could make it."

"Thank you, and thanks for taking care of Chastity last night and for all you've done since Hope's…passing."

Pam took Rachel's hand and squeezed it. "My pleasure. Chastity is always welcome at our house.

I know you're both going through a tough time now. If you need an ear…just call."

The sincere kindness in Pam's eyes thickened Rachel's throat. "Thank you."

Pam linked her arm through Rachel's, led her to the tables and introduced her to the other adults. Bill, Matt's father, had given both Matt and Jake his tall, athletic build. Rachel vaguely remembered Jake from the one time he'd tried to tag along with them to the lake. She'd never met his wife, Leann.

The Johnstons' warm welcome was overwhelming, given how badly she'd wronged them. To keep her mind off her guilt, Rachel studied the interactions between the Johnston siblings. She and Hope had never shared anything like the camaraderie and gentle, teasing barbs she observed between them.

Matt's father refilled Rachel's glass. "It's amazing what kids will come up with to get a little attention. Take those two." He nodded toward Chastity and Jessica now swinging on a wide wooden bench hanging from a massive oak branch. "They're trying to decide between getting their navels or tongues pierced."

Brad, Pam's husband, nearly tipped over his chair. "Over my dead body."

Rachel agreed. "Several of the native tribes I've worked with practice body piercing. I can show the girls pictures of the infections the medical team treated. That might change their minds."

"I would appreciate that," Pam said. "As we both know, forbidding them is the best way to guarantee they'll find someone who'll do it for them."

No, Rachel didn't know that, but she put the tip in her mental file cabinet. She had a lot to learn about being a mother. Then Pam's eyes met hers across the table, and Rachel felt an unexpected kinship with Matt's sister. But it was a friendship that could never develop. Friends didn't lie to each other.

Carol intercepted their exchange. "Pam was our rebel. Like you, Rachel, she seemed determined to stir up trouble."

Mortification stung Rachel's cheeks. Foolishly, she'd allowed herself to believe that everyone had forgotten what an immature brat she'd been.

"Remember the Mohawk?" Jake said.

Matt's father shook his head. "The one that got me was the tattoo on your—"

"Daddy, shush." Pam looked panic-stricken. "The kids don't know about that."

"We probably wouldn't have, either, if it hadn't gotten infected," Carol interjected. "But you refusing to sit down and the disappearance of my frozen bag of peas was a bit suspicious. And your insistence on going to a doctor out of town was even more telling."

The family laughed, but for Rachel the idyllic mood had been shattered. No one seemed to consider Pam a bad seed. But Pam's misdeeds hadn't come close to Rachel's, and Pam had only hurt herself.

Hope had always fixed Rachel's mistakes, but she'd also troweled on the guilt, making sure Rachel realized the effort it took and how disappointed she was in her. Their parents had responded with oppressive silence. One thing had never been in doubt. Rachel's recklessness had been a nuisance—such a bother her parents had sent her away.

"I'm proud of all my children. Jake works at the bank. Pam's a nurse with Dr. Miller's practice in town. Now that Matt's back home, all I have to do is get him married, and my job will be done."

Matt choked on his tea. Jake laughed and slapped Matt's back until he stopped wheezing. "She won't let up until you've given her a few grandkids, bro. Might as well bite the bullet."

Another shard of guilt pierced Rachel's conscience. She focused on Matt. "You've been away?"

Pam nodded. "Matt was a football star before—"

"In college," Matt interrupted. "Rachel knows that." The others around the table exchanged looks. What did Matt not want her to know?

"I moved home to take the job at Johnstonville High when my old coach retired. I might have stayed gone if I'd known Mom's evil plan." His teasing grin was a shade too tight.

"Do you follow sports, Rachel?" Jake asked.

"Baseball. I'm a Braves fan."

"You catch many games?" Bill asked.

"I have season tickets."

Pam's husband whistled. "Expensive."

"But worth every penny. I use them to motivate the kids in my neighborhood. If they stay drug free, out of gangs, and work hard to earn good grades, I reward them with tickets to a game."

"Does that work?" Pam asked.

"It's been so successful I've had to recruit businesses from the surrounding communities to sponsor blocks of tickets at progress report time."

She caught Matt's speculative gaze. "Inner-city kids?"

"They're often the ones who can't afford to attend."

"You're missing games while you're here," Jake said.

"I've left the tickets in good hands."

"You've never followed football?" That earned Jake a fierce scowl, and from the way he jumped, Rachel suspected Matt had kicked his brother under the table.

"No. As a missionaries' kid, I didn't have an opportunity to watch or play sports. I didn't get into baseball until I was older." And after Matt, she hadn't watched a single football game. She'd always been afraid she'd see him on the field, or worse, with some cheerleader in his arms after a game.

Bill's cell phone rang. He glanced at it. "Looks

like the mayor doesn't get a day of rest even on Sunday. Excuse me." He left to take the call.

Matt's dad was the mayor?

The bantering continued, but the atmosphere had changed. Was it because of the phone call? Or the conversation before it?

By late afternoon Rachel was emotionally exhausted from being on guard. It was a relief when Pam rounded up her kids.

After she and Chastity said their goodbyes, Matt walked them to the car. He leaned in the window while she buckled her seat belt. His handsome face was close enough for her to see the silver flecks mingling with the blue of his irises, close enough for her to be overwhelmed by the scent of sunshine, aftershave and man. Close enough for her to lean forward and brush his mouth with hers—if she dared. But she didn't.

"Thanks for coming," he said.

Her heart and respiratory rates increased. "I—We had a good time," she replied huskily and surprisingly, meant it.

Chastity pushed the button to lower the convertible top, making Matt spring back and breaking the connection between Matt and Rachel.

"See you at school tomorrow, Coach."

"But not in detention."

"No, sir. Second offenders get litter patrol, and I'm not real keen on picking up trash."

"And third offenders get stuck cleaning the boys' locker room after practice," he warned.

"Eew. Gross."

"You have no idea," he added with a comical face.

He had an easy way with the kids that Rachel envied. Would she ever be that relaxed and comfortable with her daughter?

Rachel drove away, watching him in the rearview mirror. He was still standing where she'd left him when they turned the corner. Chastity deserved a family *like* the Johnstons, but giving her this one meant taking away so much more. Everything Chastity believed about herself was based on lies.

Why did doing the right thing feel so wrong?

CHAPTER FIVE

CHASTITY BURST THROUGH the front door Monday after school and stopped to stare at the pile of boxes in the den.

"Hi. Have a good day?"

Rachel's greeting earned her a drop-dead glare, then Chastity threw her book bag on the sofa and tromped off. Rachel's excitement over their afternoon together crashed and burned.

She may be new at this parenting thing, but she'd had enough run-ins with teens at the center to know she must be firm and stand her ground. Girding herself for the encounter ahead, she rose slowly.

She walked down the hall and blocked Chastity's bedroom door with her palm before it slammed in her face. "Chastity, what's wrong?"

"Nothing," Chastity snapped back, then sat at her makeup table and turned her back.

"Listen, kiddo, I won't tolerate disrespect. Either you adjust your attitude or all deals are off, and I'll pack you up and move you to Atlanta today."

The girl spun around, radiating defiance. "I'll just run away."

Rachel tamped down her panic. She'd learned from the counselors she'd worked with that threats to leave were often empty. She couldn't back down again, or this would become a way for Chastity to control her. She'd have to talk tough and try to be convincing.

"If you run away I'll report you, and if you're lucky enough for the cops to find you before some thug rapes you or forces you into prostitution, then you'll spend time in juvenile detention. That means you won't be coming home to your friends. You'll be locked up. And just so you know, asking Jessica's family to help you would get them charged with contributing to the delinquency of a minor." At least she thought it would.

Chastity's eyes widened, then she gulped. "You wouldn't report me. Or them."

"Yes, I would. I love you. Your mother entrusted me with your care. I'm going to do my best to keep you safe—by whatever means at my disposal. Stunts like the other night's when you took off without telling me where you were going, when you'd be home or how to reach you will not be tolerated."

"You'd be able to reach me if I had a cell phone." More defiance, but this time with manipulation thrown in for good measure.

"I'm not rewarding you for bad behavior. If you

keep this up, you'll get the opposite—grounded for the rest of our time here." She inhaled slowly, then exhaled, grappling for patience, strength and the right words. "Let's try this again. What's wrong?"

Tense silence stretched until she believed she'd have to enforce her threat. "I had a shitty day," Chastity blurted. "And then I came home and you were packing."

Rachel debated reprimanding her for swearing but feared it would put up another wall. "You knew we'd be packing. So what went wrong before you got here?"

Chastity slicked on a fresh coat of black nail polish. "My English teacher is having problems with her pregnancy. She has to stay in bed, so today we got our new teacher for the rest of the year. He made me look like an idiot."

The automatic urge to defend her child roared to life. But Rachel reined it in. She needed facts first. "Was it Matt?"

"No. Mr. Gold is some fresh-out-of-school weirdo who thinks he knows everything."

"How did he make you look foolish?"

"He made me read out loud in front of the class."

"Reading aloud is pretty standard stuff."

"My other teachers never make me do it. I suck at it."

"Suck how?"

Chastity shifted restlessly and wouldn't meet Rachel's gaze. "I just do."

The reaction seemed over the top. "How did acting up here solve your problem at school?"

Chastity shot her a fierce scowl but remained mute.

"If reading aloud is an issue for you, then your best bet is to speak to the teacher privately. I'll go with you if you like."

"No," she answered a little too quickly. "I'll handle it myself."

"If you change your mind, let me know. Now, I need help getting things down from the attic before you start your homework. Please." She tacked on the last politely but firmly, letting Chastity know her assistance wasn't optional.

The teen sighed as if greatly put out. "I'll mess up my nails."

"Then you can redo them after homework. If you have time."

Chastity followed Rachel into the hall. Rachel ignored her sullen attitude and pulled down the attic stairs. "The attic is too hot and dimly lit for us to examine the contents up there. So I'll pass the boxes down to you. Stack them along the wall in the dining room, then later, we'll go through them and sort the contents into keep and donate piles."

"Whatever," Chastity muttered with zero enthusiasm.

Rachel ascended the ladder and headed for the neat pile of boxes in the far corner. She carried them one by one across the plywood floor and handed them down without doing more than a cursory check for spiders.

When she returned with the eleventh box, Chastity was gone. "Hey! Where'd you go?" No answer. "Chastity?"

"What's all this?" came the muffled reply, the previous belligerence missing from Chastity's tone.

Rachel looked through the opening and spotted the teen sitting on the floor with a pile of photographs scattered around her. Rachel descended the steps. Her breath snagged in her chest when she recognized the shots.

Each time they'd vacationed together Rachel had asked bystanders to take pictures of the three of them. And sometimes Hope had used Rachel's camera to take pictures of Rachel with Chastity. Rachel had always gotten extra prints made and mailed the duplicates to Hope. And here they were. Crammed in a dusty box in the attic, their edges yellowed and curling from the heat.

"You've never seen these before?"

"No. There are a lot of them. You're in most of them."

Rachel sank onto the floor beside her. "You, your mom and I used to vacation together."

"I kinda remember that. I wish we hadn't stopped."

"Me, too, kiddo. I guess your mom got too busy with work and volunteering."

"She said *you* were too busy for *us*." Eyes so much like Rachel's glared accusingly at her.

Rachel shook her head. "No. Never."

"You could have come here."

How did she explain Hope had banned her from Johnstonville? "Your mom didn't want that."

"Why?"

What could she say without blackening Hope's name? Rachel shrugged and dodged the question by reaching into the box. The grinning gap-toothed face staring at her made her chest ache. "This was your sixth birthday."

"How can you tell? There are no candles."

"You were pony-crazy that year. I spent days making that pony-shaped cake. The candles were in the mini banana bread loaves decorated like hay bales that you can't see in this shot."

"You baked my cake?"

"Every year."

They went through the entire box, culminating in Chastity's eighth birthday—their last family vacation. In photo after photo the love in Rachel's face was plain to see. Was that why Hope hadn't shared the pictures with Chastity?

That, in addition to the visiting ban, made Rachel wonder if Hope had been trying to erase her from Chastity's life. But no. Hope had been too good-hearted to do that. Hadn't she? She'd helped Rachel too many times to be that petty.

"Mom said you were probably chasin' a man and couldn't be bothered with family."

The unjustness of the unexpected attack robbed her breath. She struggled for composure and the right words. "I wasn't. And for the record, I don't chase men."

"But you have before."

What kind of tales had Hope told? Had her virtuous sister lied about more than Chastity's parenthood? "Once."

"Once?" Chastity's disbelief was obvious. "Mom said—"

"Chastity, I've only chased one man in my life, and I caught him." Rachel immediately regretted the outburst. The last thing she needed was for Chastity to ask more questions, but Hope's betrayal stunned, hurt and angered her.

"So where is he now?"

Rachel frowned at Chastity's smart-alecky tone. "I wasn't the right woman for him."

"Did he dump you or turn out to be a jerk? Was he married? Or gay?"

"No. He was perfect. Too perfect for somebody like me."

"What's that supposed to mean?"

Rachel didn't relish rehashing her mistakes. Chastity wasn't old enough to understand. Maybe one day…but not tonight. "It means I haven't always made the right choices."

Chastity rolled her eyes. "Mom never made mistakes."

Did the edge in Chastity's voice mean she'd had as much trouble with Hope's perfection as Rachel had? "Everybody makes mistakes. Some mistakes are more obvious than others."

"Try selling that idea to the principal."

A smile tweaked Rachel's mouth. "Just do your best, okay? And always try to do the right thing. That's all you can do."

Chastity flipped through the earliest photos one more time. "I don't remember any of these trips."

"When we have more time I'll tell you about them. I have more pictures back at my place."

"You do love me."

Shocked, she leaned back. "Of course I do. I have from the minute I learned about you."

"Mom said—" Chastity stopped and ducked her head, her hair fell forward, shielding her face. "I thought you didn't love me because I'm not perfect like Mom."

Rachel's heart ached. She tucked a dark lock behind Chastity's ear, and the teen looked up with a face full of regret. "Neither am I, Chastity. Not even close."

"I'm sorry for saying you're not my real family."

Rachel's throat tightened. "Apology accepted. Remember, nobody's perfect. We all make mistakes. We all say things we shouldn't. It happens."

Chastity blinked her over-bright eyes and shook

off Rachel's hand on her shoulder. "I better start my homework. Can I keep these?"

"Absolutely. I'll get an album for them tomorrow if you want, and after school we can fill the pages."

"That would be cool."

Together they returned the photos to the box, then Chastity carried them to her room. Rachel heaved a sigh of relief. This was the kind of relationship she'd yearned for with her dau—niece. She hoped more would follow.

THE DOORBELL RANG Tuesday morning as Rachel was pouring her first cup of coffee. She checked the clock on the microwave. Pam was early for carpool. And usually she just tooted the horn.

Shoving back her hair, Rachel crossed the den and opened the front door. Matt stood on the porch. Her stomach took a nosedive to her bare feet.

"G'morning. Is Chastity ready?" His gaze ran over her, and she wanted to hide. He'd caught her at a disadvantage. Again. She must look awful. She'd barely slept last night after discovering Hope's betrayal.

"Where's Pam?"

"Johnathan woke up sick. She's taking the morning off to stay with him. Jessica was supposed to call Chastity to let her know that I'm the DD and my ETA."

"I haven't heard the phone ring. I don't know if Chastity's ready. I'll check." She stepped away from the door, and he followed. She didn't know how to politely ask him to stay outside. He glanced past her, his gaze landing on the pile of boxes. "What's all this?"

"Stuff to donate. I need to find a charity that will take it."

"It won't fit in that fancy red convertible you're driving. How will you get it there?"

"I'll figure it out."

"I can help you haul it. But not tonight. I have Scouts."

"Scouts? Aren't you a little old for that?"

"I'm a troop leader."

Of course he was.

"The church sponsors a thrift shop in town. I'll come by tomorrow night and help you carry all this over there."

Alarm bells rang in her subconscious. "That's not necessary. The car's a rental. I can probably trade it in for something larger."

"Suit yourself. The offer stands."

Why was he being nice when she'd done nothing to deserve it?

The bedroom door burst open behind her. "'Mornin', Coach," Chastity called out, then hustled through the kitchen, grabbed a breakfast bar, a small bottle of orange juice and joined them.

She wore slightly less makeup than usual—a positive change.

"Good morning. Let's head out." His gaze locked on Rachel's. "Later." And then they were gone.

She sincerely hoped she wouldn't see him again today. Adrenaline drained from her, and regret took its place. Matt was great with kids and generous with his time. He would have been the perfect husband.

For Hope.

THE HOUSE PHONE rang as Rachel stepped out of the shower. She grabbed a towel and hustled to the kitchen to answer it. "Hello?"

"Rachel, it's Pam. I'm in a bind, and I need a favor."

Why would Matt's sister call her? "What kind of favor?"

"Matt probably mentioned I'm at home with a sick child this morning. Mom's my usual backup, but she has an appointment she can't miss. I need someone to run Dr. Miller's office until Mom can take over for me here and I can get in to work. Lunchtime. No later."

Getting involved with Hope's community didn't seem like a good idea. And one-on-one time with the townsfolk was risky. But how could she refuse? Pam had been so good to Chastity.

"Pam, I'm not licensed in North Carolina."

"I know you can't do a lot of things, but it would

help tremendously if you could answer the phone, triage the patients and prep them. Stuff like that. Just the basics."

Rachel cringed. Yes, she had done that plenty of times in the past both overseas and at the clinic. But still… "Doesn't he have other staff who can pitch in?"

"It's a one-man/one-woman office. Please, Rachel. He's not busy this morning, but a male doctor shouldn't see female patients alone and all that legal garbage. In return I'll help you sort Hope's stuff. Matt says you're working on a donation pile for the church. I knew Hope well enough to know what she'd want to save for Chastity."

Blackmail. And, unfortunately, it was effective. Admitting defeat, Rachel reached for the pen and paper. Matt's name and number were scrawled on the top sheet beneath the neighbor's. She fought an odd urge to brush her fingers over his writing and flipped to the second page. "Tell me where I need to be and when."

She jotted down the address and directions, then checked her watch. In a town as small as Johnstonville she could be there in twenty minutes. "I'm on it."

"Thank you! Oops. Gotta run. Johnathan's heaving again."

The line went dead. Rachel hoped she wouldn't regret this.

RACHEL SAGGED IN relief when Dr. Miller hung the closed-for-lunch sign on the office door.

"Glad that's over," he said with an engaging smile. He was in his midforties and not unattractive. There was no Mrs. Miller in the picture—or so more than one of his patients had informed her. Rachel didn't need to know that, and she wouldn't speculate on why he wasn't married. It wasn't her business, and she wouldn't be here long enough for that to change.

"I'm sorry I wasn't more help. I didn't even get vitals on most of the patients.

"No apology needed. I'm the one who told you I'd work anyone in who called. I never know when a patient will be a genuine emergency, so I don't turn them away. You barely had time to take their names, pull their files and get them to the treatment rooms for answering the phone. Besides, I'm not so old that I've forgotten how to use a blood pressure cuff or thermometer, although I admit to being a little rusty," he added with a rueful shrug. "You are certainly good for business, Rachel."

A warning prickle crept up her spine. "You're not usually this busy?"

"Not even close. We're a quiet little office. Only two of today's work-ins were actually ill. The rest were here to check you out." He leaned a hip against the counter. "So let me see if the gossips got the gist of it right. You lived here before with your sister." It was a statement, not a question.

Nerves snarled in her stomach. She should have known if the patients would gossip *to* her, they'd gossip *about* her. "For six months many years ago when I was in high school."

"Then Hope moved to Atlanta and worked in a big firm. She rented her house because she couldn't sell it and returned two years later, a widow with a baby, claiming big business wasn't for her. But you weren't with her."

She tried not to let her uneasiness show. "I stayed to attend college."

"Must have been hard for Hope, having a premature infant with no husband for emotional support. How early was Chastity?"

Rachel had no idea what Hope had told everyone. The lie had been a sore point for her sister, and she'd refused to discuss it. Making up something would be dangerous—especially with a doctor. Rachel had to be very careful.

"I don't recall exactly."

The door opened, and Pam rushed in. "Oh, good. Rachel, you're still here. I brought lunch. We can share while you catch me up on the morning. I heard it was hectic."

Rachel had never experienced claustrophobia in her life, but she suspected the desperate need to escape clawing through her right now might be how it felt.

"Thanks for lunch, but I promised to pick up

something for Chastity today, and if I intend to be home before she gets there I need to get going."

"That's too bad." Pam seemed genuinely disappointed. "I'll come over as soon as I can, and we'll sort Hope's things, and you can tell me about some of your adventures."

"Great." She grabbed her purse and made a hasty exit. No doubt about it, the citizens of Johnstonville knew more about Hope's cover story than Rachel did. She wanted more details and had no way to get them except by listening to gossip.

CHAPTER SIX

RACHEL HEARD A car turn into the driveway and headed for the front door eager to go through the pictures with Chastity again while they put them into the scrapbook she'd bought.

The door opened before she reached it. But Chastity wasn't alone. Jessica was hot on her heels, and Matt shadowed them both. Her pulse leaped. What was *he* doing here?

"We have to work on our social studies project," Chastity said before Rachel could ask.

"'Beauty Around the World,'" Jessica added. "My mom said you might have pictures from your trips abroad that we could use about what women do to make themselves pretty in other cultures."

Rachel mentally connected the dots. "I do."

"You have them with you?" Chastity persisted. "You only brought a duffel bag. With three outfits in it." She sneered at Rachel's attire.

Rachel ignored the dig about her wardrobe. She pointed skyward. "My pictures are up there, in the Cloud."

She'd learned the hard way that a remote server

was the only way to guarantee her pictures and documents made it home. Flash drives got lost, broken or, in some cases, confiscated by paranoid governments. "But I don't have a computer, and I need one to sign into my account and download the pictures."

"You could use mine," Chastity offered. "I'll get it." Then she darted toward her room.

Jessica followed, leaving Rachel alone with Matt. Tongue-tied, she stared at him and wished she had something intelligent to say, but her conversation vault was empty. His blue eyes were alert and watchful. Was he holding something behind his back?

"While this *is* a school project, their underlying motive is to gain ammunition in their case for piercings, in case you haven't guessed. Mom caught them looking at pictures of navel jewelry."

"I suspected as much." The album grew heavier in her hand. She had to get rid of Matt before Chastity brought out the pictures. If he saw them he might notice the resemblance between Rachel's younger self and Chastity today. "Thanks for bringing her home."

"I have strict orders to make sure you don't mind Jess staying until Pam gets here. If you do, I'll take Jess to my place."

Where was that? So she could avoid it. But she couldn't ask. "She's welcome. Anytime."

He glanced toward the dining room. "No progress on packing?"

"Nope. I covered for Pam this morning."

Dark golden eyebrows hiked. "At Dr. Miller's office?"

"Yes."

One corner of his mouth lifted, sending a corresponding wisp of desire through her. "That must have been interesting."

Not the word she'd choose to describe the interrogations she'd endured. "Yes."

"Now I know why Pam insisted you'd need chocolate." His wink made her pulse skip, then he produced a bakery box from behind his back. "Brownies. For you and the girls."

She remembered the time he'd brought his mother's homemade brownies on one of their long-ago dates, and an assortment of other small gifts on each meeting thereafter. It had been the first and only time anyone had spoiled her like that. Rachel snuffed the memories and accepted the box. "The girls will love them. Thanks for… everything. See you around."

"Trying to get rid of me, Rachel?"

She willed herself not to blush, but the warmth in her face told her she'd failed. "You must have things to do…papers to grade or something."

"I'm the coach, the athletic director and sometimes a substitute teacher or detention monitor. I don't grade papers. *And* I'm forbidden to leave without inviting you to our church softball game tomorrow night."

More time with the Johnstonville grillers, as she'd dubbed the nosy patients. "I appreciate the invite, but I can't. Stuff to do." She jerked a thumb toward the pile in the dining room.

"I can't take 'no' for an answer. Chastity usually attends our games."

"Softball games?" Chastity chirped as she returned with her laptop. "Love 'em. We'll be there to cheer you on. I want to introduce Aunt Rachel to my friends. Ooh, you brought brownies?"

"Yes. Pam will be here around six," Matt said. "Work hard, girls." He tossed a wave and left.

"Is that the photo album?" Chastity asked.

"Yes. I bought pens and decorations, too. We can turn this into a scrapbooking project."

Chastity squealed with excitement, set the brownies on the coffee table and took the scrapbook from Rachel. "Cool. Jess, you have to see these pictures!"

Nerves bunched in Rachel's belly. Teens talked. A lot. "We can work on the scrapbook another time. Focus on your project today."

"Pictures first."

"Work first. Play later," Rachel insisted. "Fix your snacks while I download the pictures."

Groaning in chorus, the girls retreated to the kitchen.

Rachel sagged. Her plan to avoid Matt seemed

destined to fail. So why did a prickle of anticipation over seeing him again flood her veins?

"THIS IS GOING to be the best presentation ever! Thanks, Aunt Rachel," Chastity said as she closed her laptop and rose from the kitchen table.

"You're welcome."

"Some of those pics were nasty," Jessica added, neatly stacking their papers. "We'd never let our belly buttons get infected like that. Would we, Chaz?"

Rachel seized the opportunity to test her parental skills. "If you're going to a place that breaks the law by piercing underage kids, then how can you be sure they'll follow the health department's regulations?"

The girls shared a grimace, then Chastity said, "Good point."

"So we'll put off our piercings for a few years. No big deal," Jessica added.

"Right. Let's work on the scrapbook now," Chastity said.

Rachel's excitement overruled her reservations about sharing the pictures with Chastity's friend. And cousin. She followed them to Chastity's bedroom.

Chastity stopped in the doorway, blocking Rachel's path. "Could you like...leave us now?"

Taken aback, Rachel stopped. "Don't you want my help with chronology?"

"I think we can figure it out."

Deflated, she considered insisting, but that could erase the points she'd earned by helping them with the project. She and Chastity had made progress this afternoon, but she couldn't expect to recover years of lost ground in one day.

"I'll start dinner. Call if you need me."

"My mom's bringing dinner," Jessica called out. "She'll be here any minute."

"I didn't know that."

"She texted me that you needed her help with something."

"Yes, I do. Well…I'll leave you to your scrap-booking."

Feeling excluded, Rachel returned to the kitchen and set the table for four. At least she wouldn't have to worry about Matt dropping in since he had Scouts tonight.

By the time she'd stirred the last scoop of sugar into the freshly brewed iced tea, Pam was calling from the front door. "Yoo-hoo. Anybody home? Food's here."

Rachel met her in the den. "Hi. You didn't have to bring dinner."

"I owe you for this morning and for keeping an eye on Jess this afternoon. I brought fettuccine Alfredo and garlic roasted broccoli from the girls' favorite restaurant."

"Yummy," Jessica said from the hall.

"Ditto," Chastity added. "Can we eat in here and watch TV?"

"Sure," Pam answered before Rachel could. The girls trooped into the kitchen, loaded their plates and disappeared.

Pam whispered, "Sorry for taking over, but I also brought a bottle of wine. I figured we'd need fortification to go through Hope's things. If the girls are in there we can sip, chat and sort in peace."

She pulled the bottle from her tote, went straight to the drawer for the corkscrew, then the cabinet holding wineglasses. She filled two to the brim. She caught Rachel's look. "I'm making myself at home, aren't I? It's just that Hope and I often got together while the girls did homework if Brad and the boys were at practice."

"So you and Hope were close?" Rachel asked, trying to be casual about it while they served themselves.

Pam paused. "As close as anyone got to Hope, I guess. She was kind, generous and pious, but she held something back, you know? Of course you do. You're her sister."

Rachel sipped her wine and didn't correct her. Because she hadn't known Hope well enough to know she'd been reserved with her friends. The wine was slightly sweet and a little tart, and the pasta was flavorful. Despite that, Rachel had no appetite. It was uncomfortable to befriend Matt's sister and Hope's friend, especially while lying to her. But she ate anyway, hoping to gain insight into the fictional side of Hope's life.

"Did she ever talk about...her marriage?" Rachel ventured.

Pam shook her head. "No. Absolutely not. After she initially told me what happened, we avoided the topic. I think she might have been embarrassed by falling head over heels for a guy on a cruise, then impulsively marrying him as soon as they hit dry land. I mean, that wasn't like Hope at all."

"No," seemed a safe response. Rachel had been the impulsive one. She chewed and sipped, leaving Pam to carry on.

"It was tragic for him to die in the fire just days after they returned home and even before she knew she was pregnant *or* had time to change her name."

More questions answered. She hadn't realized her sister was so creative.

"I always thought she was more shell-shocked than grief-stricken over his death, if you know what I mean," Pam continued without waiting for Rachel's reply. "They barely knew each other. It's not like they'd been married for decades, and she couldn't imagine life without her soul mate."

Rachel took it all in. "No. I guess not."

"I mean, it takes years for infatuation to become true love—you know, accepting someone, flaws and all, and choosing to love them anyway."

Did it? What she'd felt for Matt had seemed like love. The way he'd made her feel had certainly set the bar unreachably high for the men she'd dated since. "You could be right."

"It's a shame you weren't on the cruise with her. You could've slowed down the relationship."

Rachel made a noncommittal "Mmm" with her mouth full of pasta.

"What did you think of him?"

Caught off guard, Rachel chewed slower, giving herself time to think. She'd lived with Hope until moving into the dorm. If Hope and her pretend new husband had been home days—*how many days?*—before he died, then theoretically Rachel would have met him.

"Like you said, everything happened so quickly. I didn't have time to get to know him."

"No, I guess you wouldn't. Not with school and all. It's a good thing you weren't there when the fire broke out or else Chastity might not have anyone now. Except us, I mean. She's like another daughter to me."

Hope's story was coming together, but it still had too many holes for Rachel's comfort.

"And Chastity is the spittin' image of your father and grandfather, so I don't have to ask you if she looks like Adam."

Who was Adam? Rachel opened her mouth, then bit her tongue. That had to be the name Hope had given her pretend husband. "Chastity definitely resembles the Bishops."

Then Pam paused, looking slightly uncomfortable. "Rachel, you can't take offense when people ask personal questions."

The change in subject made Rachel's head spin. "I'm sorry?"

"Today at the office. I heard the snoops made you a little…testy."

"We were busy. I didn't have time for gossip."

"You were busier than we've ever been. I saw the appointment book. But try to understand, not much happens in Johnstonville, and you've been around the globe. People want to know all about your exotic life. Most of us only dream of seeing anyplace else."

"I suppose so. Shall we tackle Hope's things now?"

Not that she wanted to. But it seemed like a lesser evil than having Pam turn this into a conversation about Rachel.

"You bet." Pam refilled their glasses, then rose, gathered her and Rachel's dishes, rinsed them and put them into the dishwasher. "Sorry again. Hope would do the same at my house."

"No problem." But tonight had taught her one very important lesson. She would have to be careful around Pam. Hope's friend would likely catch the tiniest slipup.

Two hours later Pam stood back and parked her hands on her hips. She surveyed the neat boxes and bags of Hope's belongings piled on the bed. "You should move into this room. That way you won't have to share a bathroom with Chastity. I love that girl, but she can be messy."

Rachel recoiled at the idea of sleeping in the bed her sister might have shared with Matt. "I can't do that."

"Too soon? I'm sorry. Even though you were far away and we never saw you, she was your sister. You must have been close."

She and Hope never shared the usual things sisters shared, like makeup tips or secrets. Sure, they'd slept in the same tent or whatever rough accommodations they had on missionary postings, but with the decade age gap, sleeping space was about all they'd had in common. And then Hope had left the traveling behind to go to college in the States. She'd only occasionally returned to work with their parents during summer vacations.

Pam's lips pursed in sympathy. She draped an arm around Rachel's shoulders. "I shouldn't have suggested it."

She must have taken Rachel's silence for grief. Was it grief? How did she feel about losing her only sibling? She didn't know. She was still kind of...numb. But her feelings—or lack of them—were not something she'd pick apart with company.

She eased free by picking up a bag of clothing and carrying it to the dining room, calling over her shoulder, "It's okay. Thanks for your concern and your help."

"You and Chastity will be fine," Pam said, joining her and depositing more in the donate pile. "It'll just take time. Parenting a teenage girl is a challenge anytime. But being thrown in at the deep end…well, I don't envy you."

Best to stick with the truth. "I'm looking forward to it."

"That's the right attitude." Pam scanned the stacks. "You're okay with donating this to the church thrift shop?"

"Yes."

"Then I'll come back with my minivan over the weekend and help you get it there."

"Great."

Pam made no move to leave. Instead she stood with her head tilted, observing Rachel. "FYI, when I came home from college and heard about the pranks you'd pulled…I was jealous. You were so darn imaginative. I wished I'd thought of them."

Rachel gaped. "I was horrible."

"You wanted attention. And my kids have taught me that sometimes negative attention is better than no attention at all. Putting the goat herd in Mr. Mc-Gruder's yard because he refused to mow, even though his grass was taller than his picket fence, was priceless. He still talks about it at the nursing home."

"I, uh…was never charged with that."

"Rachel, who else would know how to herd goats except someone who lived in countries where shepherds still did that?"

Rachel kept her lips sealed, but she suspected the guilty flush burning her face said a lot.

"And I know for a fact that you rocked my brother's world for a while."

The comment hit like a punch to the solar plexus.

"Much as I love him, Matt has always been such an uptight, rule-following, perfect specimen that Jake and I couldn't compare to. It was nice to see Matt act like a normal human being and kick it up, have some fun. Thank you for that."

Rachel fought to conceal her horror. Pam was thanking her for being despicable.

"Matt was a nice guy."

"He still is, but he's too serious. Too buried in his job and his Scout troop to have much of a life. All work and no play…kind of like Hope was. So I'm glad they didn't hook up. But enough about our hyperperfect siblings. Let me round up my drama queen and get out of your hair."

The Weavers blew out of the house, leaving Rachel with a sinking feeling she'd wronged someone she would very much like to have as a friend. But friendship with any of Matt's family was impossible.

"THERE'S JESS," CHASTITY said before bolting off and leaving Rachel alone on the edge of the ball field.

From the crowded bleachers ahead, dozens of sets of eyes tracked her steps. She hated arriving late to things. The urge to retreat thumped heavily in her chest. But she fought it and strode forward, feigning confidence she didn't feel. One thing quickly became evident. There were no vacant seats. She was an outsider. Again.

Their tardiness could have been prevented if Chastity hadn't waited until five minutes before they were due to leave to tell Rachel they were supposed to bring a dish for a potluck picnic with Jessica's family after the game. The only thing Rachel could concoct with no notice was a fruit salad.

Through the chain-link fence she saw players huddled in the dugout around someone seated on the bench, then the huddle broke and the bench-sitter rose. Matt. Her stomach did a familiar loop-de-loop.

Matt led the team onto the field. A navy T-shirt emblazoned with the church's name stretched across his broad shoulders, and faded jeans hugged his thighs and butt. She averted her gaze and caught Carol standing nearby, watching her. Only then did Rachel realize she'd stopped to ogle Matt. Embarrassed, she choked out, "Hello, Carol."

Matt's mom smiled and nodded at the glass bowl in Rachel's hands. "That looks delicious.

We'll put it in our cooler. C'mon. I've saved you a seat."

Two minutes later Rachel found herself sandwiched between Carol and Bill Johnston. To her left the men talked tractors, farming and politics. On her right Carol and her friends discussed recipes. Rachel had nothing to contribute to either conversation.

"Do you cook, Rachel?" one of the women asked.

"Not often."

Carol patted Rachel's hand. "Your mother probably didn't have time to teach you in the places where y'all were stationed."

"No."

Another woman leaned forward. "Some of our church members have been on mission trips to third world countries. I can't imagine living there all the time."

"It's different," Rachel replied. "You learn what real necessities are."

Shouts from the sidelines snagged Rachel's attention. Chastity and three other girls cheered, cartwheeled and flipped.

"Has Chastity mentioned cheerleading camp yet?" Carol asked.

"No."

"She will. The flyer came yesterday. Jessica's going."

"When is it?"

"Mid-July."

"We'll be in Atlanta by then."

"That's a shame. I'd love for Jessica to have a friend at camp."

A whistle blew, drawing Rachel's attention back to the field—and Matt. He stood on the pitcher's mound. Their eyes met and she couldn't breathe, then he turned back to the plate. He threw the first pitch. High and outside. Luckily, his catcher caught the ball.

Again, she caught Carol watching her watch Matt and diverted her gaze toward Pam in left field. It was going to be a very long evening. And whatever she did, she could not let Carol know that her son still made Rachel's pulse race.

CHAPTER SEVEN

MATT WINCED AS yet another ball sailed over his head. Disgusted by his performance, he punched his fist into his glove and kicked the mound. This game couldn't end soon enough.

They were getting their butts kicked because of him. He couldn't concentrate with Rachel on the sidelines. But there wasn't anyone on the roster who could take over for him.

The runner sprinted to first, then rounded second wide-open. Matt carefully jogged over to back up the cutoff throw to the third baseman. He had a second to be proud of Pam's strong arm as the ball came from the outfield. Tom caught it and dived for the bag. The runner slid. The collision between the runner's knee and baseman's skull knocked Tom backward with an ominous thump, followed by a snap. The base runner's howl rent the air.

As a player, then a coach, Matt recognized the sound of breaking bones. The runner doubled up, his face contorted in agony. But Matt's primary concern was for his Sunday school teacher, Tom, who lay flat on his back, his legs sprawled unnaturally. He didn't get up.

Silence descended over the previously rowdy crowd. A flash of movement caught Matt's peripheral vision. Rachel streaked from the stands. In seconds she was on her knees beside Tom, her knuckle against his breastbone. "Sir, can you hear me? Sir?"

No answer. She pointed a finger at the writhing runner. "Lie still. Do. Not. Move. You hear me?"

At the command in her voice, the guy stopped squirming. Again, she rubbed a knuckle in Tom's chest and called him once more. Tom twisted to get away from the stimulus, then roused, albeit groggily. When the runner tried to rise, she pressed a hand on his shoulder. "I told you not to move," she said. "I'm Rachel. I'm a nurse. I'm going to take care of you until the paramedics arrive. But first I need to see to this guy. What's your name?"

"Lee," the runner grunted.

"Lee, you're going to be okay. I know you're hurting, but just give me a minute."

Her gaze slammed Matt's. "Call an ambulance. Tell them two casualties. One probable concussion. One compound fracture. And I need the first-aid kit. Stat."

He glanced at the men. Tom looked woozy, and his eyes were unfocused. A knot was already rising on his forehead. Then Matt spotted the crimson staining the other guy's gray sweatpants—pants that were tented out at an odd angle where his shin had been. A nasty break.

"Got it." He sprinted for the dugout, shouting instructions to his mom to call 911, relaying Rachel's words because that would be quicker than digging his phone out of his gym bag. Then he grabbed the white metal box and returned to Rachel's side. He knelt and opened the kit.

"Keep him seated until the ambulance arrives," she ordered Matt, pointing to Tom. "Clear the crowd," she said to a bystander. "I need blankets and something stiff to make a splint," she told another man.

The people she'd singled out hustled to do her bidding. She surveyed the kit, donned gloves, withdrew the scissors and cut the bloody pant leg. Matt had seen a lot of nasty injuries, but torn flesh and jagged bone was gruesome enough to send a couple of onlookers bolting to the fence.

Rachel showed no sign of having problems with the grisly sight. The guy twisted. "Lee, be still. You have a compound fracture. Moving will do more damage. Do you hurt anywhere else?"

Matt couldn't understand the garbled answer, but Rachel must have, because she nodded. "Can you feel your toes?"

The calm surety in her voice as she continued providing care surprised him. The Rachel he remembered had been excitable, and she'd kept Matt on an adrenaline roller coaster. But this Rachel's composure never cracked.

Transfixed, Matt watched her in action as she wrapped the wound and splinted the leg with a folding car window sunshade, all the while talking to the victim to keep him calm. Finally, Matt heard an ambulance siren at a distance.

Rachel scanned her surroundings, then pointed at a bystander. "Open the double gates and direct the ambulance back here."

The guy took off.

"Help," someone cried from the stands.

Matt spotted a woman in her sixties clutching her chest. Before he could react, Rachel put a hand on the injured man's shoulder. "You're going to be okay. Sit tight until the gurney gets here. They'll give you something for the pain as soon as the ER doc clears it." She rose and looked at Pam who'd joined them. "Monitor them? Yell if anything changes."

Pam nodded, and Rachel sprinted toward the stands. Matt couldn't hear the conversation, but he saw Rachel tending to the woman. Then the ambulance screeched onto the field, stopping only yards away.

Just as the doors opened Rachel was at his side barking medical jargon in a matter-of-fact tone that sucked Matt back in time to the field when he'd been the patient. When bone and ligaments had torn and twisted and his dreams had died. Because he'd been thinking about Rachel.

The paramedics loaded the fracture patient as a second ambulance roared up. Rachel hovered between the bumpers answering questions as Tom and the woman were loaded. Rachel practically vibrated with energy.

Pam stood beside him. "Holy moly, she's good. Had them triaged before I got there."

Matt was impressed, too. Rachel had handled three serious casualties as if they were nothing. She spoke to each victim and gave each a thumbs-up before stepping back. The ambulances doors closed and the vehicles pulled away.

Chastity grabbed her elbow. "That was so cool!"

Rachel seemed to snap back to the present, the energy draining from her. "Just doing my job."

Someone applauded. The rest of the crowd joined in. Rachel's face turned scarlet. The woman who'd once done everything she could to get attention was clearly uncomfortable with it now. One thing was clear. Rachel was still an adrenaline junky. Now she played with broken bodies instead of guys' hearts. And he needed to keep his distance from her before she led him down the wrong path again.

But damn, she was impressive.

SATURDAY MORNING RACHEL congratulated herself on having avoided Matt for two whole days.

It hadn't been easy with Chastity so deeply entrenched in the Johnston family's activities, but with a little luck and planning Rachel had managed to have other things to do during those "together" times. It wasn't a lie. She had mounds of paperwork to complete to settle Hope's estate.

Today Chastity wanted to spend the day at Jessica's, finishing their report which was due on Monday. After learning from Pam that Matt was at their house helping Brad with something, Rachel had suggested Chastity ride her bicycle the short distance.

She heard a vehicle turn into the driveway and checked her watch. Pam was early to take the donations to the thrift store. Rachel hustled to open the front door. Her welcoming smile collapsed when she spotted Matt's pickup instead of Pam's minivan. She hoped Pam had borrowed the truck, but then she recognized the blond head in the driver's seat, and she had to fight the urge to shut the door and pretend she wasn't home. Her luck in avoiding him had apparently run out.

Matt climbed from the cab looking like an advertisement for a men's outdoor magazine in his jeans and white T-shirt that showed off his pecs and biceps. Once again, he'd caught her at less than her best. Anticipating a day of work and sweat, the totality of her beauty regimen had amounted to pulling on her rattiest clothing, brushing her teeth and loosely braiding her hair.

"Where's Pam?" She hadn't meant to sound ungracious, but Matt's jacking eyebrows told her she'd done just that.

"Good morning to you, too. Pam's van has a flat tire. I've been deputized to carry your load to the church thrift shop."

Rachel winced. "I'm sorry you got roped into this. You shouldn't give up your only day off. I can wait until Pam's available."

"The church's big sale is next weekend. They'll need time to sort and price your items."

Stuck. "Then, thanks," she forced out, hoping her smile didn't look as artificial as it felt. "Come in."

And if she had any luck left he'd run out of room in his truck before they emptied the dining room.

Matt followed her too closely for comfort. She felt the heat radiating from his body and smelled his spice and citrus cologne. A weed of desire sprouted in her belly, kicking her into action. She launched into motion, grabbed a box and turned. He blocked her path. They did an awkward left-right-left dance step in the narrow space before he backed out of the way and let her pass. She beelined for the door.

Outside, she gulped a cleansing breath of the late-spring flowers and someone's freshly mown lawn. It did nothing to slow her jittery pulse.

Why did Matt still trip her triggers? Her time with him might have been sweet and intense, but it was also connected to the most painful period of her life. If anything, his familiar scent should repel her.

He came out behind her, jarring her from her analysis. Eager to get this day behind her, she set her box in the truck bed and returned for another, careful this time to avoid dancing in doorways. Soon they'd managed to empty the dining room, but the truck bed was only half full. Anxiety gripped her stomach at the thought of going to the last place she wanted to be alone with him.

"That's it?" he asked.

"There's more in Hope's bedroom."

She motioned for him to precede her. He entered the room, paused and looked around. With curiosity? Or familiarity? His neutral expression gave nothing away. But the question nagged her like a hangnail. Had he shared Hope's bed? Had he stroked her ivory flesh and thought of Rachel's tawny skin? Had he combed his fingers through her sister's baby-fine blond hair and recalled Rachel's thicker, darker locks?

Had he ever thought of her at all?

"All of it?"

Again, his voice jerked her back to the present, making her aware of a burn behind her sternum. *Heartburn from too much coffee. That's all.* "Just the boxes."

"No furniture?"

"No. I... I'll probably sell it and put the money aside for Chastity."

"You didn't find a will?"

"No, and neither her bank or lawyer has one. I guess she never expected..."

His lips tightened. "None of us do at her age."

He abruptly turned and, biceps flexing, lifted the largest box. His elbow grazed her breast as he brushed past her. Sparks shot through her veins like a volley of bottle rockets.

Get a grip, Rach. She hefted the heaviest box, hoping the extra exertion would override her reaction, and followed him out. No luck.

Ten minutes later Hope's personal belongings were gone. The items saved for Chastity occupied a single box on a shelf in the closet. Rachel scanned the space. The white-on-white decor looked sterile. There was nothing here to remind her of her sister. She tried to picture Hope in this lifeless room...and couldn't.

"Ready?" Matt asked. "There's a storm front moving in. I'd like to unload this before it hits."

She nodded because her throat was doing that odd spasm thing again. She grabbed her keys and wallet, followed Matt out, then climbed into the cab beside him. The tight airless compartment felt crowded, even though there was no clutter scattered around the four-door cab.

Different day. Different truck. But it smelled the same. Like Matt. The memory of his old truck, of cool vinyl against her bare back and his hot body pressed to her breasts ambushed her.

"You're still a neat freak, I see," she blurted to banish the image.

"You going to mess it up?" His crooked smile and the humorous glint in his eyes hurled her into the past—back to the day she'd realized she wanted to be the kind of girl who could be right for Matt Johnston.

Memories rolled through her like a rock slide. Then he faced forward and put the truck in gear, breaking the spell. She took a long, slow calming breath. "I don't get my jollies out of creating chaos anymore."

"Glad to hear it. For Chastity's sake."

The silence in the cab gave her too much time to think, to remember. "Did Hope ever mention Chastity having trouble in English to you?"

"No. Why?"

"Chastity said the new English teacher was giving her grief. I just wondered."

"Aaron? He seems like a nice guy. Young. Enthusiastic. I suspect it's Chastity's attitude more than anything else that's causing problems. A new teacher is one more change to her right now."

"Yeah. If it comes up again, I'll make an appointment with him. Right now she doesn't want me to."

"If she can handle it on her own, that would be for the best. Kids lack conflict-resolution skills these days. Too many electronics. Not enough human interaction." He glanced at her. "Sorry. My soapbox."

"Mine, too, because it's true."

Matt stopped behind one of the old stores fronting Main Street, reversed the truck and parked under a sign that read, Donation Drop Off. He climbed out and knocked on the door. It opened, and an older woman's face lit up.

Rachel's nerves knotted in recognition, halting her outside the truck's door.

"Matthew Johnston. What brings you here, m'dear?"

"Rachel brought some of Hope's things to donate."

The woman's smile vanished. Her lips thinned and curved downward. She wasn't happy to see Rachel, but why would she be? During Rachel's time here she'd cut out and painted thirty cardboard cats and staked them out in the woman's front yard with a sign that said Crazy Cat Lady.

The hard gaze swung back to Matt. "I hope you're smart enough not to get tangled up with her again."

Humiliation burned Rachel. Long memories like Miss Burns's were the reason Rachel and Chastity could never stay in Johnstonville.

"I'm sure you and the church are grateful to receive the items Rachel is donating. How about you go back inside and write up her receipt?"

The woman pinked at his gentle chastisement, pivoted and disappeared into the building.

"Don't make enemies because of me, Matt," Rachel said, but a small bud had opened inside her when he'd defended her.

"She needs to remember her manners." His speculative gaze hit Rachel. "You never told me what she did to make you put those signs in her yard."

"I took a shortcut through her yard once on the way home from school. She threw a hissy fit, claiming I scared her cats. She had a dozen."

His lips twitched as he turned to prop open the donation door. Unloading Hope's boxes prevented further discussion. By the time they finished, Rachel was hot and sweaty but glad to have the job done. She stepped outside to let the breeze cool her overheated body. The empty truck bed yawned.

Items her sister had spent years accumulating were going to be scattered among strangers. It was almost as if they were erasing decades of her sister's life. Erasing Hope. But what else was she to do?

A heavy sensation settled on Rachel's sternum. Feeling antsy, she strode to the edge of the parking lot. She hoped she wasn't coming down with something. The intermittent tightness in her throat combined with the pressure in her chest was becoming a nuisance.

She shook it off and faced Matt. He hadn't even

broken a sweat. "Thanks for your help. I think I'll walk home."

He looked skyward. "Storm's coming."

She couldn't get back in that truck with him. Not now. "Contrary to popular belief, I won't melt in the rain."

He didn't smile. "It's six miles, Rachel."

"I can easily walk that in a couple of hours, and I need the exercise. I've been a couch potato since getting here."

"Rach—"

"Thanks again, Matt. See ya." Before he could say more, she headed down the street at a fast pace. She expected him to call her back. She was glad he didn't. At the corner she encountered another victim from her past. "Hello, Mrs. Beecham."

The woman's scowl cut grooves in her face deeper than the Grand Canyon. "Go back to wherever you came from. You're not welcome here," she groused before ducking into the church store.

"Guess she hasn't forgiven me for filling her gaudy water fountain with bubble bath," Rachel muttered. The bubble mountain had covered half the yard. A photograph had made the local paper. Rachel had used biodegradable soap, and it hadn't killed grass or anything. Yeah, she'd been a real prize back then. Hope had been a saint to put up with her childish behavior. Which circled her thoughts back to her sister whose belongings she'd just dumped like trash for strangers to paw through.

Why had the saintly sister died? And why hadn't Hope's anal-retentive, chronic-planning ways extended to drafting a will or buying life insurance? At least enough to cover her funeral?

The lawyer said the church had paid for the service. Rachel would repay them. She refused to be beholden to anyone—especially anyone in Johnstonville.

But damn Hope. Damn her for not preparing better. For not making sure Chastity had money for college and a way out of this one-horse, judgmental town. Damn Hope for not being her usually overcautious, granny-driving self and avoiding an accident. The pressure on Rachel's chest increased. She sucked in a deep breath and walked faster.

How in the hell had Hope been careless enough to run off the road and hit a tree? Rachel hadn't needed any of the details the lead cop had provided. The moment he'd said single-vehicle-versus-tree, her brain had filled with mental images she didn't want. She'd worked too many similar scenes.

Had Hope dodged an animal or been forced off the road by a drunk driver crossing the center line? The officer said there'd been no sign of another vehicle. No skid marks. No evidence of a sideswipe. Nothing.

Had Hope been texting? Surely her rule-following sister wouldn't be that stupid? Had they found her phone in the wreckage? If so, the officer hadn't mentioned it. Had Hope fallen asleep at the wheel?

Another idea flickered in Rachel's subconscious. Denial couldn't smother it. Had the lie which Hope had been living become too much of a burden for her to bear? Had Hope taken the easy way out and left Rachel to clean up after her big sister for once?

A hot coal seared Rachel's stomach. It burned her throat and stung her eyes. She picked up her pace. No. *No!* Her sister wouldn't do that. The Bible she loved to quote said suicide was a sin. Hope had a beautiful daughter to live for, to provide for, and to watch grow up. Hope would never abandon Chastity like that.

Would she?

The pressure building in her torso made it difficult to breath. She took a moment to self-assess. Her heart rate was well above normal, but she wasn't having a heart attack. The pressure was anger. Anger at the police who hadn't figured out the cause of the accident, because, damn it, every accident had a cause. Anger at God or whoever had orchestrated the tragic event. Anger at Hope.

Damn her for leaving Rachel to throw out the things she'd cherished as if they were nothing more than leftover wrappers from a fast-food meal.

Damn her for denying Rachel five years of watching Chastity grow up. Five years of nothing but emails and brief phone calls. Eighteen-hundred-plus nights of not being able to hold Chastity, to laugh with her, to dry her tears. To be her friend.

That hadn't been their deal.

This current situation certainly wasn't their deal.

Thunder rumbled overhead. She looked up, and a drop splattered on her forehead. Retribution for cursing the heavens? Then lightning split the sky, and the bottom fell out of the clouds. Rachel was drenched within seconds.

Serves you right for questioning His ways, her parents and sister would have said. She soldiered on, her rage at the police, her sister and the heavens burning in her chest. But how could she not be angry and resentful?

The wrong sister had died.

Rachel cursed Hope for putting her in a position where failure would be more than just a personal screwup. She was terrified she wasn't up to the task of mothering Chastity. Her daughter deserved better. Hadn't Hope said that countless times before?

Chastity needed a stable mother. And Rachel was anything but. She worked erratic hours and gallivanted around the globe to dangerous hot spots on her vacations. She volunteered in the armpit of her community on her days off. That was no life for a teenage girl.

Damn Hope. Damn her. For violating their bargain. For dying too soon. For leaving her daughter alone to work out problems with a bully teacher and a clueless aunt who didn't know how to be a mother to the child she'd given birth to.

And how sad and unfair was that?

Another bolt of lightning hit nearby with an ear-popping bang. The smell of ozone filled the air. Rachel pressed closer to the building. The lingering heat in the bricks did nothing to warm the ice in her core.

"When I said I'd do anything to spend time with Chastity, this isn't what I meant!" She hurled the angry words at the dark clouds above, then looked around quickly to see who'd overheard. But the streets were deserted.

The pain and pressure in her chest erupted in a pitiful sound. "I didn't mean that!" she whispered.

LIGHTNING SPLIT THE HORIZON, followed by a truck-rattling rumble of thunder. "Crap."

Matt turned on his wipers and headlights and took his foot off the gas. He couldn't leave Rachel to walk home in a lightning storm. He might be an adult, but he wasn't so old his mother wouldn't tan his hide for putting someone at risk. And he wasn't an asshole.

Making a U-turn, he retraced his path, but he didn't see Rachel. He slowed to check stores to see if she'd sought shelter, but the stores were dark and locked up tight. Another jagged bolt split the air, followed by a loud boom. When he reached the thrift shop, he circled back, going slower this time to check cross streets. Three blocks down he spotted her pressed against a wall. She must have been hustling to have made it this far.

He pointed the truck in her direction. The minute the headlights hit her, she pushed off the building, ducked her head and started walking. He pulled up alongside her and lowered the passenger window. Cool, damp air rushed in. The temperature had dropped ten degrees in five minutes. Rachel was soaking wet with her arms hugging her torso and her hair a slick, wet rope down her back. She kept her eyes forward.

"Rachel, hop in."

She glanced at him, then shook her head. "I'm already drenched. Can't get any wetter. Thanks, but no thanks."

She should know better. He shot into an empty parallel parking spot ahead of her, stomped the brakes and threw the truck into Park. "There's lightning. Get in."

"I'll ruin your leather seats."

"Would you rather be electrocuted? Damn it. Get in." He hadn't meant to yell. Or curse. But it worked. She inched his way. He grabbed the blanket he kept in the back and spread it over the seat.

She climbed in and slammed the door. Her lips

were practically blue from the cold. He put up the window. When she reached for her seat belt the pointy tips of her nipples tenting her T-shirt lassoed his gaze. Heat ignited in his groin, and a firestorm of memories licked through him.

He still remembered the exact shade and taste of her nipples, the feel of those satiny nubs on his tongue and the smell of her when he'd buried his face between her breasts. Yet he couldn't recall the same about any of the women he'd been with since.

Maybe *he* needed a cold shower. Instead, he turned up the heater. For Rachel's sake. Though getting her warm wouldn't hurt his sanity, either.

"Wrap up." His voice was a barely audible growl. When she didn't move fast enough he snarled, "Do I need to do it for you?"

She shot him a furious glare. Her eyes were red and swollen. Had she been crying? The idea hit him like a shoulder charge to the gut. Then denial immediately doused that reaction. Tough-as-nails Rachel crying? No way. But…he had to ask.

"You okay?"

"Peachy," she snapped. The choked-out word confirmed his fears. He hated tears. He'd endured them enough back in Pam's emotional days, and occasionally he had to deal with an overly sensitive student or player. The number one lesson he'd learned was talking about it only made it worse.

Let it go. Drive.

"Then why are you crying?" The words escaped before he could heed his own advice.

"I'm not." She tried to hide it by facing the window.

"Liar."

That earned him one of those if-looks-could-kill scowls. "It's none of your business, even if I were." She grabbed the door handle, but the kid-safe locks he kept engaged for hauling nieces and nephews stopped her. "Let me out."

Another flash lit the sky a second before thunder shook them.

"Not in this weather. If you won't think of yourself, think of Chastity."

She hugged the blanket and averted her face. What could have upset her? Surely not donating Hope's stuff? Rachel hadn't shown one hint of grief to this point. But he couldn't come up with anything else.

"Hope would be happy to know her things were going to someone who needed them."

"I'm sure. She'd do anything for an-anyone."

Had her voice broken or had that rumble of thunder distorted it? He caught a brief glimpse of pain-filled brown eyes, before she ducked her head and fussed with the blanket. "Take me home, Matt. Please."

The irregular rise and fall of her chest and that same ol' hint of vulnerability that had hooked him years ago snagged his attention. He was glad he was wrong about her being a coldhearted bitch who'd snatch her grieving niece away from her support network, but keeping his distance would have been easier if he hadn't been.

Giving her a moment to pull herself together, he tracked the torrents of rain turning his window into a blinding curtain even the wipers couldn't hold back. Her subdued sniffles and the surreptitious swipes of her cheeks were getting to him. Keeping it all in was a hell of a lot harder than letting it all out—something he understood all too well.

He'd never once let his family or friends know how much losing Rachel or his football career had hurt. Both incidents had nearly emasculated him. Each made him question who he was and what his purpose was on this planet. But only he knew the turmoil he'd gone through.

Did Rachel have anyone to talk to back home? She had no one here. Except Pam. Maybe. But Pam and Hope had been close, so his sister wasn't an impartial listener. She'd heard Hope talk about Rachel's distance. They all had.

Another quiet sniff ripped right through him. He gripped the wheel tighter. He needed a distraction.

"I heard you called to check on each of the victims from the softball game," he said.

She shrugged. "Protocol."

He suspected it was more than that. "Thanks to your rapid response, they'll all be fine."

"G-good."

Aw. Hell. Knowing he'd regret it but unable to resist, he yanked up the armrest between them and turned in his seat. "Talk to me, Rachel. Like you used to."

"The weather sucks."

The deflection was so similar to her prickliness years ago he almost smiled. "That's not what I meant."

"Can we just go?"

"It's normal to miss her."

Her ragged breath filled the otherwise silent cab. She needed comfort, and that's all he was offering. Or that's what he told himself when he hooked an arm around her shoulders and pulled her stiff body across the seat.

"Matt, don't," she protested and squirmed in the band of his arms, but he held tight.

"You and Chastity have each other to lean on." If anything, she grew more tense. "What if—"

"'What if' what?"

She tilted her head up. Worry filled her brown eyes and pleated her brow. "What if I fail her? What do I know about being a mother? Or about teenagers? I had all these fantasies about how well we'd get along, but…it's not going too well."

The admission punched him in the gut. Her fear of failing to live up to others' expectations had been one of the qualities that had ensnared him the last time. She'd hidden it from others behind a rebellious facade, but for some reason she'd shared her true feelings with him. Hope and her parents had set high standards—standards she'd confessed she couldn't meet. Her honesty about that had bound them together in a way he'd never experienced before or since, because even though he'd never confessed it to anyone, he'd shared that same anxiety of not being good enough.

His father had been the high school's football hero, but he'd given up a college scholarship and an almost certain chance at a pro-football career when Matt's mother became pregnant with Matt. From the time Matt had hit peewee league his father had lived vicariously through each of Matt's achievements. And Matt had done his best to repay him for the sacrifice he'd made. But then he'd disappointed them all—his father and the citizens of Johnstonville who'd been expecting him to put their little town on the map.

"You need to be her parent, not her friend. You'll find your feet. We survivors always do." Hope-filled eyes met his. And held. Desire crowded out the defeat lead-weighting his stomach. His pulse thumped in his ears and his groin. He should push Rachel away, but he couldn't. Why did she affect him like no other woman?

Only one way to find out.

He pulled her closer. Her lips parted on a gasp a

split second before he covered them. Then it happened. That shooting star sensation that he hadn't experienced since Rachel had kissed him fourteen years ago, then a new meteor shower rained down on him.

After a heartbeat's hesitation, she leaned into him. He stroked her soft bottom lip with his tongue, then her hot wet flesh met his with a deft counterstroke that decimated him. *This.* This was what he'd been searching for.

He cupped her wet head and kissed her deeper, trying to recapture years' worth of denial. She wasn't close enough. He lifted her from the blanket and settled her in his lap. Her clothing saturated his, but he didn't care. His only concern was that Rachel kissed him back. Her hands fisted in his shirt. He cradled her face, relearning the curve of her jaw, her ear, her neck, her shoulder, her surprisingly firm biceps. And then he cupped her breast. Her quick inhalation sucked the air from his lungs. Then she pressed into his palm, a taut nipple prodding him. He stroked it with his thumb, and a moan filled his mouth. Hers? Or his?

Her hands splayed on his chest, kneading and giving rise to more heat and passion than he could handle here. In his truck. In the street. In the middle of downtown. Sobering slightly, he reluctantly released her mouth and rested his forehead on hers. Her panted breaths warmed his lips. Rain or not, the stores would be opening soon.

"Rachel, honey, we can't do this here."

She blinked slowly, then bolted upright. Her eyes widened with horror. She scrambled back to her side of the cab and glanced around. The windows had fogged on the inside. Rain still coated the outside. No one could have seen them. But that looked suspiciously like shame darkening her face.

"We can't do this at all, Matt. I can't handle another fling. And I'm not staying in Johnstonville long enough for it to become anything else."

And he wasn't leaving. This was his home. The people here had stood by him when he'd crashed and burned. And then there were the expectations for his future... He had obligations. Desire fizzed like a doused wildfire, but a persistent ember smoldered. "Johnstonville's a nice place to raise a family—if you're not always looking for mischief."

Her face paled. "I will not stay here. And I don't want Chastity raised here. I'm counting the days until we can leave this judgmental, grudge-holding town." She yanked the door handle. It remained locked. "Please, let me out."

Unless he changed her mind about staying, he had no future with Rachel. Did he want one? Maybe.

And maybe he needed his head examined.

"I'll take you home." He hit the defrost button. The second he could see through the windshield, he put the truck in gear. Tension filled the cab the entire ride back to Hope's house.

As soon as he stopped in the driveway, she reached for the door handle. "When you get back to Pam's, could you ask Chastity to call me when she needs a ride home?"

"Rachel, I work with teens every day. I'll help you figure things out with her."

That earned him a suspicious frown. "Why?"

"Because it's the right thing to do. For Chastity's sake. And because Hope would want me to." Did he imagine her flinch? He released the childproof locks. She vaulted from the cab and sprinted for the house. He watched her until she was safely inside.

It was halftime. He could walk off the field defeated and let her go, or he could regroup and see if the chemistry between them was more than just nostalgia for the woman who'd been his first love. If he chose the latter, he would need one hell of a good playbook. And probably a cast-iron heart.

Who was he kidding? He'd never been a quitter.

CHAPTER EIGHT

RACHEL BOLTED INTO the house, slammed the door and sagged against it, banging her head on the jam. "Stupid. Stupid. Stupid."

"I am not stupid!" Chastity snapped from the hallway.

Rachel startled and straightened. "Sorry. I was talking to myself. What are you doing here? I thought you were working on your project at Jessica's." She reached out to flip the light switch. Nothing happened. She flipped it again. Zilch.

"Power's out. And the boys were making too much noise. So we went over to Mrs. Johnston's."

"Matt's mom's?"

"Yeah. Then the power went out there, too. We couldn't use the internet. Where have you been?" The hysteria in Chastity's voice was impossible to miss.

"I was taking things to the donation site. You knew I was doing that this morning."

"But Mrs. Weaver was getting her tire fixed."

"Matt took me."

"Why didn't you tell me? Nobody tells me anything. You could have called or left a note," she railed back.

"I'm sorry. I didn't expect you to come back so soon. How did you get home? You didn't ride your bike in the storm, did you?"

"I said I wasn't stupid. Mrs. Johnston brought me. I didn't know where you were. Your car was here. And you weren't. If I had a cell phone, I could've called you."

Here we go again. Stay calm. Don't overreact. "The house phone—"

"Is digital. It doesn't work when the power's out."

"You're not getting a cell phone," Rachel stated as firmly as she could.

"Jess has one."

"You're not Jessica." Rachel wanted to slap a hand over her mouth. How many times had she begged for something and been denied with similar words from her mother?

Chastity flailed an arm toward the dining room. "Why are you in such a hurry to get rid of Mom's stuff anyway? It's not like it would've killed you to wait until I could help."

"I'm sorry. You said you didn't want to." Part of that, Rachel suspected, was because Chastity wasn't ready to accept her mom's passing. But Rachel refused to force Chastity to discuss her loss before she was ready.

"Plus, I have to do something productive with my days while I'm here."

"Get a job."

"It wouldn't be fair to an employer when we're leaving in a few weeks."

Chastity folded her arms and jacked up her chin. Fury gleamed in her overly lined eyes. "I don't want to go."

"Our deal was I agreed to stay until you graduated eighth grade. You promised."

"What if I fail and I have to stay for summer school?" Belligerence replaced her panicked tone.

"Is that likely?"

Chastity's only answer was a shoulder roll.

"Do I need to set up conferences with your teachers?"

"No! Mind your own business."

"You are my business now, Chastity."

"I don't want to be. I want to stay here and go to cheerleading camp with Jess."

Rachel sighed. She'd been warned this would come up. "We've been over this. I have a job. They need me."

"Mom was right. You only ever think of yourself. You are never going to be as good a mom as her." Then she spun around, stomped into her room and slammed the door.

The arrow hit its target. Rachel pressed a hand to her aching chest. She might never be as good a mother as Hope. But that didn't mean she wouldn't try. She started after Chastity, then stopped when she realized she had no idea what to say. She'd let Chastity calm down. Maybe later she'd have the perfect words.

But today had made two things very clear. First, as much as she wanted to avoid Matt, she would have to accept his offer of help with Chastity because she had no idea how to handle a temperamental teen.

Second, she needed something to do besides think about Matt's kiss. The perfect distraction was something she had to do anyway—try to find out why Hope had died. Otherwise, she would let her mind continue to be occupied with thoughts of Matt and end up getting her heart broken again.

Because she still wanted Matt.

And she still couldn't have him.

PAM HOVERED IN the doorway Sunday morning. "Are you sure you don't want to go with us?"

Rachel smothered her urge to recoil. Going to church with Matt's family and sitting in the pew beside them when she was living a lie seemed like hypocrisy. "I need to make a few phone calls while Chastity's out of the house."

Curiosity lit Pam's eyes. She gave Rachel a moment to elaborate. Rachel didn't. Pam looked a bit hurt, which only amped up Rachel's guilt. "Well, if you're sure…"

"I am. And thanks for taking her. It's good to keep as much normality in her life as we can."

"Right. And if you need any help…with anything, I can stop by after church."

"Thanks. I've got it."

"Okay, then. Do you mind if Chastity comes home with us after the service? The girls need to put the finishing touch on their presentation."

"Sure. Sounds great."

Still, Pam hesitated. Then her van's horn blew. She jumped. "Impatient kids. They love their Sunday school youth group. See you later."

Rachel waved them off. She waited until they were out of sight, then grabbed her keys, hopped in her car and headed for the Johnstonville police department. Sunday or not, police departments had to be open. Didn't they?

She located the small white brick building and went inside. The place was as quiet as a tomb, but the lights were on, and the entry was unlocked. "Hello?" she called out.

A uniformed forty-something woman ambled in from a side room with a mug of coffee in her hand. "Can I help you?"

"I'm Rachel Bishop. Hope Bishop is—was my sister. I'd like to find out what I can about her accident."

"The accident was over a month ago."

The critical tone filled Rachel with shame. "I

know. I just…" Words failed her. How could she explain what she didn't understand?

The woman's expression softened. "It's all right, hon. I know it's hard to face losing a loved one."

Rachel didn't correct her. She hadn't sought facts before because… Maybe she hadn't been ready to hear them. "I'm sorry to say I don't recall the officer's name who called me."

"Of course you don't. Not after a shock like that. Officer Reed's the one you need, and he's at church. Then he spends Sunday afternoons with his grandmother at Shady Oaks. I can have him call you first thing tomorrow."

She didn't want to wait but had no choice. "Thank you. Can I get a copy of the report today?"

"I'll print it out, but you really should talk to Officer Reed." She tapped keys on her computer. A printer spewed paper. She pushed the report and a pink message pad across the counter. "Leave me your name and number, and I'll have him call you."

Stymied by the dead end, Rachel did as requested. She didn't want to return to the empty house and be reminded of her failed attempts to get through to Chastity yesterday afternoon or the eager way the teen had raced back to Matt's mother's place once the rain had stopped and the power had been restored. Rachel drove around town instead and found herself in front of Hope's office. Who had been dealing with Hope's clients in her absence? The guy Hope had worked for had retired years ago. Had another CPA taken his place? She didn't know because she'd never asked.

Rachel was forced to admit that she'd been as guilty as Chastity at avoiding certain topics, because she wasn't ready to accept that Hope wasn't coming back, either. She added yet another item to her "to deal with" list—checking to see that Hope's client files were passed on to the appropriate persons. Maybe Hope's lawyer would know.

A truck that looked like Matt's passed by. Her breath hitched and her body reawakened. The old man driving wasn't Matt. But seeing the vehicle had reminded her of Matt's kiss—something she wanted to forget.

RACHEL HAD SEEN a lot of wrecked vehicles. Several crumpled worse than this one. But none had nauseated her the way viewing the remains of Hope's car did.

Bile rose in her throat. She inhaled and exhaled slowly, trying to settle her churning stomach and agitated nerves. A bad way to start her Monday, but this was the only time Officer Reed had to meet with her, and if she wanted answers, then she had to tough out this encounter.

"Restrained passenger?" she asked.

"More than that. Stuck."

Startled, she whipped around to the officer who hadn't been on the Johnstonville force when she'd lived here. He'd called soon after Chastity left for school this morning and informed her that he'd not only written the report, he'd been the first on the scene. He'd suggested they meet at the salvage yard so he could talk her through the accident.

"What do you mean stuck?"

"She had on her seat belt, and judging by the friction burns on her neck, it functioned properly. But she also had her right hand jammed between the seat and console. Like she was reaching for something. Paramedics had to cut her bracelet to get her out. It looks like it got hung up."

A bracelet? Both Hope and their parents had condemned jewelry—even earrings—as vanity items. The only jewelry she'd been allowed had been a watch—and even that had to be plain and practical.

"Your report said she wasn't speeding."

"That's right. I followed up with the guys in the garage to confirm. They said the mark on the speedometer glass shows impact below posted speed for that stretch of road, and as I told you on the phone, the taillights and lack of skid marks indicate she never applied the brakes. She hit the tree hard enough to force the engine into the passenger compartment. The steering column crushed her chest."

She tried to erase the mental image but couldn't. "Weather wasn't a factor?"

"No, ma'am. Clear day. Dry roads."

"Sun in her eyes?"

He shook his head. "Southbound."

"Accidents don't happen without cause."

"Not usually."

Frustration built. "Did you look for her cell phone? Maybe she dropped it. I've been on a lot of calls in which searching for dropped phones caused accidents."

"Same here. I looked, and then my partner did. We didn't find a phone or I'd have used it for the ICE contact."

Who had been Hope's "in case of emergency" contact?

"Everything we found when we processed the scene was bagged," the officer added. "Did you pick up her belongings yet?"

"The salvage yard manager gave me a box when I arrived." She hadn't been able to bring herself to go through the contents. Hope's purse, laptop and briefcase had been listed, along with numerous inconsequential items. The manager had assured her each item found had been documented. "I read the contents list. No phone."

"The car's been searched. But if you want to go through it again, I have gloves—"

She flinched. "I'll take your word for it."

She'd treated patients trapped in vehicles before and dealt with bodily fluids on almost every shift. But that was her sister's blood on the upholstery and the steering wheel. A chill raced over her, and goose bumps sprang up on her arms. She tried to rub them away. The constriction of her chest returned. She couldn't go through Hope's car. Not today.

"The coroner said there were no drugs or alcohol in her system. You can call him if you want confirmation."

She shook her head, then forced herself to ask, "Deliberate?"

"I sincerely doubt it. My best guess is that her front tire left the road, and with her right hand hung up she couldn't recover. There's a pretty deep drop-off along that section of pavement."

"That's not in your report."

"No, because it's a guess. I try to stick to the facts in my reports. Only your sister and the one who called her home really know what happened."

But his guess made sense. That left the question of the bracelet. Why would her sister suddenly start wearing jewelry? "Thank you for your time, Officer Reed."

"Again, my condolences. I hope you find your answers. Hope was liked and respected in our community. This one's going to bug me for a while."

Rachel returned to her rental and opened the door. Hope's scent wafted out. She staggered back and looked around. But Hope wasn't here. The box containing her belongings on the passenger seat must be emitting her scent. She cleared her throat. The sun was bright. It made her eyes burn and water. She slid behind the wheel and donned her sunglasses. It didn't alleviate the sting.

She looked at the box. Then popped the trunk, climbed from the car and transferred Hope's things to the back. Then she put down the convertible top to clear the air and headed for Hope's house.

Her cell phone rang before she could get there. She fumbled in her pocket for it. She didn't recognize the number, but it was a local area code. "Hello."

"Rachel. It's Matt." Her stomach did its usual flip. "I need you to come and get Chastity."

Panic grabbed her. "Is she sick? Hurt?"

"No. She's been in a fight."

"*What!* Why?"

"She won't say. She's in my office. In the gym. You remember where the gym is?"

"Yes. I'm on my way." She swung the car around and headed for the school.

"I've told the office you're coming. You don't need to sign in. Come through the double doors. Go left. You'll see me."

Rachel made it to school, parked beside the white activity bus and raced into the gymnasium. Her footsteps echoed off the cinderblock walls. Matt stood in a doorway at the end of the long hall. She instantly recalled his kiss and his touch. Her pulse kicked wildly, and her steps slowed. She had to ignore her response and focus on the reason she was here. Chastity was apparently a chip off the old block when it came to finding trouble.

"How did you end up with her?" she asked.

"We needed to separate the girls." Matt indicated his office with a tilt of his head.

One look at Chastity's militant expression and she knew the teen was guilty of whatever the charges. "What happened?"

Chastity turned away.

"Tell her," Matt growled in a warning tone.

"My lame-ass junior partner for our end-of-the-year chemistry project told the teacher in front of the whole class that she couldn't work with me."

"What's a junior partner?"

"We have to work with the stupid sixth graders."

"Okay. And why can't your partner work with you?"

Chastity looked at Matt. He nodded. "Her mom says she has to stay away from you and anyone associated with you."

Rachel's stomach sank. She knew she wasn't going to like the answer but asked anyway, "Why?"

"Beth's mom told her you were a tramp, and she can't have your sinful habits rubbing off on her daughter. So I gave Beth what she deserved. I popped her right in her nasty mouth."

Horrified, Rachel tried to catch a breath. Her worst nightmare was coming true. Chastity was being tarred with Rachel's reputation. It would only get worse if people found out she was Chastity's biological mother. She had to get out of this damned town ASAP.

"Chastity. You can't hit people just because they're assh—idiots."

"You want me to let her talk trash about you? Family's supposed to stick up for each other."

Matt's scowl made Rachel excruciatingly aware of her lack of parenting skills. She decided it was time she took Matt's advice and acted like a parent instead of Chastity's friend. It lit a fire of worry in her stomach because she could very well make her daughter hate her.

"There are better ways to handle obnoxious people. Just ignore them."

"Like you did when you trimmed the principal's shrub into the shape of a penis because he was a dickhead who rode your case when you went to school here."

Shame engulfed Rachel. "Not one of my finer moments. I wanted my parents' attention and did stupid things to get it. None of it worked. As your mom often told me, just because someone acts like a prick doesn't mean you should stoop to their level."

"How will they learn if I always 'turn the other cheek'?"

"Teaching them is not your job. Kill 'em with kindness instead. When they get a reaction out of you, *they* are controlling your behavior instead of you controlling it. It irritates them more when you ignore them." Rachel could have sworn she saw approval in Matt's eyes, but it was gone too fast to be sure. "What do I need to do, Matt?"

"Chastity's suspended for three days. Sign her out in the office. I'll make sure she gets her assignments. You make sure she makes up the missed work."

"Got it."

His frown turned to the teen. "And, Chastity, when you return, you get a week of litter patrol."

"But, Coach—"

"I warned you what would happen if you got in trouble again."

"You said if I ended up in detention."

"This is worse. Much worse. You assaulted another student. I should bump you right up to locker room duty."

"No! I'll straighten up. And I'll do litter patrol."

Rachel put a hand on Chastity's shoulder. "Let's go."

"But what about my presentation with Jess after lunch?"

Rachel glanced at Matt. He shook his head. "You should have thought of that before you hit that girl."

"But Jess might fail—"

"I hope she'll forgive you."

Chastity pivoted on her heel and stomped out.

"Lesson number one," Matt said when Chastity

was out of hearing range. "If you threaten it, follow through."

Feeling as if she'd handled everything wrong, Rachel looked at him. "This sucks."

"Yes. It does. But you're getting the hang of it. You did well."

His praise was nice, but it didn't make her feel any better.

Her daughter had been forced to defend her honor once. She couldn't stay in Johnstonville and risk it happening again.

"WHAT IN THE devil happened at school today?" Pam demanded as she entered the garage.

Matt straightened from the engine compartment of the old MG he was helping his brother-in-law restore. "What do you mean?"

His sister shot him a spill-it look, one she'd learned from their mother. "Don't play dumb with me, Matthew Johnston. Jess called me at work, nearly hysterical because Chastity wasn't there to do her part in their presentation, and Jess had to do it alone. She said Chastity disappeared before lunch, and she's nowhere to be found now."

Alarm prickled through him at the idea of the girl missing. "She's not at home with Rachel?"

"No one is answering the phone at Hope's—I mean, Rachel's, and I didn't get her cell number."

Maybe they'd gone shopping. Or had Rachel

packed up the kid and left town? She'd looked devastated by this morning's incident.

He debated claiming teacher/student privilege, but he knew Pam wouldn't fall for that. "Chastity's chemistry partner refused to work with her, but the teacher insisted the girls work out their differences in the privacy of her office. Beth claimed her mom said Rachel was a tramp, and she feared her loose morals would rub off on her kid."

"Oh, shit." Pam covered her mouth, then looked around to see if any of her kids had overheard her cursing. "Who's the mom?"

No point in evading. Pam was as persistent as a mosquito. "Liz Bass."

Her husband chuckled beside Matt. "Your old girlfriend. Figures."

"Chastity smacked Beth and was suspended. The principal's trying to keep it quiet since she was provoked, and there were no witnesses other than the teacher."

"Poor child. First she loses her mom and now this. And all because you dated Liz, that vengeful, jealous bitch."

"Hey! How is this my fault?"

"You were young and stupid. And while we're on the topic, you never should have let Rachel get away. She's the only woman you've ever dated who got that stick out of your butt."

He should probably keep his mouth shut, but

he wasn't going to take the rap for something he didn't do. "I didn't 'let' Rachel go. She left me."

Pam blinked. "Really? You never said."

"It was none of your business. Still isn't."

"He's right, babe," said Brad.

Pam sent him a scowl that promised he'd regret the comment. "What'd you do to make her dump you?"

"I don't know."

"That's not exactly something a man brags about, dear," Brad chimed in again.

Pam shot another glare at Brad. "Well, where'd Rachel and Chastity go?"

Good question. "Rachel doesn't report to me, Pam."

She snatched her keys off the counter. "I'm going over there."

"I'll check on them on my way home. I picked up Chastity's assignments, and I need to drop them off."

She checked her watch. "You haven't yet? It's almost nine."

"I lost track of time." Matt wouldn't admit he was procrastinating. He hadn't worked out his game plan for convincing Rachel to give them another try. Today's debacle hadn't helped. He'd been doing his damnedest this morning to be a stern teacher, and all he could think about was how Rachel had tasted and felt in his arms and how close he'd come to making love to her Saturday.

He washed his hands and headed for his truck. He was doing the right thing, he told himself as he drove toward Rachel's. He'd promised to deliver Chastity's assignments, and that's all he would do tonight. He wasn't going to kiss Rachel. Or take her in his arms. Or—

Aw, hell, who was he fooling? The burning need to see Rachel was directly connected to the defeat he'd seen in her eyes before she'd left him. He needed to reassure her that she'd handled her niece correctly. And, yes, he'd been dragging his feet because he'd wanted to drop by after Chastity had gone to bed.

The red Mustang wasn't in the driveway, and the house was completely dark. He pulled in anyway and rang the bell. No response. He knocked. Still nothing.

Had she skipped town despite her promise to let Chastity finish out the year?

Had she bailed on him again without any explanation?

It shouldn't matter. They were nothing to each other now. No promises had been made. They'd kissed. That was it.

But it did matter. He wanted more from Rachel Bishop. Much more.

CHAPTER NINE

"Take the bedroom," Rachel told Chastity as she unlocked the door of her tiny apartment. "I'll sleep on the couch."

"Why are we here? I mean, Mom was right. Aunt Rachel, your place is a dump. And it stinks. Couldn't we have stayed in a hotel or something?"

Rachel tried not to take offense. She crossed the room and adjusted the thermostat. "It's smells because it's been locked up for almost six weeks. Once the air conditioner circulates the stagnant air it won't stink. And my apartment may be in an old building, but that doesn't mean it's not clean and paid for."

"What are we going to do now?"

"We're going to bed."

"But it's early!"

Rachel ignored the protest. "We're starting early in the morning. We need to check out schools and look for houses."

"I hope you don't mean in this neighborhood."

"No. My boss lives in a nice suburb. I hope we can find a house there."

"The house in Johnstonville is paid for. We could stay there for free."

"Then, when we sell it, you'll have enough to pay for your college education."

That earned her an eye roll. "Who says I'm going to college? I hate school."

"I can't make you go. But I will tell you that more doors are open if you have an education. Without a degree you're looking at minimum wage, *if* you can find a job. As much as you've talked about wanting to see the world, you'll need to be able to finance that."

Chastity gave a dramatic sigh worthy of a silent-screen actress. "Do we have to talk to the home-less guys again when we go out?"

"Yes. They won't hurt you. I know them." And for the price of the Chinese take-out dinners she'd given to them on her way in she could trust them to keep an eye on the rental car. But she wouldn't share that info with Chastity.

"When can we go home?"

"After we house hunt. Even if we found the per-fect one tomorrow, the paperwork takes time. We need to start the process now if we want to move in this summer. You can't go back to school be-fore Friday. We might as well do something pro-ductive, rather than sit in the house and stare at each other." She wished they didn't have to return to Johnstonville.

"You should buy a car, so we wouldn't have to keep the rental."

"If we find a house, I will."

Her cell phone rang. Who would be calling after nine?

"It wouldn't cost much to add me to your cell plan," Chastity suggested with a sly look. "My birthday's coming up."

"Not for months, and you've done nothing to earn a phone."

Rachel's answer sent Chastity flouncing into the bedroom. The door shut just short of a slam.

Rachel pulled her phone from her pocket. Seeing Matt's number on the screen did crazy things to her vitals. "Hello, Matt."

"Where are you?"

His voice shimmied through her. "Atlanta."

Seconds ticked past. "Are you coming back?"

Her mouth dried. The tension in his voice made it sound as if he cared. But he shouldn't. "Yes, but we need to check out the school situation here."

"I'm at your house. I brought Chastity's work."

"Thank you. If Hope gave you a key, you can put it inside." She wasn't fishing. *She wasn't.*

"I don't have a key."

A warm flush of relief rushed over her. "Then leave everything on the porch. We'll get it when we come back."

"When's that?"

"Sometime Thursday."

More silence. "Tell Chastity Beth was suspended, too—for instigating the fight."

"Will her mother press charges?"

"I'll see that she doesn't."

First, her child going to bat for her and now, Matt. "Thanks for that and for getting Chastity's work. I'll make sure she completes it. Good night."

Rachel disconnected. Fourteen years ago Matt's willingness to take her side and fight her battles had made her fall in love with him. She couldn't risk a recurrence.

"WHAT'D YOU THINK?" Rachel asked as they returned to the car. She hoped this school had made a better impression than the first one which had driven Chastity to silence.

Chastity turned wide, panic-filled eyes to her. "This one's even bigger than the first one. I can't go here."

"This is a private school. It has a large campus because it's kindergarten through twelfth grade. All the kids wouldn't be in your class or even your building. And believe it or not, the public school isn't that big, either."

"Compared to Johnstonville, it is humongous. I can't change schools, Aunt Rachel. You have no idea how hard it will be for me to…fit in at a new one."

Empathy clutched her chest. "Yes, kiddo, I do. In my twelve years I attended seventeen different schools—many in countries where English wasn't the first language."

"You don't understand. I'm not like other kids. I don't…adjust well."

Anxiety over moving from the only house she'd ever known was to be expected. "You'll do fine, Chastity—especially here. The teacher/student ratio is great in both schools."

Not looking convinced, Chastity knotted her fingers and stared out the car window.

"Let's go find our house," Rachel suggested, hoping to elicit some response.

Chastity remained mute during the short ride to Marcia's neighborhood. Her tension was palpable. Rachel wished she had the magic words to calm the teen's fears. But she didn't. She stopped the car in front of a cedar-sided two-story home with a for-sale sign in the front yard. "How about this one?"

"It's all brown. No grass or flowers. All trees and shade. No sunshine for a garden."

"True." Rachel rolled on without reminding her she'd specified no garden and halted by the next real estate sign.

Chastity's face scrunched. "It's ugly. Looks like stacked shoe boxes. Too modern."

And so the ride continued past two more houses.

Chastity found fault with each of them with excuses as lame as, "The neighbor's house is another gross box."

"You wouldn't be living in the neighbor's house, Chastity."

"But I'd have to look at it every day."

Frustrated, Rachel put the car in motion. If Chastity was going to be difficult, then Rachel might have to choose their home without the teen's approval. That wouldn't be an auspicious start.

There were only two streets left in Marcia's neighborhood, and Rachel had about given up on finding a house when she rounded a curve and spotted a Craftsman-style cottage with gray shingles, white trim and a stone foundation. And a for-sale sign out front. Everything about this one called out "Welcome home" to Rachel. She hit the brakes at the end of the sidewalk.

"I love the covered porch all the way across the front and the big pillars," she offered to get the ball rolling.

Chastity lowered the window, showing interest for the first time. "I like the flowers and the porch swing and the white fence around the whole yard." Then she frowned. "But there's no driveway."

Rachel had been too entranced to notice. The street was wide, but she wasn't sure about parking a vehicle on it overnight. "This is a corner lot.

Maybe it's on the side. Why don't you grab a brochure from the box, then we'll check?"

Chastity did as Rachel asked without hesitation, and returned to the car. "It has four bedrooms, three and a half bathrooms and a bonus room," Chastity read while Rachel drove around the corner. "Does that mean I could have a ping-pong table?"

Enthusiasm. Finally. "I didn't know you like ping-pong."

"Jess has a table. I'm pretty good."

The picket fence led from the front yard to the driveway on the side, enclosing a decent-sized area that included a vegetable garden.

"Look at the sunflowers," Chastity said. "They're *gigantic*! They must be ten feet tall!"

Several rows of dinner-plate-sized blooms marked the border of the vegetable patch. The driveway led to a two-car garage. More fencing enclosed the backyard.

"There's room for me to park my car when I get my license." Rachel heard the smile in Chastity's voice. "And the backyard's big enough for a dog. Could we have one? I've always wanted a dog."

So had Rachel. But her vagabond childhood hadn't allowed for one. And since she volunteered so many hours and lived in the tiny apartment, she hadn't felt it fair to the animal to get one now. "Maybe. Should we call for an appointment to see it?"

"Why can't we just knock on the door?"

"The owners hired a real estate agent so strangers wouldn't do that."

An angst-laden sigh filled the car. "In Johnstonville we could knock. Call. I want to see it."

Rachel punched in the number, spoke to the agent, then relayed the bad news. "We can't see the house until tomorrow. The owners are having some kind of dinner party tonight. Want to keep looking until then?"

"I like this one."

"Me, too, kiddo. But just in case the inside's not as wonderful as the outside, let's ride through the rest of the neighborhood. See what else there is around."

"If we have to." Rachel didn't think she'd ever be able to keep up with Chastity's mercurial attitude fluctuations.

They covered the final street, with Rachel pointing out her boss's house, but none of the other homes appealed as much as the cottage. They rode past it one more time before heading for her apartment.

"I need to pick up some takeout."

"Don't you ever cook? Mom was a great cook."

The barb hit home. "Yes, when I'm at home. But other than a couple cans of chicken noodle soup, I have no groceries in the apartment, and there's no point in stocking up if we're leaving soon. Besides, I like taking Bill and Fred something."

"The homeless guys? Why?"

"Because you should help others when you can." Something she hadn't understood as a child. But she tried to do it with more moderation than her parents, who'd given up everything, and she tried to respect others' choices—something her parents definitely had not done. "The guys, in turn, will help me by keeping an eye on things."

"Don't they have a shelter or something they can go to?"

"There are shelters, but some people aren't comfortable around crowds. Bill and Fred prefer their alleys."

"Why don't they just get jobs?"

How did you explain homeless veterans to a teen? "They had jobs once. Then bad things happened in their lives, and they…didn't recover from them."

"Mom always said you're never a loser until you quit trying."

"And she was right." Hope had been full of wisdom she'd gained from living around the globe with their parents—wisdom Rachel hadn't been smart enough to absorb at the time. "But sometimes people run out of energy to keep trying."

Had Hope?

They settled on Italian food, delivered the meals to Bill and Fred, and returned to Rachel's to eat. Chastity took a big bite of her chicken Parmesan, then blurted with a full mouth, "If I have to go to a new school, I *need* to go to cheerleading camp."

Rachel bit her tongue in vexation, her appetite wavering. Was everything going to be a battle? "Chastity—"

"No, really. If I make the cheerleading squad at my new school, I'll have instant friends. I'll fit in. I'll be popular. Even the teachers will help me…adjust."

A good argument. "Even if I let you go to cheerleading camp, as a freshman there's no guarantee you'd make the squad."

"But I'd at least have a shot. Both schools have varsity and junior varsity cheerleading squads, so I'd have double the chance of making one of them. *Pleeease*, Aunt Rachel."

Those big brown pleading eyes slayed her better judgment. "I'll make you a deal. If you stay out of trouble and keep your grades up for the rest of the year, then I'll let you go to camp."

"Seriously?" Chastity bounced on her seat. "Really?"

"Really. But no trouble. None. Zilch. Nada. If I get called to school again—"

"You won't. I promise. I'll be good. I won't even let bitches like Beth get to me."

Rachel hiked an eyebrow at the curse word. Chastity grimaced. "Well, she was one."

"I don't doubt it. But you behave. Got it?"

Chastity grinned. "Got it."

Rachel felt her excitement building. She'd never owned a home, and as far as she remembered, neither had her parents. To own one now and share it with Chastity was a long suppressed dream she'd never allowed herself to believe could come true.

Agreeing to camp meant more time in Johnstonville. But it would be worth it to have her daughter living under her roof.

PAM OPENED THE door to Matt Thursday evening. "What are you doing here?"

He wouldn't let his sister's lack of welcome deter him from his goal. Until thirty minutes ago, he'd planned to mow his lawn this evening, but then he'd run into his brother-in-law who mentioned that Rachel was coming to dinner. Mowing could wait.

"I saw Brad at the hardware store. He said he needed help with the car. I brought dessert." He presented the cake he'd bought from Johnstonville's only bakery.

"Amaretto cake with almond buttercream frosting? You know that's my favorite." She narrowed her eyes, then asked, "Even though you're bribing your way into a dinner invitation, you are welcome to join us. C'mon in. I won't even tell Mom you bought a store cake instead of asking her to bake one."

"She doesn't make Amaretto cake."

"No. She doesn't." Pam carried the cake to the

kitchen, opened the box and stole a finger swipe of icing. Her eyes rolled back in pleasure, then she patted his cheek. "Have I ever told you how much I love you, big brother?"

"Hmm. I'm not sure."

Pam whacked him with a pot holder. "Rachel's due any moment."

"What has she said about Atlanta?"

"Nothing yet. That's what tonight's about. Chastity called Jessica a couple of hours ago raving about the trip. Jess 'bout cried her eyes out when she got off the phone. She doesn't want her best friend to move away. So I invited Rachel and Chastity to dinner. You want her to stay, don't you?"

The way Rachel unsettled him was too personal to share. So he stuck with his favorite coaching advice: show no fear. Admit no weakness. "I never said that."

"You could ask her."

So much for his sister not reading his defense. "I don't even know if I'm interested in a relationship with her again."

"Oh, please. You can't keep your eyes off her."

Pam wouldn't quit until he gave her something. "There's still chemistry between us, but I don't know if it's worth pursuing."

"To quote you when you coach your team, 'If you want something bad enough, you find a way. If you don't, you find an excuse.' We have to find a way to convince them to stay."

He didn't tell her he was already planning his offensive drive.

"Hey, you big goon, are you with me or not?"

"I'm in. For Jessica's sake. And Mom's. She loves that kid like she's her own granddaughter."

Pam snorted and rolled her eyes, clearly not buying his deflection. "Get out and let me finish dinner. Brad's in the garage with his four-wheeled mistress."

Matt joined his brother-in-law.

Minutes later Brad called out, "Earth to Matt."

"What? Did I miss something?"

"The same request three times. If you'd told me you were more interested in seeing Rachel than helping with the timing belt, we could've been inside watching *Sports Center* and drinking a beer. No offense, man, but you're useless with the wrench tonight."

"Sorry."

"Forget it. Let's wash up. Dinner should be ready soon."

The minute Brad opened the door from the garage to the laundry room Matt heard Chastity's excited chatter. He subdued the urge to beeline to the kitchen and waited impatiently for his turn at the washroom sink before joining the gathering around the breakfast bar.

"The house is awesome!" Chastity was telling Pam and Jessica. "Aunt Rachel says I can have the whole upstairs to myself. There are two bedrooms, a bathroom and a bonus room up there. The bonus room is big enough for a ping-pong table *and* a home theater. Aunt Rachel's bedroom and office would be downstairs. And the house has a fenced yard and a garden with sunflowers taller than my head and a screened porch and a huge patio with an outdoor fireplace." She paused to gulp a deep breath. "It would be so cool to have parties there. Jess, you could come and stay and we could go to the aquarium and baseball games, and the Coke Museum and all kinds of stuff. Oh." Chastity bounced in her chair. "And Aunt Rachel said I can get a dog."

That was the most he'd heard Chastity say in all the years he'd known her. She wasn't wearing her usual caked-on makeup, either, and her hair hung down her back in a shiny sheet instead of being teased into a tangled mess. She looked like a normal thirteen-year-old instead of a wrinkle-free thirty-year-old. It was a nice change—one he hoped stuck.

"*If* we get the house," Rachel interjected, then her eyes met his, winding him. "The owners haven't accepted our offer yet, Chastity."

"They will. And then you'll have your first house ever! And we can buy a car, too. I get to help pick it out."

Everyone in the room was smiling at Chasity's enthusiasm. Everyone but him. Matt's gut churned, and his muscles quivered as if he'd overdosed on energy drinks. Rachel glanced up and caught his gaze. Every cell in his body snapped to attention. She looked good tonight in a white top and jeans that hugged her hips. And for the first time since her return, she looked rested, relaxed and happy.

He hoped the owners didn't accept her offer. He didn't want her to go. Not yet. There'd be other houses. Maybe closer to Johnstonville.

"Aaand..." Chastity paused for effect and drum-rolled her fingers on the table. "I can go to cheer-leading camp."

The girls' shrieks of excitement nearly shattered Matt's eardrums. At least the pain in his ears had the fringe benefit of distracting him from his crazy palm-sweating reaction to Rachel's proximity, to the sparkle in her eyes and the healthy flush on her cheeks.

"I said you could go to camp *if* you stayed out of trouble and kept up your grades," Rachel corrected. Then she flicked a glance at Matt from beneath thick lashes. For a moment he stared back into her dark eyes, and all he could think about was that kiss in his truck. How she'd tasted. The softness of her breasts pressed against him. Then her eyebrow hiked, and it hit him that she was seeking his approval of the way she'd handled the situation. He couldn't manage more than a dip of his head because of his suddenly stiff neck. All his blood had drained into his jeans.

"I swear it, Aunt Rachel. I'm going to be as perfect as Mom."

In an instant the mood in the room changed from jubilant to somber. Chastity's lip wobbled. Rachel's smile inverted. She reached across the counter to cover the teen's fist. "Nobody expects you to be perfect. Because none of us are."

Jessica slid off her bar stool. "Let's go look at dogs on my computer. Maybe you can get one before you move, and I can help you train it."

Rachel's lips parted, but before she could comment, Chastity yanked her hand away and the girls raced from the room. Matt knew one thing for sure. Camp would keep Rachel here through July. Surely by then he'd know what he wanted from her? Was it just to scratch curiosity's itch or more?

Pam slid a glass of wine in front of Rachel. "Those two will be miserable without each other. Have you considered looking for a job in or around Johnstonville?"

Rachel fiddled with the stem of the glass. "I love the job I have. And I miss it."

"Maybe there's something similar nearby?"

"My team is my family, and I don't want to lose them. I feel bad enough sticking them with the extra duty while I'm here."

Matt didn't know how to describe the climb-out-of-his-skin desperate feeling her statement evoked. "Mom will miss her, too."

Rachel's gaze swung his way. "What do you mean?"

"Wherever Jess goes, Chastity usually follows. Chastity's like an unofficial grandkid."

Rachel's gaze fell to a fisted hand. "I knew Carol watched them sometimes, but I didn't realize it was that…often."

"We'll all miss her," Pam added. "You know Brad and I are her godparents?"

Rachel's eyes widened. "No. I didn't."

"We promised before God to love and protect her. We're willing to adopt her if you don't want—"

"No!" Rachel objected. "I want Chastity with me. I appreciate your offer, but no thank you. I've already petitioned the courts to legally make her mine."

"We love her. We want what's best for her," Pam insisted.

Rachel straightened, her shoulders going back, her chin lifting and cheeks flushing. Matt recognized her going-to-battle posture even if his sister didn't, and he wanted to warn Pam to back off before she scared Rachel away.

Rachel stood. "I want what's best for Chastity, too, and I believe that's a life with me. No one else will love her as much as I do. We are moving back to Atlanta. If you invited us to dinner to coerce me into doing otherwise, then we'll go home now. I don't want anyone making the transition any more difficult for her than it already is."

An uncomfortable silence filled the room.

"I'm sorry, Rachel," Pam said, capitulating. "I wouldn't do anything to hurt her. She's lost so much already. You both have. It's just…we're going to miss her. Please stay for dinner."

Pam and Rachel's gazes held. Rachel nodded.

Then the stove's timer beeped. Pam bustled around the kitchen, draining the fettuccine, mixing it with her famous cream sauce and broccoli and putting the heaping pot in the center of the table. She rang the old brass dinner bell and Johnathan, Ben and the girls stormed in from somewhere in the house. Their excited conversations filled the silent room.

"Everybody sit. Dinner's ready," Pam announced with a tension in her face and voice Matt hadn't seen before.

Matt elbowed his nephew out of the way and seated himself directly across from Rachel. Admittedly, it hadn't been a subtle maneuver. His brother-in-law coughed "Smooth" into his napkin. Matt's neck heated. He tried to concentrate on being grateful as Brad blessed the food, but then his toes bumped Rachel's under the table. Simultaneously, she startled, and static electricity shot up his leg.

How could she walk away from whatever they

had without seeing if they were still as combustible as they'd been before? He couldn't. He'd never felt more connected to anyone in his life, and he had to know if it was more here than nostalgia.

"Will you use Hope's furniture?" Pam asked after all the plates had been loaded and the scrape of forks was the only sound filling the room.

"Some of it. It's a big house, and I've been living in a one-bedroom apartment. I'll let Chastity decide what to move and what to sell."

"Moving is expensive. We'll help you. Matt and Brad can lend muscle and their trucks. And Bill has an enclosed trailer."

"I'm sure the guys appreciate you volunteering them without asking," she added with a rueful smile. "Thanks. I'll let you know if we need help when the time comes."

But she wouldn't call. He heard it in her distancing tone, and he knew without a doubt that if he let Rachel leave Johnstonville, he'd never see her again. A strange disquiet invaded him. He wasn't in love with her this time, he assured himself. The devastation wouldn't be the same.

Or would it?

"Rachel, I wish you'd reconsider. I'm sorry." Pam held up a hand. "I know you said don't try to change your mind, but Johnstonville's a great place to raise children. My boss and I will put out feelers in the medical community to see if any of the hospitals are hiring helicopter nurses. And as mayor, my dad knows everybody and everything about the area. He'll help. We will be a great family for you and Chastity if you'll let us."

Rachel gasped, then wheezed. Her eyes watered as she struggled to clear whatever she'd choked on. Matt rose to help—Heimlich, pat on the back, whatever she needed—but she waved him off, then dabbed her eyes with her napkin and cleared her throat. He waited for the explosion. Pam had violated her request. Would Rachel grab her niece and storm out of the house? The old Rachel would have. But the current Rachel didn't look ready to explode. She looked...sad?

"I—I appreciate that," she croaked. "But don't look for jobs for me. Chastity and I are excited about our new house. Aren't we?" she asked the teen who nodded, her expression uncertain.

"I mean it," Pam reiterated. "There's so much for you here." She made a say-something face at Matt, but he'd respect Rachel's wishes not to put Chastity in the middle. The kid already looked stressed.

"Pam, let it go," he ordered in his sternest voice.

He'd fight for more time with Rachel, but it would be a private battle between the two of them. He'd crashed and burned in front of thousands before. If he tried and failed again he wouldn't be left with even a sliver of pride.

Winning an opportunity to explore their relationship would be like planning for a championship game. He'd strategize around his greatest weapon—their explosive attraction. And then he'd have a backup plan in case his first line of attack failed.

It was time to turn up the heat on Rachel Bishop. And he was looking forward to the second half.

CHAPTER TEN

RACHEL HAD NO appetite Saturday morning as she sat across the table from Chastity wondering what she could do to turn the teen's mood around. Ever since dinner at the Weavers' Thursday night, both she and Chastity had been dancing uneasily around each other.

She feared the Weavers had eradicated the progress she'd made in convincing Chastity to relocate. Even more, she feared losing Chastity to a family who'd openly stated their desire to have her when Rachel was just on the verge of getting her daughter back. Rachel's appointment with Hope's lawyer on Monday morning couldn't come fast enough. She had to ensure her claim on Chastity was secure.

The simultaneous peal and vibration of her cell phone spooked her. She fumbled the unit out of her pocket and checked the screen. A Georgia area code. The real estate agent's number. Her mouth dried. The woman's news could make things better...or worse—much worse, if they didn't get the house Chastity had fallen in love with.

"Are you going to answer that?" Chastity asked when the phone rang a third time.

Rachel took a deep breath and pushed the button. "This is Rachel."

"Rachel, Lisa. Are you sitting down? You've got your house," she continued without waiting for a response. "The owners didn't even make a counteroffer."

Rachel's extremities prickled with excitement. She looked at Chastity's curious face. "We got the house. *Our* house."

The ensuing piercing squeal was music to Rachel's ears. Then Chastity sprang from her chair and danced around the kitchen.

A chuckle traveled through the phone. "I can tell Chastity's excited. Are you near a computer so you can e-sign the documents?" the saleswoman asked, bringing Rachel back to earth.

In all the excitement over putting in an offer on the house, she'd forgotten to bring her computer with her from Atlanta.

"Can I use your laptop, Chastity?" she asked.

Chastity smacked her forehead. "I left it at Jess's cuz I thought I was going to be there today. Why?"

"Lisa needs to email us some forms."

"What about Mom's? You said it was in the box of stuff from her car. I know her passwords."

Trepidation squeezed Rachel's throat. She'd been reluctant to turn on Hope's computer and retrace what had likely been her sister's last steps. But what choice did she have?

"It's in her bedroom closet," she told Chastity, and the girl raced off. "Lisa, send the documents. I'll read over them and return them to you as soon as I can."

The click of keys filled Rachel's ear. "Done."

Chastity hustled back into the kitchen with Hope's computer. Her fingers flew across the keyboard.

"Do you have access to a printer?" the agent asked. "If so I'll send something to entertain you and Chastity until move-in day."

"Let me ask Chastity. Do we have access to a printer?"

"Sure. Mom's laptop's connected to our home network." She spun the unit around.

Rachel's dread of touching Hope's computer wasn't rational. But it was real. Her palms were damp, her pulse was too fast, and her hands weren't steady. "We do, Lisa."

"Excellent. Another file on the way."

Suppressing her strange reaction to touching the keys her sister had likely touched on her last day alive, Rachel entered her email password. She had mail waiting—a lot of mail. Skimming down the list, she clicked on the Realtor's, then downloaded and opened the files.

"I have them," she confirmed.

"Good. If you know how to e-sign, then I'll let you get to it."

"I do. Thank you, Lisa."

"Rachel, congratulations. You and your niece have a new home. I'll be seeing you soon."

Her niece for now, but as soon as the paperwork went through, Chastity would officially be her daughter. Again. Emotion crushed her lungs. "Thanks again," she choked out, then disconnected and clicked the print button.

At the sound of the machine spewing pages, Chastity hustled to her bedroom and returned seconds later with her bounty.

"This is so cool. Lisa sent a floor plan of our house and a page of furniture cutouts. Little sofas and beds and stuff."

Rachel smiled at Chastity's enthusiasm. What a wonderful way to get Chastity even more excited about moving. "We can get a head start on furniture placement instead of waiting until we get there and moving things multiple times."

"I'll cut out the pieces." Chastity raided a kitchen drawer for scissors, leaving the stack of house photos on the table.

Rachel sifted through them and stared at the images. A sense of pride and satisfaction invaded her. Yes, she'd screwed up as a teen, but years of hard work and trying to become the best person she could be had finally paid off. This was her "do-over." She'd soon have everything she'd ever dreamed of—a home of her own and her daughter back.

The sound of an engine outside caught her attention. "Are you expecting company?"

Chastity shook her head. "No. Jess came down with that virus her brother had, and we had to cancel our lake trip."

"That's what I thought." Rachel rose and headed for the front window. Matt's truck was backing up the driveway. Her stomach sank.

"It's Matt with a lawn mower and a bunch of other yard equipment on a trailer. Did he mow your mom's grass?"

"No. Mom hired a service," Chastity answered without looking up from her project. She stuck her tongue between her teeth and tilted her head at an angle as she carefully cut the paper. She looked so adorable Rachel wanted to squeeze her. But that wouldn't be welcome. Not yet. One day soon, she hoped it would be.

Rachel's gaze swung back outside. The grass did need cutting. Then Matt faced the house, stripped off his shirt and pitched it into the cab. Muscles flexed, including thick biceps, rounded deltoids, wonderful pectorals and a six-pack abdomen as he unlatched and lowered the ramp on the back of the trailer. An agitated beehive of hormones swarmed in her lower belly.

"Do we have a lawn mower, Chastity?"

"Nope."

That meant Rachel couldn't insist on mowing her own lawn and send him home. Not that she knew how to operate the machine anyway. She'd probably end up severing a foot. Not a pretty sight, as she knew from one of her air ambulance runs.

"It's nice of him to help," Chastity said, still engrossed in her cutting.

No. It wasn't. It was trouble. Definitely trouble. The sting of desire burned through Rachel. If Chastity weren't around she'd probably stand here for the duration with her nose pressed to the glass and watch the forbidden fruit in her yard.

"Why did he take his shirt off?" Chastity asked, joining her at the window.

Rachel blinked and hoped her lusty reaction wasn't obvious. "I guess he's trying to keep cool. It is in the lower eighties already today and humid. Or maybe he's working on his tan." Although his golden skin already glistened.

Chastity watched him for a minute. "He has a pretty good body. For an old guy."

Rachel winced. "He's not that old."

"Says you." Then he stretched and flexed in a fabulous display of his perfect physique. Chastity's expression turned to one of disbelief. "Tell me he's not doing all that...posing for you."

Flabbergasted, Rachel stared into the accusing brown eyes and feigned innocence. She suspected that was exactly what Matt was doing, and she didn't want to lie. There were already too many of those floating around like helium balloons waiting to pop. So she played dumb. "Posing for me?"

"He was Mom's boyfriend. *Him* hitting on *you* would be sick."

"Chastity, he and your mom only dated."

"But they discussed marriage, and to get serious enough to even talk about that, they had to have been…intimate."

A thought Rachel didn't want to contemplate. But it was enough to squash her budding arousal. "That I don't know."

"Aunt Rachel, please, tell me you wouldn't take Mom's rejects."

How could she explain that Matt had been hers first without complicating an already complicated situation? She couldn't. "No."

"Good. Because that would be really disgusting. I don't think I could handle it." Chastity flounced back to the table, leaving Rachel to wonder how she could convince Matt to stop tempting her. And how she could stop herself from being tempted.

"Are you going to help with this or stand there gawking all day?" Chastity called out.

Rachel forced herself away from the window, congratulating herself for not taking one last peek.

When she reached the table Chastity had the second floor layout in front of her. She'd already put beds and dressers in place and a sofa and TV in the bonus room. She'd cut out a rectangle and wrote "pinp-ponp" table on it. It took Rachel a second to realize she meant ping-pong. And the desk image was facedown with the word showing in reverse through the back of the paper.

She must be very excited to be in such a rush. Smiling, Rachel reached across and flipped the image, but said nothing about the misspelled words.

"It takes up the same space frontward or backward," Chastity snapped.

Rachel took one look at her red face and said, "You're right. I was just trying to help."

"Forget it. I don't need your help."

Taken aback by the overzealous reaction, Rachel blinked. "I thought we were going to work on this together.

"You do it." Chastity shot to her feet.

"Chastity, I told you, the upstairs is yours. I want your input."

"Then I'll do my part in my room. You do yours in here." Chastity gathered her pieces and left.

Rachel stared after her and tried not to be hurt. She didn't understand Chastity's mood swings or her hypersensitivity. Being a parent wasn't as easy as she'd thought it would be.

And neither was staying away from the front window. She ached to go out and talk to Matt. In the past he'd had a way of calming her and helping her find solutions. But doing so today would only complicate things with Chastity. So she stayed inside.

MATT LATCHED THE trailer's ramp gate and splashed some bottled water over his chest and shoulders in an attempt to rinse off some of the grime he'd accumulated. He glanced toward the house to see if Rachel was watching, but he didn't see her at the window. She hadn't come out—not even when he'd weed-eaten the flower beds close to the foundation.

Her car was here. She should be home. If not, his cheesy display had been wasted. But he worked out as hard as his players, and he was proud of the results. And if the chemistry between them was his best weapon, then he had to strategically use his assets the same way he'd put the ball into the hands of his strongest players.

He dried off, pitched his towel onto the floorboard and headed up the sidewalk. Had she gone for a run?

He lifted a fist to knock, but the door opened before he made contact. Rachel stood in front of him. Her quick response told him she'd been watching. Good. A rush of adrenaline eradicated his tiredness.

She wore low-riding jeans and a yellow sleeveless polo that revealed she took as much care with her physical condition as he did with his. His visceral reaction to her hadn't lessened. She still got to him, making him nervous and tongue-tied.

"I mowed your grass," he announced, then wanted to kick himself for stating the obvious.

"Thank you. But you shouldn't have. Chastity says Hope employed a service. I'll pay you for your time."

Her gaze roved his chest, then traveled down to the damp waistband of his jeans. She swallowed and her cheeks flushed, then she yanked her gaze back to his face.

Plan working. He crushed a smug smile. "The only payment I'll accept is a cold drink."

She hesitated so long he thought she'd refuse. "Put on a shirt before you come inside."

"I'm sweaty."

"Chastity's here."

That decimated his seduction strategy. "I thought she went camping with Pam's brood."

"Jessica came down with the virus her brother had. The trip's postponed."

He had to scramble for another approach. Rachel wouldn't be home alone tonight. That meant no intimate meal for two at his house. He'd have to come up with something else. Something that included Chastity. He hated involving the kid if this was a temporary itch and nothing long-term, but how else would he know than to try?

"I'll bet Chastity's disappointed. I can take y'all to the lake for the day. I have a boat."

Rachel literally backed a step. "Good for you. But still, no thanks."

That had sounded like bragging, hadn't it? How did she turn him into a tongue-tied adolescent?

"I meant, we could take her tubing or fishing or whatever teenage girls like to do."

"Matt. No," she repeated with finality.

"Why not?" He was pushing too hard. But quitters never achieved their goals.

Rachel's brow pleated. She glanced briefly over her shoulder, then stepped onto the porch, pulling the door closed behind her. "She witnessed your little display earlier, and it freaked her out. She said you'd better not be 'posing' for my benefit, and it would be 'sick' if I dated her mother's boyfriend."

Busted. "I wasn't Hope's boyfriend."

"Tell that to the kid who heard you discussing marriage with her mom."

Stymied, he shifted his jaw. Time out. He needed to retreat to his locker room, aka home, and rethink his strategy. Because now he had not one female to win over, he had two. So much for keeping the kid off the field.

"Wake up, Aunt Rachel. Wake up!"

Chastity's urgent plea penetrated Rachel's sound, hard-to-come-by sleep. "Wha—? What's wrong?"

"I need a ride to church."

Rachel rolled over and groggily blinked at the clock. Eight. What time had she finally dozed off? It seemed like only minutes ago. Matt's display yesterday had disrupted her sleep with hot, sweaty sex dreams. Her face burned at the memory of how hot. She hoped she hadn't made noises or talked in her sleep.

"I usually go with Jess, but she's still sick, and now so is her dad and other brother. The whole family's staying home. You have to take me."

Alarm eradicated the last remaining cobwebs from Rachel's brain. The idea of attending church in Johnstonville where she'd be surrounded by those she'd wronged did not appeal. She'd probably burst into flames on the threshold.

"Can't you miss this week?"

"No. My youth group's leading the service. I have to be there to do my part."

Only then did Rachel notice the teen was already dressed—and tastefully at that. Her hair hung in a glossy straight curtain, and her light makeup was suitable for someone her age. Progress. "Chastity—"

"Good grief. If you can't handle it, I can call Mrs. Johnston."

Panic brought Rachel upright. Would not attending make her seem like an unfit parent?

"Mom never missed church," Chastity grumbled as she turned for the door.

Rachel could have kicked herself for bringing a black skirt back with her from her apartment. Otherwise she'd have an excuse to skip church.

She swung her feet to the floor, dreading the hours ahead. "I'll need a shower first."

"Yes, you will. You have an hour."

Ninety minutes later Rachel found herself standing alone in the vestibule, wishing she were anywhere but here. Not even the organ music emanating from the sanctuary could mask the heartbeat pounding in her ears. Chastity had abandoned Rachel the minute they'd entered the arched double doors. The hour was still young enough that only early birds trickled in.

Rachel flinched each time the door opened. Would the next arrival be someone with a long memory and a grudge? The man who'd given her the service bulletin watched her as she debated slipping out the side entrance. Would Chastity notice if Rachel didn't stay? Probably. She'd been pretty intense this morning. Silent. Edgy. Rachel made her way toward a back pew, hoping she'd be invisible to most.

"Rachel!"

The call of the familiar female voice startled her. She spotted Matt's parents coming toward her. Carol took Rachel's hand. "I'm so glad you made it. Chastity is so excited about her solo."

"Her solo?" Rachel parroted dumbly.

"She didn't tell you? She's singing her first solo during the service today," Carol said. "She's been practicing like crazy at my house."

Chastity was even closer to the Johnstons than Rachel had suspected. Her birth family knew things about her that her own mother didn't. "She hasn't mentioned it."

"I'll bet she wants to surprise you."

"That girl sings like an angel," Bill added.

She hadn't inherited that talent from her birth mother.

Carol snaked her arm through Rachel's. "Sit with us."

Refusal raged within Rachel, but she couldn't think of a polite way to escape. "Thanks."

Rather than make eye contact with the other congregants, she took in the stained-glass windows and the satiny wall hangings as she let Carol lead her down the center aisle. She noticed the organist was only a teenager. The closer they got to the altar, the more claustrophobic Rachel became. This beautiful, perfect building was a far cry from the primitive ones in which her parents had worked. Some of those hadn't even had walls.

Carol stopped and motioned Rachel into the third pew from the front. She wouldn't be able to hide up here. Rachel sidestepped in. Then she dared to lift her gaze and came face-to-face with Matt. In the same pew. How could she sit beside him? Her fight-or-flight response kicked in, ordering her to retreat. But she couldn't. Carol and Bill hemmed her in.

Matt glanced up from the bulletin in his hand and did a double take. The polite smile froze

on his face. His lips parted in surprise. Then he
rose, nodding.

"G'morning, Mom, Dad... Rachel. You came
for Chastity's solo?"

Did everyone but her know about that?

"I came because Chastity asked me to." She
sat, trying to keep her elbows tight to her side and
her eyes forward. The Johnstons had left her little room for personal space. The sound of crum-
pling paper drew her attention to the bulletin she'd
crushed in her fingers. She exhaled and counted
heartbeats, trying to force herself to relax, but how
could she when she was superconscious of the
warm, delicious-smelling man beside her wearing
crisply pleated navy pants and a baby blue shirt?

Her palms were damp, her pulse racing and her
mouth dry. She felt like a hypocrite under a spot-
light.

The music ended. Only then did Rachel notice
the church had filled. A young man of approxi-
mately sixteen stepped to the pulpit and offered
a decent, if wobbly, welcome speech, then said,
"Let us pray."

Rachel mechanically bowed her head. Matt's
hand nudged hers. Startled, she glanced at his open
palm. He wanted to hold hands? In church? With
her? With people watching? Was he deranged?

Then Carol clasped Rachel's other hand. Rachel stiffened. Apparently, the Johnstons held
hands when they prayed. And for her to refuse

would only draw more attention—the last thing she wanted. Matt's long fingers enfolded hers. His grasp was gentle. Warm. Firm. Familiar. And arousing. Heat seared her palm and traveled like a lava trail to her tummy. Memories swamped her. She and Matt had held hands often back then. He'd been the first and last person she'd enjoyed that simple touch with, and it had usually led to more. Much more. Naked.

Piety was the farthest thing from her mind as she struggled to regulate her breathing so that Carol would not notice the quickening cadence. Lust in church. So wrong. So inappropriate. She could practically hear her father's scolding tones.

Then Carol released her, and Rachel realized the prayer was over, and she'd missed the whole message. The choir rose. Rachel searched the robe-garbed group and spotted Chastity. Then the young organist launched into a tune, and Chastity lifted a microphone. From the teen's first pitch-perfect note, Rachel hung on to every beautifully sung word. Once Chastity's initial nervousness faded from her expression and voice, the sheer joy on her face and confidence in her stance made Rachel's eyes sting and her heart swell with pride.

Why hadn't Hope mentioned that the daughter they shared was musically gifted? Why had Chastity never once in all her emails or phone calls mentioned she loved to sing? How could Rachel not have known something this important about the child she'd birthed?

Carol's elbow nudged hers. Rachel blinked and saw the tissue Carol offered. Only then did Rachel realize tears streaked her cheeks. Embarrassed, she blotted. Gulped. Breathed. As Matt's dad had said, her daughter had the voice of an angel. That hadn't come from her mother or maternal grandparents.

And then Chastity sat down, a look of relief and elation on her face. Another teen girl took the pulpit, and the sermon continued. The beautiful moment was over, but the pride suffusing Rachel didn't dissipate. She turned to Matt. A smile curved his lips. He nodded.

Then the organist began the next tune, and the congregation rose. Rachel was a beat behind in doing the same. A rich baritone filled her left ear. Matt's. Carol's smooth alto did the same on her right.

Chastity had been blessed with gifts from the Johnstons. Gifts Rachel could never match.

Matt caught her hand once more and tugged, urging her to sit. She glanced side to side and realized the song had ended, and the congregation was already seated. *Nothing like drawing attention to yourself, Rach.* She abruptly sat. She had to pull it together. Hard to do with Matt beside her. She tugged free.

Rachel's parents' devout commitment to spread

their religion had taken so much from her. A normal childhood, the opportunity to form lasting friendships and, in the end, her parents' lives. She'd sworn she'd never become a church member anywhere again.

Her mind raced. She couldn't deny Chastity the opportunity to do something at which she excelled nor the chance to share her gift with others. That meant Rachel needed to find a church for Chastity as soon as they relocated. But how could she send her daughter to church and not attend herself? She couldn't.

But she would never allow the church to consume her or Chastity as it had her parents. How would she ever find the perfect balance when she'd never experienced it in her life?

She didn't have a clue. But for Chastity's sake she had to figure it out.

LATE MONDAY MORNING Rachel stared at the older man sitting across the desk from her and fought to conceal the panic nearly suffocating her.

"I'm sorry to have to ask for clarification, but that initial visit on my first day back in Johnstonville is a blur. I read and signed so many forms, I can't recall what we covered." She'd been jet-lagged, numb with the news of Hope's death, and terrified of failing her daughter. "We completed all the paperwork granting me guardianship of Chastity and to apply for adoption, didn't we?"

"We did."

"Pam Weaver said she and her husband were Chastity's godparents. Can they contest my guardianship?"

"Historically, the church has viewed godparenthood as an obligation to raise the child should something happen to the parents. Today, it merely means your sister chose them to support her in Chastity's spiritual and moral upbringing. It is not a legally binding agreement. Unless you give the Weavers or Social Services reason to believe you'd be an unfit parent, it would be frivolous and costly for them to take action."

She tried to find comfort in his words. And failed.

"But as far as the state is concerned, I'm okay?"

"Yes, because you are her only blood relative."

No. She wasn't. Matt and his entire family were blood relatives. And sadly, they were probably better suited to be Chastity's guardians than Rachel. But they could never love her as much as Rachel did.

"You're sure?"

"Miss Bishop, you told me you are gainfully employed and that you have a substantial amount of cash in reserves. Is that still true?"

She'd invested most of her salary over the years because she refused to give away every dime like her parents had. She'd also vowed never to be anyone's charity case again, totally dependent on others for food, shelter and clothing.

"Yes. But I'm liquidating some of my investments to buy a house."

"Providing a stable environment for the child is good. I wouldn't worry."

But how could she not? She knew more than he did. And if her secret got out and the Weavers or Matt decided to fight for Chastity, Rachel could lose every dime she'd saved in the resulting legal battle. Because she would not give up her child a second time.

She nodded, her neck stiff. "What else do I need to do?"

"Nothing except exercise patience until the paperwork goes through, and, of course, continue to prove you're the most qualified candidate to care for the child. Speaking of papers, here are yours. I've kept copies." He slid a manila envelope across the desk. Rachel put it in her purse.

Why had she agreed to cheerleading camp? If she hadn't, she could have been safely out of Johnstonville in just over two weeks. Could she revoke her promise without damaging hers and Chastity's relationship? No. And if Chastity's behavior reverted to rebellion, then the Weavers might well question Rachel's ability to parent.

That meant she had seven more torturous weeks to get through. Seven weeks of trying not to screw up, of trying to keep Chastity from screwing up, of trying to keep the truth dead and buried. Almost two more months of worrying before she and her daughter would be free of Johnstonville and the past forever.

She'd have to convince Chastity to move after they closed on their house, then they would come back only for camp. That would keep the promise but limit the threat of exposure.

CHAPTER ELEVEN

PROVE YOU'RE THE most qualified candidate to parent the child.

The lawyer's advice was the only reason Rachel had allowed herself to be conned—*convinced*—to take Pam's place working a Meals on Wheels lunch shift with Carol Johnston on Tuesday. Rachel believed in donating her time to good causes but was leery of entering the homes of people who might remember her less than fondly and even more wary of spending two hours with Matt's mother.

"All of these folks are homebound," Carol said as she maneuvered the church van through the center of downtown. "Some have no visitors except us. Most are incapable of preparing meals for themselves. We'll deliver three meals today—a hot lunch, something simple like a sandwich for dinner and a sausage biscuit or muffin for breakfast. Tomorrow's crew will do the same."

"What happens when you can't deliver?"

The sadness on Carol's face was unmistakable. "We try to make sure that doesn't happen."

"But if it does, does each recipient have a supply of nonperishables on hand? I'm sorry," Rachel hastened to add when Carol's eyebrows rose. "I'm not trying to tell you how to do your job, but if weather or illness prevents a visit, then a supply of nonperishables could be beneficial."

Carol nodded. "You raise a good point. I'll present it to the auxiliary. This virus has taken out a good portion of us volunteers. And Pam's had her hands full with the kids getting sick. I insisted she stay away from our clients rather than risk spreading the illness."

"I'm sorry Pam's having a tough time." But illness in the Weaver home meant Rachel would get more time with Chastity. Selfish of her? Definitely.

"Families should look out for each other. It's a shame that our clients don't have that support."

Rachel looked out the window to hide any guilt on her face. She was robbing Chastity of exactly that support system.

"You don't have to travel to third world countries to find those in need, Rachel."

"I know. That's why I live where I do and volunteer at the inner-city clinic."

Carol studied her. "Chastity mentioned you feeding those homeless men when you took her to Atlanta. Hope never mentioned that you volunteered locally. Only that you lived in the slums and traveled to areas too dangerous for them to join you on your vacations."

The injustice of Carol's comment took her aback. Why had Hope painted her in a bad light? "I didn't start volunteering abroad until *after* Hope and Chastity stopped vacationing with me."

That earned her a long, searching look. "Did Hope give you a reason why she ended the visits?"

"She said Chastity preferred traveling with her best friend's family."

Carol's frown deepened. She rode for a moment in silence. "Hope vacationed with Pam's brood once three years ago. I can't blame her for not repeating the experience. As much as I love my grandchildren, trying to rest and relax around them is impossible. They're high energy, always in search of excitement." Her fingers flexed on the wheel, then she shifted in her seat. "Do you think Hope might have been a bit jealous of you?"

Caught off guard, Rachel blurted, "Jealous? Of me? She had everything. Everything that mattered."

"Your life is full of travel and adventure. You're the one Chastity talked about. Every time you called or sent a package, your niece gushed to Jessica and anyone who'd listen for weeks. I doubt Hope enjoyed that."

Saint Hope, jealous? That seemed unlikely. But it was something to think about.

"Don't get me wrong. Hope was a sweet girl. She tried very hard with Chastity. But personality-wise, they are very different. Hope was so cautious, a homebody, and Chastity…" Carol's smile radiated love. "Your niece has an adventurous soul."

Like her momma. "Yes. She does. I always rode the roller coasters with her at amusement parks while Hope guarded our things."

"That's a perfect metaphor for their temperaments." Carol turned down a road lined with small, square mill houses and huge oak trees dripping with Spanish moss. "Was Hope happy with Chastity's father?"

Shock dried Rachel's mouth. She wanted out of the vehicle. "I don't know. I wasn't around much to see their interactions."

Not a lie. She had no idea how Matt and Hope had been together.

"I'd like to believe she was happy for the short time she had Adam. That maybe she…unwound a little. Like Matt did with you."

A familiar vise banded Rachel's chest. She knew she should say something, but she couldn't find the words.

"I'm not asking for details, Rachel, but Matt was different when he dated you. Happier. More relaxed. He talked about something besides football. Like a college boy is supposed to. Even though he was hurt when it didn't work out, I was happy he had that time with you."

Carol had no idea how wrong she was to be grateful. "We…um… We had fun."

"I hope you'll find someone special. Not just

for your sake, but for Chastity's, too. I hope Matt will, too. Someone who'll be a good mayor's wife."

Another shock of alarm bolted through her. "Mayor's wife?"

Carol rolled one shoulder. "The Johnstons founded this town. One or the other of them has been mayor on and off since the incorporation. And being a mayor's wife has…well, certain pressures and expectations. When Bill retires Matt will likely follow in his father's political footsteps. Between work and the kids, Jake and Pam are too busy."

Horrified, Rachel glanced at the woman beside her, then quickly out the windshield. She'd known Bill was the mayor, but she'd never considered Matt as a future candidate.

Yet another reason to keep her secret. If word got out that Matt had slept with a seventeen-year-old all those years ago, his political ambitions could be ruined. No one would care that Rachel had lied about her age. People would only see the four-year age gap and the baby they'd created—the one Matt hadn't claimed through no fault of his own.

"Any chance that someone will be you?" Carol prompted.

"No. No chance at all," Rachel replied a little too quickly. It shouldn't hurt to say it, but the weight on her chest was undeniable. "I'm not mayor's wife material."

"Please don't hurt him again. He thinks I don't know how badly your breakup affected him. But a mother always knows. Just as I knew he and Hope weren't meant to be. They just didn't have that spark."

Once again, Rachel was speechless. No way was that relief coursing through her.

Carol stopped the van in front of a small house. "Chastity says you work twenty-four hour shifts. Have you thought about who'll watch her while you work? She's not old enough to stay alone yet— especially somewhere she doesn't know anyone."

Prickles of uneasiness worked along Rachel's extremities. "My boss lives in our new neighborhood. Marcia has a son and daughter close to Chastity's age, and she's promised to help me find child care. She's one of the nicest, most dependable people I know. Chastity will always have someone nearby she can trust."

"Promise me you won't leave her home alone."

The genuine concern in Carol's expression touched Rachel. "I won't."

"Pam says you miss your job. If you'd like to go back to work, or need to, before the end of school, Chastity could stay with us. And you could hammer out the details of her care while you're there."

And risk being accused of abandoning her child? "That's a generous offer, but I've taken family leave from work, so I can stay with Chastity and help her transition."

"The offer's on the table if you change your mind."

"Thanks." But she wouldn't change her mind. She couldn't afford to.

"AUNT RACHEL, WHERE are you?" Chastity shouted as she blasted through the door after school.

Rachel dropped the shirt she'd been folding and raced from the laundry room, certain something disastrous had happened. "What's wrong? Are you okay?"

"Of course. Do you have a bathing suit?"

A quick visual exam revealed Chastity was intact and not in jeopardy. Adrenaline drained. "A bathing suit? No. Why?"

"Because tomorrow's a teacher's workday. No school. We're going to the lake with the Weavers."

Rachel's stomach swooped like a dive-bombing raptor. "Aren't they sick?"

"Not anymore. They're picking us up in the morning."

"Chastity, you should have asked me first."

The comment earned her an exasperated sigh. "You're the one who said you have nothing to do with your days. We have to take a lunch, and you'll need a swimsuit. Let's go buy you one. And I'm picking it out. You're fashion-challenged."

Rachel winced. She didn't want to go to the lake, but she wouldn't dare let Chastity go alone and risk the Weavers undermining Chastity's current enthusiasm.

"The mall's forty minutes from here, so we'd better go now."

"What about homework?"

"I'll do it in the car."

Shopping with her daughter was something Rachel had often dreamed of doing but never thought she'd get to experience. She grabbed her purse. A trickle of excitement tempered her dread.

Chastity diligently did her homework while Rachel drove. At the mall Chastity pointed to a store. "Let's go there. That's where older people shop."

"Ouch," Rachel mumbled. The kid was rough on her ego.

Inside, Chastity perused a rack and handed Rachel a flowered suit worthy of a retirement home. "I'm not wearing that."

A frown curved the girl's lips. "Mom has—had a swim dress like this."

Oops. Rachel held up a simple black maillot. "How about this?"

"That might work." Chastity grabbed three more and pointed toward the fitting rooms. "I want to see each one."

Rachel fought a chuckle over Chastity's bossiness and ducked into a stall. The first suit was cut lower in the front than she'd realized and higher at the legs. Feeling as if she might spill out if she bent over, she reluctantly tugged at the fabric. "This one's a no."

"Let me see." Chastity ripped the curtain open. She gave Rachel the once-over and made a circle in the air with her finger. Rachel dutifully turned. She hadn't owned a swimsuit in years. There'd been no need. And she felt...exposed.

"You have a decent figure. But that suit's too Hoochie Momma. And you look like a ghost. We should hit the tanning booth after this."

"No."

"Why not?"

"I'm not interested in melanoma."

Chastity rewarded her with another eye roll. "Whatever. Next."

The curtain rattled closed. And so it went for the endless stream of suits Chastity brought her to try on.

"I like that one," Chastity pronounced finally.

Rachel twisted to look in the mirror at the plunging back of the bright orange tank. It almost dipped to her crack. "I don't know..."

"Why not?"

"It's cut really low in the back, and the gathers draw attention to my butt."

"You have a nice butt, and the suit covers everything important."

Damned with faint praise. "I don't think—"

"That bright color looks good on you, and the

others are too sexy. You don't want to look sexy. Coach Johnston will be there."

And just like that, the balloon of fun Rachel had been floating on popped. She definitely did not want to go to the lake now. But unless she woke up sick, she had no choice. All the way home she prayed she'd catch the virus going around before morning.

"LET'S GO! LET'S GO! Let's go!" Chastity shouted before bounding out the front door.

The girl was nothing if not enthusiastic. Rachel smiled and shook her head. Dreading the day ahead, she grabbed the cooler, beach bag and towels and headed out slowly. Seeing Matt and his truck with a long, low boat behind it parked at the end of the driveway stopped her in her tracks. She hadn't expected him *here*.

He stood by the open passenger doors. Chastity had already climbed inside. He strode toward Rachel.

His swim trunks and tank top accentuated the thickness of his quadriceps, his lean hips, flat belly and the breadth of his shoulders. Every cell in her body snapped to attention.

Why couldn't she have awoken sick?

"Good morning, Rachel."

His deep voice rumbled over her, scooping up a big pool of heat and depositing it in her abdomen. She couldn't read his expression behind his darkly tinted lenses, but she felt naked in her swimsuit and the black crocheted cover-up that barely hit the tops of her thighs. Her toes curled in the flip-flops Chastity had insisted she purchase.

"'Morning. I thought Brad was picking us up."

"Not enough room for everybody in his truck. Here, I'll take that." He reached for the cooler. She didn't release it fast enough, and their fingers brushed. A burst of static electricity jolted her.

He retraced his path and set the Igloo in the truck bed. She caught herself checking out his tight, firm behind and mentally kicked herself. Then she looked up directly into Chastity's puzzled face. *Get a grip, Rach.*

Matt gestured to the towels and her bag. "Better keep those in the cab or they'll blow out."

He waited by the truck. Her sluggish synapses finally connected, and she realized he was holding her door. Good ol' Southern charm. Face burning, she scrambled into the cab and hoped he wasn't looking at her butt.

Why hadn't she bought the tent-like swim dress Chastity had chosen initially?

"Can you swim?" he asked Rachel as he slid behind the wheel.

"Yes. But it's been a while."

"Ever water-ski or wakeboard?"

He smelled of Matt and coconut sunscreen, a mouthwatering combination. "No to both."

"We can get her on the tow tube, can't we, Coach?"

"Sure. If she's not chicken and she can swim well enough," he said, addressing Chastity through the rearview mirror as he put the vehicle in motion. Then he turned to Rachel. "I have extra life jackets. Keep yours on until I say otherwise."

"But her tan lines—" Chastity protested.

"Won't matter if she drowns," Matt finished. Then he glanced at Rachel's legs. "You could use a little sun."

"I tried to tell her," Chastity said in a know-it-all tone.

Rachel wanted to go home. Not just to Hope's. Home. To Atlanta. Far away from the unsettled feelings Matt provoked. "Some of us don't have the luxury of playing outside for a living."

Her snarky comment earned her a sideways grin that twisted her tummy into knots. "I'm definitely blessed in that respect." He glanced into the mirror at Chastity, then back at Rachel. "I can see Chastity's very excited, but what about you? Glad you came?"

"I'm always happy to spend a day with Chastity."

He let her evasion pass. Minutes later a wide expanse of sparkling, rippling lake came into view. "I don't remember this from…before," Rachel said.

"It wasn't here. They dammed the river five or six years ago. Construction on the shores has only just begun. The new marinas and neighborhoods will bring growth and revenue to our area."

Spoken like a future politician.

He pulled into a big circle at the top of a steep ramp leading down into the water and stopped. "You can get into the boat now."

Glad to escape, Rachel clambered out. Johnathan, Pam's son, met them. He helped Matt move gear to the boat, then boarded and sat behind the wheel. Rachel climbed on board and anxiously settled in a rear seat.

"Johnathan, get Rachel a life jacket," Matt called out before backing the trailer and boat toward the water. The weird floaty sensation of rocking in the boat on dry land reminded Rachel of riding in the rickety trucks they used on her medical missions overseas. She held on tightly to her seat. Matt pulled away, leaving the boat in the water, then Johnathan drove them away from the dock.

"Are you old enough to drive a boat?" she asked the boy. He was younger than Jessica.

"Yes, ma'am. And I took the boater safety course. Uncle Matt's all about drills and safety. He made me practice every possible disaster before he let me drive solo."

"You're not going to get sick, are you?" Chastity asked from her perch in the bow.

"I don't think so." She hoped not. That would be humiliating.

When Matt returned, the teen pulled up to the end of the dock, and Matt boarded, taking the seat opposite Rachel. He planted his feet flat on the deck and splayed his knees. The narrowness of the boat had their legs almost touching. The sudden powering up of the engine as Johnathan pulled away from shore didn't throw her off balance nearly as much as Matt stripping off his shirt to reveal his incredible golden whorl-dusted torso did. She dropped her gaze. It landed on an old and faded white scar bisecting his knee.

"What happened there?" she asked.

"Old football injury. Nothing important." His tense muscles belied his dismissive tone. "You're missing the scenery."

She let him change the subject—she could get more information out of Pam. Forcing her gaze away, she looked directly into Chastity's watchful eyes. "You've come out here with the Weavers before?"

"Yep. Lots."

"Did your mom come?"

"No. She gets—*got* seasick."

"Hope didn't ride in anything she couldn't drive," Matt added.

Rachel hadn't known that. It seemed as if Matt and his family knew more about Hope and Chastity than Rachel.

Johnathan turned the boat into a cove and cut the engine. They drifted toward a group waving from the biggest inflatable raft Rachel had ever seen. It had to be ten or twelve feet across. She barely registered another boat anchored on the opposite side.

Chastity sprang up. "C'mon, Aunt Rachel." Then she launched over the side. Johnathan dived in behind her. Both swam toward the raft. Matt took the driver's seat.

"What is that thing?" Rachel asked.

"Party Island. It's where you hang out when you're not tubing, skiing or wakeboarding. Go ahead. Jump. I'll drop off your cooler and towels."

Swimming wasn't an issue. Stripping off her cover-up in front of him was. He eased up sideways to the raft.

"Can't I just climb over?"

"Too risky. You might fall between the raft and the boat hull and get mashed." He passed their gear to Brad, who rocked precariously as he stretched for each item. Matt's gaze settled on Rachel when she hesitated.

"On second thought, sit down. I'm going to give Rachel a tour of the lake," he called out. Then, without Rachel's permission, he shifted the boat into Reverse and left her chaperones behind.

Relieved that she could keep her clothes on for a few more minutes but not thrilled about being alone with him, she perched on the cushion.

"Sit here," he shouted, pointing at the seat beside him.

She shook her head. "I'm good."

"Harder to play tour guide if I have to yell."

With no way to avoid it, she rose and inched forward, clutching seat backs along her way until she reached the captain's seat. Sitting as close to the edge as she could, she looked everywhere but at the bare, bronzed torso beside her. But each time he pointed at something, his thick biceps flexed in her field of vision. Then they bumped over a wave, and their thighs and shoulders rubbed. Her heart floated up her throat.

Rachel averted her gaze and studied the shorelines. A distant red barn caught her eye. She straightened. It couldn't be. Could it? Then he drew closer and cut the engine. "Remember this place?"

She'd only seen it at night, but how could she forget it? She'd lost her virginity in the barn's loft. So had he. The first time had lasted all of thirty seconds and left her wanting something she hadn't understood. And then he'd tried again. That second, slower effort had rocked her world as had each encounter afterward. She gulped the lump in her throat. To this day when she smelled hay, she had flashbacks of that night.

"I don't remember the river."

"Wasn't here then. You know, Mom never mentioned her missing quilt."

They'd left it behind in their hasty escape when the farmer had arrived unexpectedly. She ignored the smile in his voice and the heat pulsing through her and turned to the opposite shore. "The road is underwater."

"Right. It's one of the best fishing spots on the lake. Ask Chastity. She's caught a few big ones there."

He'd been there. Rachel hadn't. "She sent me a picture of her and her catch once."

"Do you ever think about those days?"

Too often. "I try not to."

"We had some good times."

"Yes. But I did a lot of things back then that I shouldn't have. Hope was trying to help me, and I embarrassed her."

"Do you regret us?"

How did she answer that? "Shouldn't we get back to the others?"

He leveled a look on her, but with the dark glasses covering his eyes, she couldn't tell what he was thinking. "One more stop."

"Matt, I'm not really interested in a trip down memory lane."

"This isn't one."

Good. All she had to do was sit and be quiet. Soon she'd be back with her buffers—the Weavers.

MATT PUSHED THE throttle forward. He could tell from the rapid rise and fall of Rachel's breasts beneath the sexy, semi-see-through thing she wore that she remembered how good it had been between them. He just had to let nature take its course.

He had two objectives. First, he wanted some one-on-one time with Rachel to see if this fascination was just an itch he needed to scratch, and second, he needed to make sure she'd be safe in the water. He could achieve both at the park's recreational area. The sandy shoreline and roped-off swimming areas came into view. Both were deserted, as he'd hoped they'd be early on a weekday. He aimed a word of thanks at the cloudless blue sky.

"How experienced a swimmer are you?"

"I took lessons in college so I could pass the required swim test, but other than a couple of Chattahoochee River rafting trips with coworkers, I rarely have an opportunity to practice my skills."

He coasted until the bow gently bumped the beach beside the cordoned swimming area, then tossed the anchor.

"What are you doing?" Rachel asked with a tinge of alarm in her voice.

"Making sure you can swim."

"I told you I could."

"Now you're going to show me."

"Matt—"

"Leave the life jacket here. I'll be right beside you." She shrugged it off and turned. "And the dress. It'll weigh you down."

She glared—something he could clearly see since she hadn't brought sunglasses. "Is this really necessary?"

"Safety first. The water's thirty feet deep by the party raft." She reached for her hem, and his heart pumped faster with anticipation. He'd been enjoying her long, smooth legs all morning. Now he savored the curve of her hips in the hunter's-orange suit, the nip of her waist and—he nearly choked on his own spit. Her breasts hadn't been that…full before. The bump of her nipples was impossible to miss. Rachel resembled the kind of *Sports Illustrated* model's picture that his players would tape inside their lockers.

She parked her hands on her hips. "Now what, Captain?"

Her sarcasm would have been cute if he could unglue his tongue from the roof of his mouth. He shook off his distraction as he would a bad tackle attempt. "Wade ashore. We'll take a dip inside the swimming area to see what you can do."

She clamored awkwardly over the side. Her rear view was as mouthwatering as her front. There were little gathers in the spandex cinching it up her crack and outlining each perfect globe. He whistled silently, removed his shades and followed her. As sizzling as she looked in her suit and as overheated as she made him, it was a miracle the water didn't boil around them as she slushed out until she was waist deep. Then she struck out in a rusty crawl to the rope, turned and trod water until he caught up. With a depth of six feet, he could touch bottom. She couldn't.

The urge to pull her into his arms, to hold her wet body against his and kiss her hit him hard. She must have read his thoughts because her defiant expression turned wary. She backstroked, reached for the rope, missed and bobbed under water slightly—just up to her widened eyes.

He reached for her. To help. But the moment he made contact with the firm wet curve of her waist he knew that was a lie. He ached for her worse than he had fourteen years ago, and visiting their old haunt had only exacerbated the situation. He eased her closer.

"Matt," she cautioned, and he ignored her. Her slippery legs tangled with his a split second before he covered her mouth. Her squeak of protest morphed into an *"Mmm"* that rumbled through his chest. Her hands stopped treading and anchored on his shoulders—stiff-armed as if to hold him away. He was about to release her and apologize, even though he wasn't sorry, when she relaxed and floated into him, her breasts settling against his chest.

Not close enough. He snaked his other arm around her, stroked down her spine and cupped her bottom, urging her hips toward the erection threatening to puncture the seam of his trunks. She startled on contact, then wound her legs around him and locked her ankles at the base of his spine. He thought he'd explode even faster than he had that embarrassing first time in the barn when she'd helped him roll on the condom.

He savored her lips, her tongue, the bumpy roof of her mouth. She shuddered and dug her nails into his skin the way a cat kneads the one making it purr.

He mapped her waist, her back, her buttocks and thighs. She shifted against him, sending lightning bolts though his veins and raising his blood pressure into the stratosphere. His fingertips slipped beneath the elastic of her suit, found her warm crevice moist and hot. Another *"Mmm"* rumbled through him. Her hands tangled in his hair, making him glad he hadn't yet gotten his customary summer buzz cut. He liked her holding him and kissing him back.

He needed her. Needed to be inside her. Now.

No. Not now. Thoughts bubbled through the thick stew she'd made of his brain. He wanted Rachel for more than just sex. He wanted the strong, smart, brave woman she'd become. And he wanted her forever.

With that sobering realization, he broke the kiss. Resting his forehead against hers, he labored to catch his breath and do the right thing which was definitely not pulling their suits aside and taking her here in the water.

"Rachel." He cleared his throat and tried again. "Rachel, we can't do this here." He stared into her wide, desire-glazed eyes and cursed having to stop a second time. It was the truck all over again. "When I make love to you we'll be in a bed. I want time to taste every inch of you. I need more than a quick—" He couldn't use the locker room term with her. "I need...more than just sex with you."

She stiffened, eyes going wide with panic, then she scrambled away and trod water. "That's not possible. I need to get back to Chastity."

She struck out for shore with fast choppy strokes, and he let her go. He'd laid his cards on the table. Convincing her not to leave Johnstonville was going to be his toughest game yet.

CHAPTER TWELVE

MATT WAS OFFERING more than sex. And it terrified Rachel how badly she wanted it. But relationships based on lies never worked. And she couldn't risk telling Matt the truth. He, his family and Chastity would all hate her for what she'd denied them.

As soon as Matt drifted near the floating island, Rachel dived overboard. She wished she could hide out in the water. How could she look the others in the eyes knowing how close she'd been to naked just moments ago? Where was her hard-won self-discipline?

Would Matt expect to pick up where they'd left off when he took her home today? Of course, that wasn't possible with Chastity in the house—especially with how Chastity felt about Rachel and Matt getting together.

Disappointment weighted her chest. And the added fact that Matt had exercised more control than she had was mortifying. From the moment he'd kissed her, she'd been oblivious to their surroundings.

Matt ending the embrace when she'd been easy

pickings only proved he was still a nice guy. Too nice for her? Still? She'd tried hard to become the kind of woman a man like Matt deserved. Loyal. Hardworking. Dependable. Generous. Honest... mostly.

She'd had a few relationships over the years, but her inability to commit had sabotaged each of them. She held back emotionally, fearing a serious relationship could lead to marriage and children. It seemed disloyal to Chastity to have given her away and then keep another baby.

She climbed the float's ladder, crawled to the middle, fished a bottle of water from her cooler and gulped down several icy mouthfuls trying to wash away Matt's taste. She felt the others watching her.

"Everything okay?" Pam asked.

"Yes," she and Matt responded instantly and simultaneously, which pretty much negated their answer. She glanced at him and immediately wished she hadn't when desire rekindled.

"Who wants to go tubing?" Matt asked finally. A chorus of "Me" rent the air. "Rachel?"

She shook her head. "Not this time."

The men and juveniles boarded Matt's boat and took off, leaving Rachel and Pam behind.

"Spill it," Pam ordered from her built-in seat.

"The lake's pretty," Rachel dodged. "What happened to Matt's knee?"

"I'll tell you if you tell me what happened during your *tour*."

Rachel swilled more water, buying time to think. "He gave me a swim test."

Pam groaned. "Mr. Safety strikes again. That's why schools are always trying to lure him away."

"They are?"

"He's done amazing things with Johnstonville High's team. He implemented a lot of training ideas that have prevented injuries. Plus, their record, graduation rate and public works receive a lot of attention and even get him written up in sports magazines. He was the national high school coach of the year last year. But Matt's not interested in opportunities elsewhere. He'll never leave Johnstonville. It's the family mayor tradition."

Pam's version confirmed what Carol had told her.

"So, what else happened? You look…rattled."

Rachel employed every technique she'd learned to mask her reaction. "He took me past the barn where we used to…meet."

"Did you visit the hayloft for old time's sake?"

"No." Truth. "That's not going to happen."

"A girl can hope, can't she?"

Rachel's stomach lurched. "Pam, we've covered this. I'll only be here a few more weeks."

"You might change your mind and stay for the right man. I did. Mom did."

"What did you say happened to Matt's knee?" Rachel redirected.

"I didn't. But he tore it up in a football game. Old news."

Not to her, it wasn't. Then Pam removed her long-sleeved cover-up, and something sparkly on her wrist caught Rachel's eye.

"That looks like the bracelet Chastity wears."

"It should. The girls made them in Vacation Bible School last year for each other and for Hope and me, too." She extended her arm.

A bracelet. For a woman who'd never worn jewelry but who'd been wearing a bracelet when she died. Rachel examined the string of pale pink-and-white beads. Uneasiness snaked through her. "Very pretty."

"See the tiny numbers? Each bead represents a Proverb that denotes something special about the person for whom the bracelet is made. And each bead is also individually knotted on silk cording like expensive pearls. They're practically unbreakable."

Rachel, who had been accused by coworkers of having a cast-iron stomach, felt acid burning its way up her esophagus. She swigged more water. What could have changed Hope's mind about jewelry being a vanity issue? A gift made by her daughter. Was Chastity's gift the bracelet that had trapped Hope's wrist?

The only way to be sure was to look in the box

of Hope's belongings from the car, and she had to do it soon—before Chastity beat her to it. Because if there *was* a connection, Chastity could never find out.

RELIEF WASHED OVER Rachel when she spotted an unfamiliar car in Hope's driveway and a stranger on the front porch. Matt pulled the truck to a stop. The visitor's presence meant there would be no private goodbyes with Matt.

"A friend of yours?" he asked.

"No." She hurried from the cab. Matt retrieved the cooler from the truck's bed. Rachel reached for it. Their hands touched, her heart skipped. "Thanks for today."

He held on to the cooler. "I'll stay until you find out who she is."

She'd had a Matt overload and needed a break to regroup. "Chastity and I can handle a visitor."

He held her gaze. She could tell he had more to say.

"Yeah, thanks, Coach. See ya." The finality in Chastity's tone surprised Rachel. But the girl had been a very diligent chaperone today, sitting between Rachel and Matt and watching their exchanges.

His gaze flicked to the teen, then with obvious reluctance, he surrendered the cooler. "You did great on the wakeboard, Chastity."

Rachel held her breath until he got back in his truck and left.

"Miss Bishop?" the stranger called out.

Rachel pivoted. "Yes."

The woman met them at the bottom of the porch stairs. "Does this belong to you?" She extended a hand holding a cell phone.

Before Rachel could set down her load, Chastity dropped the beach bag and snatched the small device. "Mom's phone!"

The stranger's eyebrows shot up as Chastity hugged it to her chest, and Rachel's throat tightened.

"I found it between the living room sofa cushions when I cleaned Mrs. Lane's house today. You must have dropped it during your visit."

"My sister," Rachel corrected, keeping a close eye on Chastity.

"You're not Mrs. Lane's accountant?"

This woman's employer might have been the last to see Hope alive. Choking emotion swelled inside Rachel. "No. Hope was the accountant. She's no longer with us. Thank you for returning her phone."

The visitor glanced at Chastity who held the phone in trembling hands. "I'm sorry for your loss, young lady." Then she left.

"The battery's dead." Chastity's voice quavered. Her skin looked chalky beneath the tan she'd acquired today, and sweat beaded her upper lip which had a bluish tint. Her breathing was much too rapid and shallow. Signs of shock.

Rachel dumped the cooler on the porch, wrapped an arm around Chastity and steered her inside the house. "I saw your mom's charger in the nightstand."

Chastity froze just inside the door, her glassy eyes focused on the phone as she desperately punched buttons in vain. Rachel nudged her to the sofa. The teen didn't resist. And then Rachel waited for what she suspected was coming. It took seventy-four seconds for the shaking to start.

"The sound's turned off. I'm not supposed to call her when she's working. But she was late. So I called," Chastity said in a barely audible voice. "Over. And over. And over. She didn't answer," she wailed, each word increasing in volume. "I got mad. I guess she didn't have it with her. Maybe she was already—" Then the tears burst free.

Rachel pulled her daughter to her shoulder and held her. She wished she had words to ease the child's pain. But she had…nothing. She, who always knew exactly what to say to strangers in similar conditions, couldn't come up with one blessed word to comfort her own child.

That inability disturbed her more than anything, short of signing the adoption papers, ever had. For an hour she stroked Chastity's tangled hair and rocked her, her own heart shredded by the hiccuping breaths and loud sobs. Rachel's eyes stung as she silently cursed God for taking the wrong sister and putting this innocent child through hell. Matt would know what to do.

Finally, the torrent ended. She kissed the top of Chastity's head which still smelled like lake. But the showers they needed could wait. "Let's get some sleep, sweetie."

Chastity lifted red, swollen eyes to Rachel's. "Can I st-stay with y-you t-tonight?"

Love swelled inside Rachel until she thought she would explode. "Absolutely."

Within twenty minutes Chastity had fallen asleep in Rachel's arms in the narrow twin bed with the dead phone clutched to her chest between them, and for the first time since Rachel had given away her most precious possession, she got to hold her daughter while she slept.

She lay awake listening to Chastity breath, noting the hiccups growing fewer and further between, and she worried. What if her suspicions about the bracelet were correct? How much damage would it do to the child's mental health if she discovered her gift had possibly contributed to her mother's death? Could Chastity live with that?

It was a risk Rachel couldn't take. If the bracelet were to blame, she'd carry that secret to her grave. She'd been raised to believe lying was a sin and that telling the truth made everything right. But sometimes the truth could do more harm than good. And she couldn't bear to see her baby hurt anymore.

The old adage about the road to hell being paved with good intentions couldn't have been more apt.

THE SOUND OF the door closing behind Chastity when she left for school acted like a starter's pistol on Rachel's heart as it lurched into a sprinter's pace. She had to go through the box of Hope's belongings before Chastity returned home. And if the bracelet was there and broken…

She'd destroy it.

She crossed to the closed bedroom door and stopped, dread settling like a sandbag in her belly. Flexing her fingers, she dredged up her courage, then entered the white room. Hope's scent lingered, as if she'd only stepped out a few moments ago. The box sat in the center of the bed, lid askew—probably from when Chastity had retrieved Hope's laptop.

The briefcase Rachel had sent Hope for Christmas four years ago lay on the top of the contents. Rachel hadn't known Hope had used it. She set it on the bedspread to go through later. Hope's purse was next, the tan leather durable and practical. Hope hadn't been one to match accessories. One purse that suited every occasion was more her style. Rachel stacked it on top of the briefcase, then added the legal pad and calculator.

A jumble of small loose items covered the bottom of the box. A handful of black-ink pens. A dozen mechanical pencils. Paper clips. A box of mints. Coins. Then a familiar pink-and-white curve glinting beneath it all made her stomach muscles clench. She closed her eyes.

Please, let it be an unbroken circle. Please, don't let it be the one the paramedics cut off.

She lifted her lids. Her hand shook as she pushed aside a yellow sticky notepad and grasped a pink bead. Holding her breath, she lifted the strand. One end came free. Then the other. The knotted cord had been cut, and a white bead was missing between the knots. White. Pure. Like Hope. Gone.

If the officer was right, this gift had very likely contributed to Hope's death.

Bile geysered up Rachel's throat. She sprinted for Hope's bathroom and emptied her stomach into the toilet. She retched until nothing was left. Muscles quivering, she slid to the cold tile floor.

The best things in her life had been stolen from her by good-intentioned acts.

Matt.

Her parents.

Chastity.

Hope.

Pain pummeled her like a rock slide, spreading until every inch of her hurt. The grief she'd been denying welled up. She pulled her knees to her chest and banded her arms around them as loss consumed her.

Hope was gone. She wasn't coming back.

Matt knocked on Rachel's front door. He had to talk to her. She'd successfully blocked every attempt at conversation yesterday with Chastity or Pam. Luckily, since he wasn't needed as a substitute today, he had most of the day free.

When Rachel didn't answer, he knocked again. Her car was here. He tried the knob. It turned. Unlocked doors were common for locals. But Rachel wasn't a local. Pushing it open, he stepped inside and heard a muffled cry. Was she hurt?

"Rachel?" No answer.

He hustled down the hall, heard the sound again and followed it to Hope's bedroom. An open box sat on the bed with stuff scattered around it. Hope's stuff. A whimper came from the bathroom. He crossed to the open door and spotted Rachel curled in a ball on the floor by the toilet, her face pressed into a towel on her bent knees and her back against the wall.

The sour smell of vomit hit him. Had she caught the stomach virus going around? Between the towel and the dark curtain of her hair, he couldn't see her face. Then he connected the dots. She was grieving her sister. Finally.

"Rachel?"

She gasped and stiffened but didn't lift her head. "Go away."

"Not happening." He grabbed a washcloth from the towel rod and wet it in the sink. Then he knelt and tugged on her towel. She didn't let go. "Here. Take this. Wash your face, honey."

She averted her face. "Leave me alone, Matt. Please."

Her congested voice told him she'd probably been at this a while. Sympathy had always made Pam cry harder, so he'd have to try a different approach. "You're one of those, huh?"

Her chin popped up. "One of what?"

Her blotchy cheeks and narrowed puffy, blood-shot eyes torqued his heart. He wanted to hold her, to fix whatever was wrong. Instead, he yanked the towel from her hands and offered the cool, damp cloth. "The kind who always help others but can't accept help in return."

Shaking her head, she scrubbed her face with the cloth. "I don't do this."

"Do what? Have feelings like normal people?"

She scowled at him. "Lose control. Cry. I can't. Not in my line of work. Not with the stuff I see."

"This isn't work, Rachel. This is your life. You lost your only sister. You're allowed to mourn her. Frankly, you've held it together longer than I expected."

"You don't understand."

"Then explain it to me. I know I'm a dumb jock, but if you speak slowly and use one-syllable words I might get it."

His sarcasm did the trick. She struggled to her feet, refusing his outstretched hand. "This."

Her palm contained a short broken strand of beads. She'd been holding them so tightly she had round dents in her flesh. Why was she crying over a cheap plastic— Then he recognized the pink-and-white pattern. "That's like Pam's and Jess's."

"And Chastity's and H-Hope's."

He took it from her. "The clasp is missing. I can pick one up and fix it."

She shook her head. "There was no clasp. Chastity made it, then tied it on to her mother's wrist."

"Should be easy enough to rethread."

Her face crumpled, and her lips wobbled, but she pulled it together. "The officer said Hope's bracelet was hung up on something between the seat and console. He thinks her front tire left the road, and she couldn't get the car back on the road with only one hand. He said the paramedics had to cut off her bracelet to extricate her. This bracelet that Chastity made for her mother probably kil—" Her voice broke. She mashed the wadded wet cloth over her mouth.

Shit. "Does Chastity know?"

"No. And she can never find out."

"It was with Hope's stuff in the box? Right? Then we'll put it back in and—"

"No. It was *tied* onto Hope's wrist," she repeated. "It wouldn't come off without being cut. Chastity would know something was wrong." She took the beads back and held them over the toilet. "Maybe she'll never miss it."

He caught the strand halfway to the bowl. "You can't flush it. I don't claim to be an expert on teenage girls or grief, but I remember Pam yammering on and on about the bracelets and how much time Jess spent choosing the right Proverbs to fit the wearer. These were important to the girls."

"But I can't lay that kind of guilt on Chastity. I've been on scene at too many teenage suicide attempts to risk it."

He couldn't imagine the horrors Rachel had seen. "We'll tell Chastity the paramedics had to cut it off Hope to start IVs. She had IVs when I identified her bod—when I identified her." That was a sight he'd never forget.

Rachel's lips quivered. "I'm sorry…you had… to do…that. I didn't know."

"The accident scene is a couple blocks from my house. I passed it on my way home."

"You live nearby?" Her eyes widened.

She seemed bothered by the idea.

"You passed my house the day you went running. Rachel, if Chastity and Jess chose each one of the verses on these beads because they described their mothers' virtues, then it might be tough for Chastity to deal with now, but, later, fixing the bracelet could be therapy of sorts. It will help her remember how Hope lived. Not how she died."

Rachel fiddled with the strand, then met his gaze. "How do you always know what to say?"

Did he? It didn't seem like it. "I have a little more distance than you?"

"You'd lie to protect Chastity?"

Would he? "Does the officer have proof of what he told you? Did he put it in the police report?"

She shook her head.

"Then who's to say our version is a lie?"

Tears welled in her eyes, and one slid down her cheek. Nodding, she ducked her head. He brushed the moisture from her smooth skin, then he couldn't resist any longer. He pulled her into his arms and held her. This was where she belonged.

Being here this morning had reinforced the decision he'd already made. Rachel was strong for everyone else. She needed someone to be strong for her. And he was determined to be that man.

CHAPTER THIRTEEN

"HAVE YOU EATEN?" Matt asked, jarring Rachel from the warmth of his chest.

She pulled free despite an urge to linger. "No. I couldn't. Not knowing I had this waiting."

And then because she wanted so badly to return to his embrace, she launched into action, bustling out of the bathroom. She returned the bracelet to the box and covered it with the other contents. She carried the container to the closet and shoved it onto the top shelf.

Matt was right. Repairing the bracelet could be therapeutic. Even though he didn't know he was Chastity's father, he had her best interest at heart, and Rachel lov—liked him for that.

He waited at the foot of Hope's bed, watching her. She must look a wreck. While he, of course, looked good and smelled wonderful. Self-consciously, she smoothed her hands over her hair. "Thanks for stopping by."

"I'll fix you something to eat." He left the bedroom.

She chased after him and caught up with him in the kitchen. "No need. I'll eat. I promise."

"Yes. You will. After you shower." He spoke firmly, then surveyed the contents of the refrigerator.

"I'll do that after you leave."

"Go. You smell like the lake."

Rachel stood her ground. "You can't order me around like one of your players."

He straightened and piled the items he'd rummaged on the counter. "We've already established that you're a stubborn woman who can't accept help. I'm going to feed you, then take you to bed."

His blunt statement sent a cyclone of arousal swirling through her. "I don't think that's a good idea."

His spine went rigid, then his cheeks darkened and his pupils expanded. "To rest, Rachel. The circles under your eyes suggest you didn't sleep last night." One side of his mouth hitched up in a lopsided grin that made her stomach flip-flop. "Although I'm not averse to giving you a sleep aid. You always went into a fifteen-minute coma after we made love."

Desire hit her like a speeding bus, knocking the air from her lungs. It didn't help that she could see the memory and hunger reflected in his eyes.

Struggling for sanity, she pointed at the cell phone charging on the counter. "Chastity slept with me after that woman returned Hope's phone last night. She's the housekeeper for one of Hope's clients…probably the last one Hope visited that day."

"Chastity was upset?"

She nodded and reached for the device. "The battery was completely dead last night, but it's been charging since she plugged it in first thing this morning."

Rachel touched the button to turn it on, then slid her finger across the screen. Hope, who'd been too trusting, didn't have a pass code. The phone icon appeared, indicating six messages. She tapped it. Four of the messages came from Hope's home phone number. Knowing she'd regret it, she hit Play, then Speaker because the idea of pressing something that had touched Hope's cheek to hers was more than she could handle.

Chastity's petulant voice filled the room, demanding to know where her mother was and when she'd be home. In the second message Chastity whined about being hungry and Hope being late. In the third worry tinged the irritation as Chastity again demanded Hope's arrival time, and in the fourth Rachel heard Chastity's fear and panic, and it crushed her.

Matt took the phone and deleted the messages before she could stop him, then he turned off the device. "Neither of you needs to listen to those again."

He was probably right.

"Go, take your shower." He turned back to the stove, effectively dismissing her.

She debated arguing and telling him he wasn't

the boss of her, but she didn't have the energy. Shoulders dropping with fatigue and resignation, she did as he ordered. When she returned fifteen minutes later, a familiar combination of aromas filled the air. Her stomach growled loud enough for Matt to hear it and turn.

His inspecting gaze slid over her as slow and thorough as a caress, then he silently pointed at the table. The moment she sat, he placed a plate containing a grilled ham and cheese sandwich, a peeled and sectioned orange, and a glass of iced tea in front of her, then took the opposite chair. "It's not gourmet, but it's filling."

"Thanks." She took a bite of the sandwich and chewed, enjoying the buttery, gooey goodness. She didn't know what to say after her embarrassing meltdown, so she ate instead. He waited silently until she finished and pushed her plate away.

"You have people here who care about you, Rachel. I care. My whole family does. Let us help you through this."

He was going to break her heart again if he kept being so nice. "Are you planning to run for mayor when your father retires?"

Surprise set him back in his seat. "Probably. Why?"

"Then I'm bad news, Matt." She'd have to be honest. "I was seventeen when we had our affair. And you were four years older. In some states that's illegal. If that got out, it would kill your election chances."

He frowned. "You told me you were eighteen."

"I lied. I lied about a lot of things back then. I was not a good person." He had no idea how bad she'd been.

"It's history."

"History will make you or break you." A fact she knew all too well. She carried her plate to the sink, then turned and leaned against the counter. Time to lay her cards on the table.

"I'm not denying that I'm still attracted to you. I am. We both know you could have had me at the lake. But even without my history, we have too much against us to make a relationship work. Chastity can't stand the idea of us together. And I won't do anything to upset her. She's been through too much already."

"I'll talk to her."

She shook her head. "There's no point. Besides, I won't quit my job. It took me years to find a place that feels like home."

Throughout her crazy vagabond life, Atlanta was the first place that felt like home. It wasn't the city or her apartment. It was her coworkers who felt like her real family. The one thing she'd always longed for while growing up—a caring family— was finally hers. She wouldn't throw it all away.

He crossed the kitchen with athletic grace, lifted a hand and cupped her jaw. Her breath hitched.

The gentle rasp of his thumb against her mouth affected her deep in her womb. "That doesn't mean I won't try to change your mind. Yes, we have issues to work out, but I've never met a woman who makes me feel the way you do, Rachel. You're strong and smart and sexy, and I want you in my life."

"But—" A butterfly brush of his lips against hers stanched her protest and knocked her off balance. Matt pulled her flush against him. Against his heat. Against his firm muscles. Against his even harder arousal. His hands slid beneath her shirt, caressing her waist, then her back.

She should push him away. But she couldn't. Instead, she tasted his tongue, relished the strength in his hold and poured every ounce of passion she had into the kiss. When her head started spinning, she tore her mouth free to gasp for air and planted her hands on his chest, determined to do the right thing and send him home.

But his heart pounded against her palm, and his eyes melted her objections. Matt made her feel alive in ways she hadn't in a very long time, and she wasn't strong enough to fight the desire consuming her.

"If we do this, Matt...it's only for now. I will leave. As soon as cheerleading camp is over, Chastity and I will be gone. You have to accept that."

Hunger burned in his blue eyes. "You think a few weeks will be enough?"

No. Never. "It will have to be."

"We'll see." Then he swept her into his arms and carried her to her bedroom where he set her on her feet beside the bed and kissed her until her toes curled. He severed the embrace by tugging her shirt over her head, then traced the edge of her bra with one slightly abrasive fingertip. Her nipples tightened. He skimmed his palms over her hips, easing her pants down to her ankles.

She kicked them aside, then nervously stood before him in her panties and bra. She didn't think there were any obvious signs of her pregnancy other than a curve to her tummy and hips that she hadn't had before.

"You're more beautiful than you were then."

His gravelly voice and hungry eyes made her heart ache. She could not fall in love with him again, but she felt herself teetering on the brink. She pushed the feeling aside. "You're overdressed, Coach."

He stripped to his boxers in record time. The stretchy fabric tented over his erection. She wanted him so badly she couldn't wait and quickly shed her bra. The second she did he touched her flesh with his hot hands. She leaned into him, feeling the pull deep inside with each buffing pass of his thumbs. Then the wet heat of his mouth replaced his dry hands. A needy whimper escaped her lips.

She dug her fingers into his hair and held him while he suckled. Restless and on edge, she shifted her legs, trying to ease the building ache to no avail. He delved beneath the elastic of her panties, and finding moisture, he caressed her with breath-stealing accuracy, relentlessly pushing her toward a fast climax. She wanted to savor it, to come with him.

"Wait," she cried a moment too late. Wave after wave pounded through her. He barely gave her time to catch her breath before urging her toward release again. But she'd spent too many nights remembering his lovemaking, and she was eager to have him inside her. She covered him, caressed him through the cotton, then freed him. He pulled free but only to kick his underwear aside. She dispensed with hers, and while she wanted to take her time and explore the broader planes of his chest, the indentions at his hips, impatience won out. She wrapped her hand around him. He was hard and hot, and his tip was slick. She needed him inside her so badly she—

"Hold on, honey." He bent and retrieved something from his pants' pocket. It took her a moment to recognize the condom. She wouldn't get pregnant. She'd made sure of that years ago by getting an IUD. But she didn't stop him as he rolled it on. Protecting herself from other things was important—especially now that she had Chastity to worry about. The thought sobered her briefly, then he cupped her bottom and lifted her, his biceps bulging.

"Wrap your legs around me, Rachel, like you did at the lake," he ordered in a low, throaty growl that shook her to the core.

She did, grasping his shoulders, then he lifted higher and lowered her, his penis sliding home and filling her in a familiar way. He tumbled her back onto the narrow bed, and his passion-darkened eyes met hers.

"Do you know how many times I regretted never getting you into a bed?"

He'd thought of her? A warm glow suffused her.

"Me, too." He felt so good inside her, filling her. Over and over he plunged and withdrew. She buried her face in his neck and inhaled his scent. Greedy to relearn him, she mapped his waist, his spine, his buttocks, pulling and pushing herself against him until he hit just the right spot at just the right angle. The tension of her approaching orgasm spiraled tighter with every thrust, then it burst into a sprinkle of tingles that danced across her skin and traveled all the way to her toes. She muffled her cry against his neck and squeezed her internal muscles, trying to hold him and make the sensation last, but her involuntary contractions pulled him over the edge right behind her.

He bucked and groaned, then braced himself above her. Gasping for air, he eased down until his forehead rested against hers. "Am I ever going to be able to take my time with you?"

The smile in his eyes and voice filled her with

joy. It had always been that crazy-fast with them. Even when they slowed it down, her releases always came faster and harder with him than any other time. Why were they such a volatile combination?

Then her smile fell. Because she knew.

It was because she still loved him.

And she still couldn't have him.

Her flight response hit her with a bolus of adrenaline. She wanted to scramble from under him and escape before he read her feelings on her face.

But she couldn't run without him asking questions. She had to get him to leave. How? Should she feign one of the postcoital comas he'd mentioned earlier? No. That was the coward's way.

He stretched out beside her, pulling her into his arms and fusing her to the heat of his body. He nuzzled the top of her head, kissed her temple. "I apologize for going off like a rocket. It's been a while."

She didn't want to know. Nor would she tell Matt how long it had been for her. The last man she'd allowed herself to become intimate with had been a cardiothoracic surgical resident she'd believed was as focused on his career as she was on hers until he'd dropped the I-want-a-big-family-and-need-to-get-started bomb on her. Her rapid retreat had been three years ago.

Matt brushed back her hair, his expression and touch tender. "Next time—"

There couldn't be a next time.

"You have to go." She hustled around, scooping up her clothes and clutching them to her front like a shield.

He remained horizontal, his head propped on an elbow and looking sexier than sin. "Chastity won't be home for hours. You always liked round two."

Yes. She had. And she wanted it now. Dear Lord, she was in trouble. Big trouble. "I have stuff to get done before then."

His eyes narrowed. "You're remembering chores now?"

She struggled to hide her rising panic. She had to get away from him to regroup. "Please, Matt. I need...to go to the store."

Looking skeptical, he rose and searched her face. The doubt in his eyes eviscerated her. "I'll leave. But we need to talk. About us. Soon. I have to work tomorrow, but after school—"

"Chastity will be here."

Frowning, he turned and strolled into the bathroom. She could not peel her eyes from the bunching and flexing of his gluteus maximus. The urge to map every bulge and indentation—

Had to be denied. She pivoted and yanked on her clothes. How would she survive staying until after cheerleading camp without letting him know how badly she wanted him? Loved him.

She couldn't. She and Chastity would have to move as soon as they closed on the house, then

Rachel would drive Chastity back for camp. That wasn't breaking her promise.

Matt returned and dressed slowly. "Rachel." He waited until she met his gaze. "Don't get tangled up in your head. This was not a mistake."

Yes, it was. Because leaving him again was going to hurt twice as much as last time. And last time had nearly destroyed her. "I can't give you forever, Matt."

"The most important rule I tell my players is to never quit fighting for the win until the buzzer sounds." Then he left.

"I DON'T WANT to go to Atlanta this weekend," Chastity whined from the passenger seat Friday afternoon as Rachel steered the convertible onto I-85. "I want to go to the beach with the Weavers."

Pam's impromptu invitation when she'd brought Chastity home from school had taken Rachel aback. Rachel knew without a doubt Matt was behind the invitation.

She'd underestimated him.

"I want you to meet my boss's children. Her daughter is your age, and her son's a couple of years younger. Anna and Tyler have been attending the private school we visited, but Anna's transferring to the public high school next year. She might be able to help you decide where you'd like to go."

"Why couldn't we go another weekend? We were just there, and it's a long ride."

"Because my boss is off this weekend."

Making love with Matt had been a huge mistake. He'd called during his lunch period today, and she'd cowardly let voice mail pick up. She wasn't proud of that, but it wasn't fair to risk his future mayoral career or Chastity's future by giving him false hopes. She'd have to avoid him.

"You need to decide which school you want to attend, so I can get you registered and have your transcripts sent as soon as we close on the house and have a permanent address."

"But it'll be midnight when we get to your apartment, and your neighborhood's creepy after dark."

"We'll be fine. I would never, ever intentionally put you in danger."

Chastity made a face. "I wish you'd gone by yourself."

"Don't you want to see the house again?"

An eye and shoulder roll combo was her only response.

"And I thought you wanted to help me choose a car. I'm going shopping for one after we meet Marcia's family tomorrow. The rental's getting too expensive to keep."

More silence greeted her reply. Then Chastity emitted a labored sigh. "Okay. But no minivans. They are *not* cool."

"Agreed." Disaster averted, Rachel glanced at her daughter, and her heart swelled with love. She couldn't have Matt, but she could have the next best thing—his child. Then Chastity dug into her purse and pulled out Hope's phone. "What are you doing with your mother's phone?"

"I need a phone, and Mom's works. I can keep it, right?"

"I don't know why it still works. I haven't found a bill for it. Her provider should have shut it off."

"It goes on her credit card automatically."

"There weren't any credit card bills in the paperwork the lawyer gave me."

"Duh. Mom was going green. No paper bills. All email."

Rachel hadn't gone through Hope's wallet to look for credit cards or anything else. That was apparently something she couldn't avoid any longer. "Do you know her email password?"

"Of course."

"When we get home I'm going to need it. I'm supposed to notify any of her creditors of her... passing."

"So can I keep the phone?"

"Only until I close the account. But when you start high school, I'll add you to my plan and get you your own phone."

"Yes!" She fiddled with Hope's phone. "The messages have been erased."

Uneasiness filled Rachel. "Yes."

"I left a lot of messages the day she—" Chastity ducked her head. "I was really mad at her for being late."

Rachel reached across the car and captured Chastity's hand.

"Aunt Rachel, did...did Mom kill herself?"

"What!" Shocked, Rachel swung to face Chastity, accidentally swerving the car over the white line. Heart in her throat, she corrected her path. "Wh-why would you even ask that?"

Chastity picked at the seam of her shorts. "Today one of the guys at school said she probably got tired of being a Goody Two-shoes and did it to escape."

The fear in Chastity's voice shredded Rachel. "Baby, your mom had too much to live for. She never would have left you voluntarily. You were the most important part of her life. She loved you more than anything."

Chastity squirmed. "I haven't been the perfect daughter lately. We'd been fighting. A lot before... you know."

"About what?"

"Well...you, for one. I wanted to see you, and she said no."

The arrow found its mark. "I would have loved seeing you, too. What else?"

"She hated my hair and makeup."

Rachel had not commented on Chastity's tarty look, and over the past few weeks the teen had toned it down. "You have beautiful skin, and you were covering it up. And when you don't tease your hair, it's thick and shiny."

"Like yours."

"You and I take after the Bishop side of the family. What else did you fight about?"

"She wouldn't let me date. Or play video games. Or have a phone or even cable TV. She was making me a freak at school. Like I needed that."

Rachel took a deep breath, stalling while she searched for the right answers. "I know all those rules seem rigid and ridiculous, but they're meant to protect you. Some of the things I see at work and when I'm volunteering downtown—like school shootings, gang activity and kids who exercise nothing but their thumbs—I believe some of those problems come from too much electronic interaction and not enough physical or social activity. Kids don't talk to each other anymore. They text. They don't play together except video games over the internet. And because of that they don't learn how to work out their differences. And the violence… I think we're becoming desensitized to it."

"That's what Mom always said."

"I will always do what I think is best for you, Chastity. Sometimes you might not like my rules. But try to remember, they're because I want to keep you safe, and I love you."

Brown eyes flashed her way. "Yeah. Ditto."

"And, Chastity, I appreciate you not punching

that boy in the mouth for saying that about your mom. I'm sure you wanted to. I would have."

"I *really* did. But I didn't want to clean the guys' locker room." Chastity reached for the radio knob, cranking up the volume.

Great way to avoid conversation. She'd have to thank Matt. His threatened punishment had been an effective deterrent.

Parenthood was nothing like Rachel had always dreamed. It was harder, and she sucked at it. But she was getting less sucky every day. She'd have to settle for slow but steady progress.

"CHASTITY'S A NATURAL, and it looks like she's going to be as horse-crazy as Anna," Marcia said as she and Rachel watched Chastity take her first horseback riding lesson.

Rachel made a conscious effort to unclench her fists. She hadn't realized being a mother involved repeated doses of fear. "How do you watch?"

"I trust the instructor, the horse and, most of the time, my daughter. You'll get used to it. Wait until Chastity starts jumping. Then you'll really be a nervous wreck."

"I had hoped the girls would become friends, but I didn't expect it to happen instantly."

The girls had hit if off immediately this morning. When they'd arrived at the stable, Anna had asked Chastity to help her groom the mare and prepare for the lesson. Chastity, who hadn't been around horses since that birthday party Rachel had planned years ago, had quickly caught on. Then when the instructor had asked Chastity if she'd like to try riding, Anna had encouraged her.

Marcia nodded. "They have a lot in common. Cheerleading, choir, starting a new school in the fall and now horses."

"Anna did a great job of explaining the pros and cons of each school on the ride over here. Since it sounds like she's convinced Chastity to attend the public school, I should have money for riding lessons."

"I'm eager for you to move Chastity down here and not just because we miss you at work."

Guilt rushed Rachel. "I'm sorry. I know I'm inconveniencing everyone."

"Don't be. Family comes first. I'd do the same. Anyone on the team would. Chastity seems like a good kid."

Rachel wondered if Marcia would have said that if Chastity had reverted to her rebellious attire for the visit.

"I close on the house on the nineteenth. I'm hoping to be back at work soon after that. If you have any recommendations for movers, I'd appreciate that." She didn't want Matt and Brad to help. As generous as Pam's offer had been, memories of Matt in their new home would be too hard to handle.

"I'll ask at work Monday."

Rachel's cell phone rang before she could express her thanks. The ringtone spooked Chastity's horse. It sidestepped a few strides, terrifying Rachel, but Chastity held on and even grinned once the mare settled.

Keeping her eye on her daughter, Rachel answered the phone without checking the number first. "Hello."

"You ran."

Matt. Her heart danced as wildly as the horse had. She held up a give-me-a-moment finger to Marcia and quickly walked away from the riding ring.

"You conned your sister into getting Chastity out of the house for the weekend."

"Jess would have enjoyed Chastity's company at the beach. And I wanted to spend time with you."

She gave him points for not denying his involvement. "If you'd asked me, I would have told you Chastity and I had things to do here to get ready for the move. It's only a few weeks away," she pointed out, reminding him as much as herself that their affair was temporary.

"You couldn't have waited until we talked about…us."

Rachel's mouth went dry. Her heart hip-hopped. "Matt, I told you, there can't be an 'us' beyond camp."

"Rachel, if you want something bad enough, you find a way. If not—"

"Chastity and I have to finalize the school choice and get the transfer paperwork started. And I want to buy a car."

"Have you ever bought a car before?"

"No."

"Wait until you get home. I'll take you to a dealer I know and trust. Salesmen pull all kinds of tricks to make a buck."

She appreciated his offer, but she couldn't become dependent on him. "Thanks, but it makes sense to buy here where I'll be having it serviced." Another less than subtle reminder.

She glanced over her shoulder at the riding ring and saw Chastity taking another lap, this time at a slow trot. She stared hard at Rachel as she passed. "I have to go. Chastity's riding a horse for the first time, and I'm missing it. Bye, Matt."

She turned off the phone and shoved it into her pocket. The sooner she cut all ties with Matt Johnston, the better. Because wishing he could be here to see this was not an option.

CHAPTER FOURTEEN

MATT DETOURED DOWN Rachel's street on his way home from his men's group Sunday evening. At almost nine, it was too late to drop by uninvited, but he needed to know she'd made it back safely.

Rachel believed she could walk away again. He couldn't let that happen. Not only was their chemistry more potent than before, but the bracelet incident had demonstrated she would always put Chastity's welfare first. So, convincing Rachel that Chastity would be better off in Johnstonville with her friends, her church and his family as a support network was priority number one.

All he had to do was keep reminding Rachel how good it was between them and show her that his family could become hers and Chastity's. And he had to do it before she closed on the house.

A life with Rachel—*marrying* her—meant becoming an instant father to a thirteen-year-old girl. A ready-made family. The thought hit him with pregame jitters. He'd seen enough of Jake's and Brad's struggles to know fatherhood wasn't easy, even if you had slow and steady training. And none of their children rebelled the way Chastity had recently.

But he could handle it. He'd been the underdog on the field before and beat the odds. In fact, he relished it because when everyone expected you to fail, you often exceeded their expectations. With his family—his home-team crowd—behind him, he could go all the way to becoming the father Chastity needed.

Rachel had also proved she cared for him by mistakenly trying to protect him from his youthful mistake. After she'd left he'd checked the statutes. They had nothing to fear about her age fourteen years ago. It bothered him that she'd been under eighteen. But at least she'd been over sixteen— the legal age of consent in the state. Otherwise their four-year age gap could have spelled trouble. But the worst they faced now was talk—if anyone cared enough to do the math.

But before he went any further with his plans, he would have to tell her about his aborted NFL career before someone else did. He didn't want any secrets between them. And when she was ready, he would tell her he'd fallen in love with the strong, giving woman she'd become.

He spotted an unfamiliar red Toyota RAV4 in her driveway and turned in behind it. The cardboard new-car tag confirmed she had bought the small SUV even after he'd offered to help with her car purchase. That bothered him. He wanted to be there for her. If she'd been taken advantage of by an unscrupulous salesman he was going to head south and raise hell on her behalf whether she liked it or not. He climbed from his truck and headed toward the front porch.

Chastity responded to his knock. "Hey, Coach. Late for a visit, isn't it?"

"Yes. Is Rachel here?"

"She's cooking dinner. We just got home." She remained planted in his path, a slightly defiant expression on her face.

The kid didn't want him here. That sobered him. He'd been thinking about what a good father he would be to her, and she didn't want to let him in the house. Rachel had warned him, but he hadn't taken the threat seriously. Time to rethink his strategy.

"We missed you in church this morning," he ventured.

"We went with my friend Anna in Atlanta. Her church is huge. Like a thousand times bigger than ours. The youth group has a praise band and its own sanctuary and everything."

Not a point in his favor. He definitely needed to go back to the playbook. "May I come in?"

She hesitated.

"Who is it, Chastity?" Rachel called from the back of the house.

"Coach Johnston," Chastity shouted back without budging.

He heard a bang like a pot against the counter, then Rachel hustled into view. "Matt. What are you doing here?"

Her face was flushed and her voice breathy. She looked so good in shorts that showed off her legs and a T-shirt that hugged her curves. Hunger blitzed him. Even with the kid glaring at him.

"I saw a strange car and wanted to make sure you were okay."

"That's our new car," Chastity pointed out. "I helped pick it out. And we went by our new house today, too. When the owners saw us, they invited us in. I got to take pictures and everything." She pulled a cell phone from her pocket. He recognized Hope's Serenity Prayer phone case. "I can't wait until we move."

That shot down part of his plan.

"Have you texted the pictures to Jess?" He didn't feel a speck of guilt over reminding her of who she'd lose if she moved.

Chastity dropped her chin and mumbled, "Not yet." Then she turned to Rachel. "You're not burning dinner, are you?"

"No, kiddo. I left it warming. Matt, we're short on time. Did you need something?"

Rachel was trying to get rid of him. "No. Glad you made it home. Want to show me your car?"

"Another time."

Not getting her outside alone meant no kiss good-night. He tackled his disappointment, waved and headed for his truck, shaking his head over the failure of his offensive rush. He'd been shut down in the first quarter. Chastity had played a good defense, then Rachel had offered an assist. But the game wasn't over yet.

THE MAIN OFFICE was bedlam. It always was at this time of year. Parents, teachers, students and staff swarmed around like agitated bees. Matt wove his way through them intent on grabbing the file he needed, then getting out. He had a highly touted sophomore transferring in next year, and he wanted to call the boy's current coach and get the scoop on the punter's personality off the field.

He spotted a familiar head of glossy dark hair and stopped in his tracks. Rachel. He hadn't expected to see her today. She stood in the long line leading through the office door with her back to him.

Nodding to people he knew, he made his way to her. He ached to touch her. "Rachel."

She startled and pivoted to face him, her eyes going wide and lips parting. She jerked a thumb to indicate the sign hanging by the door. "'Do it now: Register for fall classes, sports physicals, summer school and driver's education.' Wouldn't it be more efficient to spread those out or enroll online rather than do everything in-house simultaneously?"

He shrugged. "It probably would be, but it's always been done this way."

"Yeah, that's what the other people in line told me. I see Johnstonville's refusal to adapt to the current decade hasn't changed."

Not a point in his favor, but inarguably true. The citizens of his hometown preferred doing things the old-fashioned way. "Did you need something?"

She hesitated. "I need to have Chastity's transcripts faxed to her new school so the counselor can put together a schedule for her. I guess I picked the wrong day, huh?"

Progress. In the wrong direction. "If you need the secretary or counselor's help, yes. If you'll let me help you, no."

A half-dozen heartbeats passed before she said, "I don't want to bother you."

"We have seven days of class remaining. The office will be this chaotic for the duration. Then the entire staff takes a much-deserved two week vacation. If you can wait until the last week of June—" Her shaking head stopped him.

"I guess I need your help. I don't want Chastity to miss out on her first choice electives."

"No problem. I've done it for my transferring athletes before. Wait over there on the bench." Mentally kicking himself for his vanity at sending her to sit by the trophy case where she'd see his team's successes, Matt headed into the office. He'd decided five years ago that if he couldn't be the best player the town ever produced, he would be the best coach. In doing so he would enable his players to fulfill the dreams he'd blown and succeed where he'd failed.

He waded through the crowd and grabbed a clipboard and a release form. Returning, he handed them to Rachel. "Sign this and I'll get her file. I'll need the counselor's name and fax number."

She scanned the pages, then signed. He made a point of brushing the back of her hand as he took the board back. His pulse and her breath hitched. He held her gaze long enough to see the hunger she couldn't hide. Then he had to let her go or risk drawing attention to their exchange. "Give me a few minutes."

He retrieved Chastity's file from the metal cabinet in the records room. It was thicker than he'd expected. Surely her recent mischief hadn't added that many pages? Then he made his way to the teacher's workroom, found an empty table and wrote up the fax cover sheet. He opened the file to select the necessary pages and put them in the proper order.

The multi-sheet IEP form on top surprised him. Only learning disabled students had Individualized Education Plans. Hope had never mentioned Chastity having a problem. Neither had Pam or Jess.

Dyslexia. The checked word jumped out at him as if it were lit by three-foot-tall neon letters. Chastity had dyslexia. He shook his head. It was a sad coincidence that she suffered from the same learning disability that had made his life miserable. But it meant he had something in common with the teen that he could use to work past her recent hostility.

He flipped pages to learn more. Chastity had been diagnosed in second grade, which gave her a better chance of learning to cope than he'd had. His issues hadn't been labeled until ninth. Her most recent yearly evaluation stated she struggled with reading—particularly reading aloud. That explained her issues with the new English teacher. Matt knew all about finding ways to distract others from his problems. Behavior was one.

September. Chastity had been born in September. Something about that nagged at him as he sorted pages. Then he remembered Pam had been celebrating her newly discovered pregnancy when he'd come home for Christmas the year he'd met Rachel. It was memorable because she'd still been in college, and his parents had hit the roof fearing she wouldn't finish.

Jess had been born in July. That made her only a couple of months older than Chastity. But Hope had claimed she'd conceived Chastity on her honeymoon in the spring. How could that be true? He counted back in his head and didn't like the answer, so he recalculated. Same answer. Hope had been single and living in Johnstonville nine months before Chastity's birth.

Just to be sure he wasn't scrambling the numbers, he did the math a third time on paper. The hairs on the back of his neck prickled. He stared at the twelve month school calendar on the wall and recounted a fourth time, still not willing to trust his calculations since the numbers sometimes switched places on him. The dates still didn't add up.

Someone must have entered Chastity's birth date incorrectly on the school forms. He flipped through the papers until he came to a copy of her birth certificate. He double-checked the date. There was no mistake.

He scanned down. The father's name was blank. Even if Hope's husband had died, wouldn't she have written in his name anyway if he'd fathered her child?

What if he hadn't? Could someone in Johnstonville be Chastity's father? He didn't recall Hope dating anyone. She'd always been at home when he and Rachel got together—hence Rachel having to sneak out. And Rachel had once claimed her sister was an old maid who lived for work and the church.

Maybe Chastity had been born very, very early. But that would have left her on the borderline of not surviving. Hope had never mentioned prematurity, and every parent he knew who had a "miracle child" talked about those unforgettable terrifying weeks of neonatal intensive care.

But if Chastity had been conceived in December… And Hope hadn't been seeing anyone… His gut churned. Sweat beaded his brow and upper lip.

No. Chastity was Hope's daughter. Not Rachel's. Or his. Even if she did look more like Rachel than Hope. The dyslexia was a coincidence. He and Rachel had used protection. Every time.

Dyslexia was the most commonly diagnosed disorder. But it was usually inherited. Did Rachel have it? Or her father or grandfather?

Images flashed through his mind like a strobe light. The photograph in Hope's foyer of the Bishop family. Rachel and Chastity shared the same dark hair and chocolate-brown eyes. But so did Hope's father and grandfather. Science had never been his strong suit, but he was pretty sure dark genes were dominant.

He recalled Rachel at his family's picnic watching Chastity with a look of intense anguish in her eyes. He'd assumed her pain was due to losing her sister.

Then he remembered how irritable Hope had become each time one of Rachel's letters arrived for Chastity. He'd thought it was jealousy over the way Chastity carried the letters around for days, reading them over and over, quoting her aunt. Why would Hope resent her sister for loving her child?

Unless she was jealous of a bond she didn't share with her daughter.

Panic clawed up his throat. Could Chastity be

his and Rachel's? Had Hope, the most honest person he knew, lied? He wasn't ready to believe that.

He snatched up the file, then stalked back into the school foyer certain Rachel would think he was an idiot for the question he was about to ask. She looked up from the trophy case. He skimmed her slender frame. Had she carried his child?

"My office. Now."

"Matt, that's not a good idea," she whispered.

"You don't want to have this conversation here."

Her eyes widened and filled with wariness, making him realize his tone had been...threatening. Without waiting to see if she'd follow, he strode toward the gym where they should have some measure of privacy. And he prayed, dear God, he prayed he'd jumbled up the details in his brain. He'd even welcome her laughing at his crazy idea.

He unlocked his office door and gestured for Rachel to precede him. She entered with obvious reluctance. He shut the door, turned the lock.

She stiffened. "What's going on?"

"Chastity has dyslexia."

She frowned. "She does?"

Not the response he'd expected. "Yes. Do you?"

"No."

"Did anyone else in your family?"

"Not that I know of." She seemed genuinely confused by the question. "Why does Chastity having a learning disability have you so bent out of shape? I'm sure the new school can accommodate her needs."

He hesitated. He'd hidden his imperfection for so long. No one knew the whole truth, that his inability to control his mind had led to the end of his career. "Because I have it. And it's usually an inherited condition."

She didn't scoff or laugh. Instead she went as still as a wild rabbit when it spots a predator. Her gaze slid toward the door.

"Is she mine?" he forced past the ball of fear in his throat.

She swallowed. The pulse in her neck fluttered frantically. A white line encircled her compressed lips, and the faintest of tremors overtook her body. "Why would you think that?"

The quaver of her voice told him more than any words could. Rachel had something to hide. His heartbeat hammered his eardrums. His mouth dried. He slapped Chastity's file onto his desk, shoved his fingers through his hair and scrambled to pull his thoughts together. He couldn't sit down. He circled the room and Rachel like a wrestler on the mat does his opponent.

"Chastity is my daughter. Isn't she?"

Rachel blanked her expression. This was the Rachel he'd seen by the ball field. Unnaturally calm in the midst of chaos.

"Chastity is Hope's daughter."

Carefully phrased, but not a yes or no. "Don't lie to me. I saw her birth date."

He waited for her to tell him he was full of shit, and there was no way Chastity was his. But again, she didn't. He struggled to remain calm, to keep his game face on. Yelling wouldn't get him answers.

"Why didn't you tell me you were pregnant?"

She pushed back her hair with an unsteady hand, then she sighed and sank into the visitor chair in front of his desk.

"Because you were Johnstonville's golden boy with an amazing future ahead of you. I was a screwup. I'd lied about my age. I had a bad reputation and nothing to offer a baby. Or you."

Her revelation tackled him even though it was what he'd expected to hear.

I have a child. A daughter. A teenage daughter.

Reeling, he wanted to refute Rachel's claims, but he couldn't. He'd come home for spring break eager to see her again and find out why she hadn't answered his letters. He'd found an empty house. She and Hope had moved away without leaving a forwarding address or phone number.

He'd asked around, hoping to find anybody who knew where she'd gone, but all he'd heard were the stories of Rachel's misdeeds and the lies about her promiscuity. The only way he could have proved them wrong would have been to confess they'd both been virgins when they slept together that first time in the barn. That information wouldn't have helped her reputation any, so he'd kept his mouth shut.

"We used protection. Did you tamper with it?"

"No. God, no." Her consternation looked real.

"Chastity was *your* daughter. *Our* daughter. How could you give her away?"

"I— We would have held you back," she whispered with misery in her eyes.

"That should have been my decision. Our decision, Rachel. One we made together."

"You were so excited about your future in football, the NFL scouts who'd been watching you, your dreams, and your dad living vicariously through you. How could I ruin that? For both of you."

She'd done a good job of justifying her bad decision. "How did Hope end up with our child?"

She blinked at him, pain carving lines into her face. "She caught me throwing up and asked if I was pregnant. I told her there was no way. We'd been careful. She drove me out of town, bought a pregnancy test and made me use it in the store bathroom. It was positive. Hope was furious. On the ride home she said that I couldn't stay in Johnstonville. My promiscuity would destroy her reputation. I had to leave before anyone found out. She gave me twenty-four hours to get out.

"I was terrified and in shock. I didn't know what to do. I couldn't go back to my parents. Not only were they in a country where infant mortality was incredibly high, they would never forgive or accept me as an unwed mother-to-be. Like your family, they believed in abstinence until marriage.

"I'd packed and was ready to walk out when Hope asked me where I was going and how I would provide for myself and a child when I didn't have a job or even a high school diploma. I didn't have any answers, but I was going to try. I knew terminating...wasn't for me.

"Hope pointed out that even if I finished high school, then I'd never find more than a minimum wage job. At that rate I wouldn't make enough for rent, food and day care. And she was right. I wasn't good enough for my own child." He barely heard the last anguished words, but her sense of defeat came through loud and clear in her rounded shoulders and the downward curve of her mouth.

"She offered to help me. She said we'd move away. She'd take a job elsewhere and see me through my pregnancy. But then I'd have to re-linquish the baby. I agreed because I didn't know what else to do. She chose Atlanta because she had a college friend at a big firm who could get her a job. Hope enrolled me in school and arranged for my medical care. Then I heard my baby's heart-beat, felt her growing. I learned she was a little girl. I fell more in love with her every day, and I knew I couldn't give her to strangers."

The tender expression on her face backed up her words.

"In my last month of pregnancy Hope told me she had everything she'd ever wanted except for a family. She said I had the power to give her that if I'd let her adopt my baby. I rejected the idea immediately."

Rachel plucked at the seam of her pants. "But I didn't know how I was going to provide for a child. I talked to Social Services, and it didn't look good. And Hope… Hope didn't let up on reminding me how unfair it would be to raise a child in poverty. She reminded me of the squalor we'd seen on our parents' mission trips and of the sickly children."

His college ring bit into his finger. He didn't like the scenario she was describing. Hope had always been kind and generous. She'd do anything for anyone, and he hadn't believed she had a manipulative bone in her body. Had he been wrong?

"Then my parents died. You have to understand, Matt. Hope got me out of the hellish, unstable life my parents had chosen. If not for her, I would have died in that village beside them. Plus, she'd bailed me out of one scrape right after another. And yet until she said she wanted my child she'd never asked for anything in return. Not money. Not thanks. Nothing.

"She promised that if I relinquished the baby to her I would always be a part of my child's life. I would get to see her grow up and be there for every birthday. So, as much as it broke my heart, after Chastity was born, I gave her to Hope. Because it was best for Chastity." Her eyes pleaded for understanding.

Matt had no name for the melee of emotions crushing his chest. "Did Hope know I was Chastity's father?"

"Yes. She guessed. You were the only guy I'd been seeing."

Betrayal lashed him. In his life he'd considered marrying two women. Rachel because he loved her, and Hope because he trusted her, believed they shared the same values and could build a decent life together.

"Hope was the most honest person I know. Why should I believe you?"

"I wouldn't blame you if you didn't. I'm the villain in all of this."

He saw the anguish and honesty in her eyes, and he couldn't disbelieve her no matter how badly he wanted to. His mind raced as he tried to sift the lies from the truth of everything Hope had told him.

"Hope said she had conceived on her honeymoon and her husband died before she could change her name on all the legal documents." Saying it aloud made the tale seem preposterous. How had he fallen for it? "There was never a husband or a cruise, was there?"

Rachel studied her knotted fingers. "No."

He should have known. Hope hadn't had an impetuous bone in her body. What a gullible fool he'd been. He paced the office. Anger boiled in his blood. He hadn't been in love with Hope, but he'd believed she was the most kindhearted, God-fearing woman he'd ever known. How could he have been so wrong?

"I can't believe I never suspected. Chastity looks just like you," he spat out in self-disgust.

"She has your mouth and chin," Rachel offered quietly. "I see you every time I look at her."

Matt sucked in a shocked breath and opened the file to look at the picture on Chastity's student ID. His own features were right there in front of him. "How damned stupid am I?"

"I've never known Hope to tell a lie other than this one. Her honesty is probably why no one questioned her story."

"This is one hell of a big one. She should have told me. *You* should have told me."

She shook her head. "We were kids, Matt. What kind of parents could we have been?"

"I was twenty-one years old. Old enough to know that I wanted to marry you."

She gasped. "I didn't know that. I thought I was just a vacation romance and that you'd forget about me as soon as you went back to school."

"How could you not know? I slept with you and I'd told you I'd been saving myself. Then I gushed on and on about you and us in my letters." He'd poured his heart out like a lovesick sap.

A confused frown puckered her brow. "What letters?"

Her confusion seemed sincere. "I wrote you at least a dozen times, telling you how I felt and asking you to marry me as soon as you graduated. You never wrote back. And then Hope told me you'd moved on."

Her eyes darkened. "I never got any letters. And if I moved on, it was only to bury myself in my studies so I could forget what I'd done."

"Who else knows about Chastity?"

"No one."

If she hadn't gotten the letters, then that meant Hope had hidden them. She'd deliberately kept him and Rachel apart. Hope had kept Chastity from him.

But then Hope had sought him out when he returned to Johnstonville. Them marrying had been her idea. Neither of them was getting any younger, and neither had found another to love, she'd said. And he'd come damned close to putting a ring on her finger.

Hope had betrayed him. But so had Rachel.

"I trusted her. And she lied to me." The words cauterized his throat.

"At least you've been able to spend time with your daughter, even if you didn't know the truth. I only saw Chastity a couple of times a year to begin with and not at all in the past five years. That wasn't what Hope had promised."

His brain snagged on one thing she'd said. "Hope and I started dating five years ago."

Rachel recoiled. "Well, I guess that tells me why she cut off the visits, doesn't it?"

The manipulative bitch. "When I moved home to take the coaching job, she approached me at church and suggested dinner. But Chastity and I didn't spend that much time together. She usually stayed with Jess when Hope and I went out."

He ought to demand a paternity test, but he didn't doubt Rachel. "Am I at least listed on her original birth certificate?"

Rachel face filled with regret. "No. I'm sorry, but I had to write 'unknown' to be able to relinquish her without your permission."

He had a daughter.

"I want to tell her she's mine."

Rachel's eyes widened in horror. "You can't."

"Why not?"

"For exactly the same reasons you told me I shouldn't move her to Atlanta a month ago. She's just lost the woman she believes is her mother. Do you want to destroy those memories? To take what little she has away from her? Matt, don't make her lose her mother a second time."

"She's *my* daughter. I want her to know—"

"The truth will only make her hate us all."

"Not all. I didn't know."

"Me, then. Don't make her hate me. She's all I have left, Matt." Her voice cracked.

Compassion swelled. He tried to squash it.

Everything she said made sense. But it wasn't what he wanted to hear. He sighed and wiped his face. Fourth quarter and he was down. Down, but not out. Not by a long shot. "I won't tell her now."

"Thank you."

"But I will tell her, Rachel. When the time is right, I want to acknowledge her as my daughter. I want her to know she has family who loves her."

"I understand how you feel, but that time might never come." The loneliness on her face tugged at something inside him.

"That's where you're wrong. The day will come when I can claim my child. You'd better prepare yourself."

Rachel eyed the file on his desk. "I still need those copies."

"No."

"Matt, I have to return to Atlanta, or I'll lose my job."

He hardened his resolve. "And if you try to take Chastity away from me again, I'll hire an attorney and I will stop you. I've already lost thirteen years of her life. The very least that will happen is you'll have to share custody. But between the hours you work and Chastity's ties here, I could even get full custody."

He hardened his heart against her shattered expression and the tears in her eyes. "Matt, please."

"I won't negotiate on this one, Rachel. I'll keep your secret for now, but as soon as I figure out a game plan that won't hurt her, I'm claiming my daughter. She has grandparents, aunts, uncles and cousins here, who love her. I won't let you deprive her of her family just because you want to run away and hide your mistake."

Flabbergasted, she sputtered, "My mistake?"

"You gave away our baby. In my playbook, that's a mistake no matter how many ways you justify your actions."

"Johnstonville has the memory of an elephant and a rigid moral code. Do you really want Ch— our daughter labeled a bastard? Do you want people to whisper that she's the child of the town slut?"

Something he hadn't considered. "You weren't—"

"You and I know that, but no one else will believe it, thanks to your ex-girlfriend and the guys she convinced to swear they'd screwed me. I don't care what they say about me, Matt. But I won't have Chastity hurt by my past. And it's already started. You've seen it."

Damn it. She was right. "You're happy to go through life as her 'aunt Rachel'?"

"Happy? No. But for Chastity's sake, I want the

past to stay where it belongs. Think of what openly claiming Chastity would do to Hope's reputation."

"Right now I don't give a f—a rat's ass about Hope."

"Hope's reputation will reflect on Chastity. If everyone finds out she lied…"

He let that sink in, hating that once again, she was right. "Why choose a name like Chastity? The kids tease her, you know."

"That was Hope's doing. I called her Noelle. She was my Christmas gift from you."

That hit him hard. "Hope wanted to remind you of your mistake every single time you said our daughter's name?"

"Apparently."

He sucked in a sharp breath. Add pettiness to the list of charges. How had he let himself be blinded by Hope's superficial goodness? She'd been the worst kind of hypocrite. Saint on the outside. Heart of a viper on the inside.

Where did he and Rachel go from here? He'd loved her once and, until today, had believed he loved her again. But could he forgive her for this? Or trust her again? He honestly didn't know. And even if he could, could his family accept her and the choices she'd made?

A knock on the door startled them. Frustrated they hadn't settled anything, he opened it. Chastity stood on the other side looking none too friendly. Seeing her hit him like a medicine ball to the chest.

His daughter.

"Somebody said they saw Aunt Rachel come back here with you." Her tone spit belligerence.

"I'm here," Rachel said before he could confirm or deny.

Chastity pushed her way into the room. "What are you doing with *him*?"

Rachel glanced at Matt briefly, her eyes flashing caution. Then she pointed to the file on Matt's desk. "I came to get your transcripts. After that I thought I'd join you for lunch." At Chastity's surprised expression she added, "You're not too old for company, are you?"

The aggression wavered. "I guess not. Mom never came. She was always too busy with her accounts or some church thing."

"Is the food still as bad as it used to be?"

A grin split Chastity's face. His grin, damn it. Chastity linked her arm through Rachel's and steered her out of the office. "Don't eat any casserole. They all taste like barf. And most of the vegetables have been cooked so long you can gum 'em. No teeth required. They should serve 'em at the senior center."

Rachel's strained laughter rippled over him. She didn't look back as Chastity led her away. Matt ached to go with them, to hang on Chastity's every word and memorize her features and gestures. But he couldn't. Not yet.

He dropped into his chair and buried his head in his hands. He had a daughter, a daughter he barely knew. Rachel and Hope had robbed him of that right. He didn't know her favorite color or food. If it hadn't been for seeing Rachel trying to squeeze into the crowded office today, he might never have discovered the truth.

But now that he had, what in the hell was he going to do?

CHAPTER FIFTEEN

RACHEL STARTLED AT the tap on her car window. Miss Wilkins, her nosy neighbor, stood outside, her wrinkled face pruned even more with concern. Rachel pushed the button to lower the glass.

"Are you all right, dear? You've been sitting out here for twenty minutes with the engine running."

Had she? "Yes. Thank you. I'm— I just have a lot on my mind."

Matt knew. And everything she feared could come true. But she would not panic.

"Are you sure? You look a little peaked. I can fix you a snack and a glass of sweet tea. That'll perk you right up."

Rachel forced a smile. "Thank you, Miss Wilkins. I appreciate your offer, but I have to handle some of Hope's estate issues before Chastity gets home."

If she and Chastity couldn't move—

Tension spiraled through her when she considered all that could go wrong if Matt forced them to stay in Johnstonville. She had to convince him Chastity was better off away from his hometown's vipers.

"Well…if you change your mind, just drop in. I'm a good listener." She stepped back, then fluttered her gnarled fingers and returned to her house, looking over her shoulder several times as if she hoped Rachel would join her.

Rachel felt as if she'd kicked a puppy. The woman wasn't nosy. She was lonely. And kind. But at the moment, Rachel had nothing left to give. She was emotionally bankrupt. Maybe later she could visit. Or invite her neighbor to dinner.

Focus on what you can control and the rest will fall into place. The mantra she'd learned from her first trauma boss had carried her through many a crisis.

She emptied her lungs in a long, slow effort to relax, then exited the car. As much as she dreaded it, she had to go through Hope's purse and wallet to see if she'd missed anything. She retrieved the box of Hope's belongings and set it on the kitchen table. Her cell phone rang, granting her a brief reprieve. Then she checked caller ID. *Matt.* She didn't want to answer it. But what if Chastity was in trouble again?

"Yes?"

"Invite me to dinner," he demanded without preamble. Her abdominal muscles knotted as tightly as those in the back of her neck. After their confrontation earlier today, she wasn't ready to face him again.

"Matt, that's not a good idea. Chastity's already

not thrilled about me meeting with you at school today."

"Tough. I want to get to know my daughter. Hope and I had dinner together a couple times a month. It won't seem strange to Chastity if you and I do the same—only more often. And this time Chastity will be there instead of being sent to Pam's."

Bitterness soured Rachel's stomach. Not only had Hope hidden Matt's letters, she'd been laying a trap to catch him for herself. "What makes you think I can cook?"

"If you can't, then I will."

"You'd cook for me? For us?"

"I have to cook for one. Why not make it three? Want me to bring the ingredients?"

"No, I…" *Don't want you here. Don't trust myself around you.* "I have it covered. We eat at six."

Then she hung up and buried her face in her hands. She'd never been good at playing games. Matt, on the other hand, as a player and now a coach, was an expert at gamesmanship. The trophies she'd seen today testified to that. And now the ball was in his hands. She hoped he didn't run them straight into disaster.

"Focus on what you can control," she repeated and reached for Hope's briefcase. The wallet would be last. Work seemed less personal, easier to manage. But she had to get through this before Chastity came home.

A little while later, she was staring at the snapshot of Hope holding newborn Chastity when the front door blasted open and Chastity charged in. Shocked, Rachel glanced at the clock. Where had the hours gone?

The teen stopped when she saw the mess scattered over the kitchen table. "What are you doing?"

"I didn't hear you drive up."

"Mrs. Weaver let me off at the end of the driveway so I could check the mail. What are you doing with Mom's stuff?" Chastity repeated, slapping the mail on to the counter.

"I'm looking for the credit card I missed. I have to cancel it."

"It's hidden in her recipe box. For emergencies." Chastity crossed the kitchen. She retrieved the card and handed it to Rachel, then glanced at the box on the table. *The bracelet!* Rachel fought the urge to dive for it.

"Are there any other cards I should know about?" she blurted in an attempted diversion, but Chastity only shook her head as she reached inside the box and stirred the loose items on the bottom.

Desperate, Rachel extended the photograph. "Look what I found. It's you and your mom the day she brought you home from the hospital. I've never seen her as happy as she was that day." The happiest day of Hope's life had been the absolute worst day of Rachel's. "It was in her wallet. She always kept you close. You can see how much she loved you. It's written all over her face."

Chastity glanced at the photo. Her gaze lingered only a moment, then she muttered, "Yeah," ducked her head and dug.

Horrified, Rachel watched her lift the broken strand and study the cut cord.

"It was supposed to be unbreakable," Chastity said flatly.

Rachel didn't want to lie. But she wouldn't tell the whole truth, either. "I guess it got broken when the paramedics moved your mom from the car to the ambulance. I thought you might want to keep it…to remember her by."

Chastity's hand fisted around the beads, and her face bunched up. Rachel didn't know if she was going to hurl the strand or cry over it. Chastity pressed her fist to her chest. "I will."

Dry-eyed, she picked up the picture, turned and went to her bedroom. Rachel followed. "Are you okay?" she asked gently.

"I guess. It just hurts, you know?" Chastity's voice was raw and her eyes red.

Rachel draped an arm around her shoulders. "Yeah. I do. Losing someone you love hurts. My parents died right before you were born. I'm very sorry they never got to know you."

"I've seen their pictures. They were a lot like Mom, weren't they? Always doing churchy stuff."

Rachel's lips twitched at the description. "Their favorite motto was, 'Love others before yourself.'"

"Mom said that a lot, too. But it's hard to do sometimes."

The teen had no idea. "Yes. It is. But no one expects you to be good at it at your age."

"Were you?"

Rachel laughed but without mirth. "No. I was a brat. There were times I thought my parents loved the strangers they missioned to more than me. And I resented it. I did stupid stuff to get their attention."

"But in your job…you risk your life to take care of others all the time."

"It took me a while to realize that giving is its own reward."

Chastity rolled her eyes. "Yeah. Mom said that a lot, too. What's for dinner?"

The bonding moment vanished. "Homemade pizza. Matt's coming for dinner, too."

"Why can't he leave you alone?"

Rachel scrambled for an answer. "I need to repay him for mowing the grass." True. Just not the reason behind dinner.

"He was Mom's boyfriend, and now he watches you all the time. It's disgusting." She punctuated the word with a *gag-me* finger pointing into her mouth. Drama.

Aiding in the development of the father/daughter bond might not be easy, but it was the right thing to do. As Chastity had pointed out, Rachel's job was risky. If anything ever happened to her, she knew no one would care for their daughter as well as Matt and his family. That meant telling the truth—part of it—even if it cast Hope in a less than wonderful light.

"Matt is a friend. He and I dated when I lived here."

"And then he asked Mom out? Eew."

"I think your mother asked him."

"Did *he* tell you that?"

"Yes."

"And you believe him?"

"I do. Matt has always been honest."

"Well, he should have said no."

"Your mom wasn't an easy person to say 'no' to. And Matt's a decent guy if you give him a chance. Let's go fix dinner."

"Do we have any arsenic?"

Rachel shot her a warning look. "Be nice."

The night wasn't going to be easy on many levels, and it was ironic that she, the one who used to incite chaos for kicks, was now being forced into the role of peacemaker.

MATT WAS MORE nervous than he'd ever been before any championship game when he rang Rachel's doorbell. Dinner with Rachel and his daughter—*his daughter!*—was like a double first date. He had to impress two females at once. In totally different ways.

Rachel opened the door. She had white smears on her cheek and left breast. He wanted to brush off both—the first with his lips, the second with his hand. He pointed instead. "You have smudges there and there."

She smiled—clearly forced—opened the door and dusted off the flour. "Come in. We're almost done."

"Everything okay?"

The worry in her eyes didn't bode well. "Other than her request for arsenic? Sure."

Not good. He lifted the cake carrier. "I brought dessert."

"Nice. Come in. We're eating in the kitchen. Dinner should be ready shortly."

He followed her. Chastity stood by the counter preparing a salad. She shot him a dark look. Rachel subtly nudged her with an elbow. "Hello, Mr. Johnston."

So formal. He missed her usual, "Hey, Coach." He'd have to be as dumb as a goalpost not to realize Chastity didn't want him here. Rachel had warned him. He watched her with a new curiosity as he set the cake on the counter. She was his. *His*.

"Hi, Chastity. I brought my mom's fudge cake. I heard it's your favorite."

Chastity shrugged. "I can't eat that with cheerleading camp coming up. The guys have to pick me up for the lifts. I can't weigh a ton."

Rachel shot her what looked to be a warning, and the teen said, "I'll be sure to thank Mrs. Johnston next time I see her."

Rachel squeezed her shoulder. "You're the right weight for your height and age, but if you're concerned about balancing your caloric intake, I'll wait until you get home from school to take my runs. You can go with me." The offer earned her a grimace.

"Ugh. Pass."

The timer beeped. "Pizza's ready." Rachel retrieved it from the oven and set it in the center of the table. A mouthwatering aroma filled the air. "Have a seat."

The kitchen table was set for three. Chastity quickly deposited the salad bowls and scooted into the middle chair. Her usual seat? Or did she not want him sitting beside her aunt?

"Thanks for cooking. It looks good."

Rachel cut the pie. "Pizza is one of the things Chastity and I used to make together when she and her mom came to visit."

"Forever ago," the teen groused.

Rachel extended her arms, palms up. "Your turn to say grace, Chastity."

Chastity took Rachel's hand, and after a moment's hesitation, his. He wanted to savor the fact that he was holding his daughter's hand, but instead, he reached across the table to take Rachel's. The connection was instant and electric. Her cheeks flushed, telling him she felt it, too.

A family. The three of them were a family. One that should never have been torn apart.

"Lord, thank you for this food. May it nourish us so that we can do your will. Amen. Let's eat," Chastity rattled off as fast as an auctioneer and snatched her hand free.

Matt didn't know whether to be taken aback or amused. Instead he added his "Amen" and waited for Rachel to serve slices.

He took a bite. If he weren't so nervous, his taste buds would be high-fiving. "This is the best pizza I've ever had."

"One of my early shift leaders was a transplanted Italian from New York. He gave me the recipe, and he showed Chastity how to toss the dough. You remember that?"

"Yeah. It was cool. But it was like…a long time ago."

"You were eight. Dom cooked for us during your last visit."

A shaft of jealousy shot through him. Who was Dom and what was he to Rachel? Coworkers didn't usually get invited to cook dinner for your family.

"Are you looking forward to camp?" he asked Chastity.

She shot him a look that said, "Stupid question." "Yes."

"Have you stayed in a dorm before?"

"No."

"Think you and Jess will get to room together?"

"Yes." Then, ignoring the sharp look Rachel shot her, Chastity shoved a huge bite into her mouth. He got the message—leave her alone. So much for father/daughter bonding. Not that he'd throw in the towel that easily.

He ate and tried not to stare. At Chastity. At Rachel. But he couldn't help making comparisons. Their gestures were so similar. The old "nature versus nurture" argument played in his head. Did Chastity have any of his mannerisms?

Chastity caught him staring midway through the meal and scowled. "Jessica's trying to decide what to do for her birthday," he said in an attempt to cover his fascination with her. "Do you have any suggestions?"

Chastity turned to Rachel. "Will we be here for it? It's the week after camp."

Rachel blotted her mouth and took a sip of drink. He recognized stalling when he saw it. "We'll do our best."

She hadn't told Chastity about their discussion. Matt reined in his impatience. He focused on Chastity. "What kinds of birthday parties have you had?"

Chastity shrugged. "I didn't have parties. Well, not recently. Mom said it was selfish to devote a whole day to yourself."

Rachel's mouth curved down. "That's a leftover from your grandparents. You'll have a party this year."

The teen almost cracked a smile. "For real?"

"Count on it."

"How did you and your mom usually celebrate?" Matt asked, determined to understand Hope and the way she'd raised his daughter. Pam had never mentioned Hope refusing to celebrate Chastity's birthday.

"We used to go visit Aunt Rachel till—" her eyes locked with Rachel's "—till we stopped. Year before last Mom and I had a dinner here. She cooked all of my favorites, and we decorated the cake together. Last year we drove to Raleigh to buy school clothes and supplies and spent a weekend at a hotel."

Rachel's expression turned defensive. "When Hope and Chastity came to visit me, we always celebrated in a big way, didn't we, kiddo? What would you like to do for your birthday this year?"

"I don't know. You always planned the coolest stuff. Surprise me."

"You got it."

"But I want Anna and Jess there."

"We'll try. You'll all be back in school then, so it might be tough."

Matt wanted to be a part of planning Chastity's party. And he wanted it to be here. But until she knew he was her father, he didn't have that right to insist.

"Can I get a job after we move?" Chastity asked.

Matt gritted his teeth on the need to tell her she wouldn't be moving. Not if he had anything to say about it.

"Why?" Rachel asked.

"Because I want to be able to pay for riding lessons and clothes and stuff so I can ride with Anna. You shouldn't have to pay for everything. And you always had a job when you were in school."

"You did?" Matt asked. She hadn't been working when he knew her.

"After we left Johnstonville, yes."

She'd been pregnant. "Doing what?"

"I got a job at a women's health clinic. Mostly cleaning and some paperwork. I worked there after school until…college."

Until Chastity had been born, he guessed. "Is that what turned you toward nursing?"

"Yes, I liked knowing I was helping people."

Their gazes held. He'd misjudged her in so many ways.

"What was my dad like?" Chastity blurted, clearly not liking them paying attention to each other.

Rachel went as still as prey—the way she had in his office. "What did your mother tell you about him?"

"Nothing. Every time I asked, she started crying and said it hurt too much to think about that sad time in her life." Chastity fussed with her fork. "But I need to know. Did he have brown hair like me?"

Rachel twisted her napkin. Matt wanted to see how she'd handle direct questions. Would she lie?

"No, he's...he had blond hair."

"So I got my coloring from granddad. That's what Mom always said. I wish the pictures hadn't burned in the fire."

Rachel quickly ducked her head and took a huge bite of pizza. He'd bet his next paycheck it wasn't because she was hungry.

"Was he good-looking? Is that how he swept Mom off her feet?"

Rachel's cheeks turned pink. She glanced at Matt. Dangerous territory. He was glad he wasn't the one being interrogated. "Yes, he was very attractive."

"Tall, short, fat, skinny?" Chastity persisted.

Rachel squirmed. "Tall and...and well built."

"What kinds of things did he like to do?"

Rachel looked so uncomfortable he ought to save her, but he didn't. Maybe she'd understand how badly Chastity needed to know her father if he let the teen keep grilling her.

"He was, um...athletic and smart."

"I figured he'd be a geek if he hooked up with Mom. But what was he like as a person? Mom said they met on a cruise, and she married him right away."

"He was a good listener. He had a way of making things make sense." The softness of her voice caressed his wounded ego, but she didn't even glance his way.

"A good listener? Ugh. Sounds like a wimp."

His thoughts exactly. But he couldn't defend himself or remind Rachel of their explosive chemistry now.

"No, not at all. He was…special."

Chastity's eyes narrowed suspiciously. "How special?"

"Special enough for your mother to fall in love with him."

"Why do you think she fell for him?" Matt asked, even though he knew he shouldn't needle her.

Rachel's eyebrows lowered. "He was generous, and he played fair. He never kicked a man—or woman—when she was down. He was ambitious and had big dreams, the kind of guy every girl hopes she'll meet when she grows up."

Chastity set her glass down with a thud. "Sounds like you were in love with him yourself. Maybe he should have married you. Maybe then he wouldn't be dead."

The angst in Chastity's voice made Matt feel like an ass for goading Rachel.

Rachel pushed away her plate. "If he'd married

me, then we wouldn't be sitting here or having this conversation. Now back to your desire for a job... Finding ways to support your hobbies is a great goal, but any extracurricular activities will be dependent on your grades. Like cheerleading camp, you're going to have to earn the right to work."

As good a segue as he was going to get. "Chastity, I saw in your file that you have dyslexia."

He caught Rachel's horrified expression out of the corner of his eye.

"You had no right to look at my file! You're not my teacher!" Chastity cried, her face turning deep red.

"I asked Matt to fax your records to your new school," Rachel defended.

"He shouldn't have read them."

"I had to sort out what the school needed and what it didn't," Matt explained. "I do it for my athletes all the time."

"I'm not one of your athletes, and my life is none of your business."

He'd screwed this up. He had to fix it. "Chastity, I have dyslexia, too. And sometimes I used behavior to hide it from others. I suspect that's what you've done lately. I could give you some tips on managing your learning style that don't involve detention."

It didn't look like his painful confession earned him any points. "I see the resource teacher three times a week. I don't need your help."

"Chastity—" Rachel scolded and Matt lifted a hold-it finger.

"I'm sorry if my knowing bothers you. But the offer stands. If you want to talk to someone who's been there, I have."

"I don't." The kid stewed for three minutes, a mutinous expression on her face. "Rachel said y'all used to date."

Matt tensed at the accusatory tone, but he put on his game face. He refused to let her see him sweat. "That's right."

"Did you dump her?"

"Chastity—" Rachel scolded again, and again Matt held up a hand. The kid was testing him and striking back.

"No. We met when I was at home from college on Christmas break. Then I went back. I wrote her, but she didn't get my letters and didn't know I wanted to see her again. When I came home on spring break, she and your mother had moved away."

"So *she* dumped *you*."

"Circumstances split us up," he corrected.

"So why did you date my mom?"

"She asked. And we had common interests—"

"Oh, please. Mom hated sports."

"Church, family and community," he continued, trying very hard not to lose his patience or his temper.

"It's sick. You dating Aunt Rachel, then my

mom and now Rachel again." She turned to Rachel. "May I be excused? I have homework to do."

Rachel sighed and laid down her napkin. "Don't you want cake?"

"No. I can't eat it. I'll get fat."

"Then you may be excused. If you need help—"

"I can do my homework. I may not be like everybody else, but I'm not stupid." And then she stormed out. Moments later the stereo blared.

Matt sat shell-shocked. He hadn't expected open hostility. "That didn't go well."

Rachel's worry-clouded gaze met his. "I warned you it wouldn't."

"I won't give up, Rachel."

CHAPTER SIXTEEN

RACHEL SAT AT the table, willing her tension to drain away, but her usual biofeedback techniques failed. The meal had been uncomfortable to say the least. Describing Chastity's fictional father in front of her real one, combined with not wanting to slip up or reveal how much she'd loved and desired Matt and how strongly he still affected her had been more than awkward.

Matt had been very patient with Chastity. She shouldn't be surprised, though. He'd been that easygoing with her when she'd been a troubled teen, too.

"I'll help you with the dishes," he offered. "It's the least I can do for putting you through that."

Not knowing how to politely refuse, Rachel collected plates, carried them to the sink and turned on the tap.

Matt brought the pizza pan and glasses. "I can't believe Hope made you get a job when you were pr—" Alarmed, Rachel shook her head, and he bit off the word. "You were trying to finish school," he finished in a lowered voice.

"She wanted me to earn some money for college and to keep me out of trouble. Besides, the doctors I worked for offered their services in return for my work."

"How long did you work?"

"Until she—" She nodded toward Chastity's bedroom. She'd gone into labor at work. "Until the day I couldn't."

His lips compressed. "Then what? You're a nurse. You must have gone to college. Despite all your shenanigans, your grades were always good."

"I worked full-time at the clinic until the January semester began. After that I worked part-time during school and full-time during vacations."

"How soon did you go back to work after…?"

"Three weeks."

Matt turned abruptly and paced across the room, his anger palpable. "My sister and sister-in-law took off three months."

Rachel carefully dried her hands, folded the dish towel and laid it on the counter. "I couldn't sit around the apartment and watch the two of them bond. That was…" Torture. Chastity's cries had literally been painful during those early days when Rachel had been waiting for her milk to come in and then dry up. "I needed to go back to work."

Remorse filled his face. "If I'd known—"

"You can't change the past, Matt. Trust me, I've second-guessed my choices more times than

I can count. If I had it to do over, I'm sure I'd re-write history."

"Would you change us?" he asked again. She didn't want to answer. How could she explain that meeting him had been her biggest blessing and, simultaneously, the most crippling curse?

"Why are you doing this, Matt? You're tearing me apart."

He stopped in front of her, cupping her chin and forcing her to look into his eyes. Her heart lurched into a rapid beat.

"Would you erase us, Rachel?"

He wouldn't quit until she gave him what he wanted. She shook her head. "No. I might change the ending, but I'd never wish we hadn't met."

The memory of the intimacies they'd shared tugged at her. She remembered his taste, his touch, his heat, and she ached for him again. He lowered his head and brushed his lips against hers. She knew they shouldn't. Not here. Not with Chastity down the hall. But she leaned into him and parted her lips. She couldn't help herself.

Matt plundered her mouth, his tongue strok-ing and evoking a flurry of emotions. The kiss was slick, wet, hot and instantly out of control. He slouched against the counter and widened his stance. Rachel leaned into him, splaying her palms over his chest. His hands stroked down her arms, then he cupped her bottom and pulled her closer until the heat of his erection pressed her belly.

He still represented everything she wanted… and everything she couldn't have. She tangled her fingers in his hair, holding him close one last time. The kiss turned salty. They couldn't do this. She couldn't do this. Not again. She dropped her forehead to his chest, surreptitiously wiping her face and fighting for breath and strength. When he tried to pull her back, she turned her head to the side and saw Chastity watching them with shock and revulsion on her face. Rachel's racing heart stalled. Horrified, she pulled away from Matt.

"You *are* a tramp, just like Beth's mom said," Chastity accused, then she turned and raced toward her bedroom. The door slammed.

Panic coursed through Rachel's veins, turning hot passion into icy fear. She put a hand to her brow, trying to think of a way to explain the intimate scene to an emotional teenager. She pointed toward the front door. "Go. Let me deal with this."

"Rachel—"

"Please, Matt, just go home. We'll talk tomorrow." Leaving him to let himself out, she went after Chastity. With a bracing breath, she tapped on the closed door. "Chastity?"

"Go away."

Rachel opened the door. Chastity glared at her. "Can we talk about what you just saw?"

"What's to say? You were all over him."

Anxiety squeezed Rachel's chest like a boa constrictor. "I guess it looked that way." Chastity responded with a snort. "I told you, Matt and I were…friends when I lived in Johnstonville."

"How good of friends? Did you sleep with him?"

Rachel debated telling her it was none of her business, but figured honesty was best. "Yes, I did."

Chastity's accusing glare made Rachel uncomfortable, but she knew how important this conversation could be to their future relationship.

"So you lied earlier when you said you'd only chased one man."

"No, I didn't lie. Matt is…was that man." That earned her another snort. "I loved him, Chastity."

"Well, he doesn't love you now. He was going to marry Mom."

That hurt even if Matt had claimed it wasn't true.

"Chastity," Matt called from the doorway. Why hadn't he left?

"You're cheating on my mother!"

"No, I'm not." Matt entered the room. "I liked and respected your mother, but I wasn't in love with her. Hope wasn't in love with me, either. We were lonely. We wanted big families, and life wasn't turning out the way we'd planned. We started wondering if we'd ever find that special person to spend the rest of our lives with. That led to the two of us talking about marriage—a marriage based on friendship and mutual respect. We would never have gone through with it, but we discussed it a couple of times."

"You're wrong." Tears streamed down Chastity's cheeks, making Rachel's throat ache. "My mother loved you. She told me she did and that she wanted to marry you. She told me you'd be a good dad."

Rachel froze. This was the perfect opening for Matt to confess the sordid truth. But it was too soon. It would ruin everything.

He sat down on the edge of the bed and put a hand on Chastity's shoulder. She shrugged it off. "Any man would be lucky to have your mother for a wife and you for a daughter."

"So why didn't you marry her?"

"I didn't love her like she deserved to be loved. Like the Bible says a man should love his wife."

"Is that why you didn't marry Rachel? You didn't love her, either?"

His gaze found Rachel's, and her heart stilled at the emotion in his eyes. Then he faced Chastity again. "I loved Rachel and wanted to marry her. And I would have, if I'd been given the chance. You know the rest."

"I think Aunt Rachel was stupid, and she dumped you."

Matt's chest rose and fell. "Is that supposed to be a compliment to me or an insult to Rachel?"

"What do you think?" Chastity radiated defiance. "I think you are surrounded by people who care about you, and your surly attitude is pushing us away. I know you miss your mom, and you're angry she's gone. It's normal to feel that way. Sometimes life sucks and it's not fair. Bad things happen to good people. But you need to wake up to what you're doing to yourself, your friends and your family. Hurting people isn't the best choice."

Rachel opened her mouth to temper Matt's harsh words but remained silent when Chastity bowed her head and nodded. "I know, but Mom messed up everything by dying. She used to help me with my homework and talk to my teachers... She should have been paying more attention to the road." Then she burst into tears.

Matt wrapped his arms around her, and surprisingly, Chastity didn't push him away. He held her while she sobbed. "You'll always love her and always miss her, but that will get better with time. I promise."

Rachel felt an unmistakable twinge of jealousy that he knew exactly how to handle an emotional teen. She stood helplessly lost looking on, her own heart aching with grief for the relationship she and Matt hadn't had and the one she'd denied him with his daughter. She even ached for Hope, despite the wrongs her sister had committed against them. She couldn't fault her sister for doing what she'd thought was best for Chastity because Rachel had done the same.

Finally, Chastity's sobs ceased. She straightened and wiped her face. She looked at Rachel. "I don't want to stay in Johnstonville. Everywhere I look I'm reminded of Mom. And kids at school joke about her being such a Jesus-freak that she killed herself to meet him."

Appalled, Rachel shook her head. "I told you that's not what happened."

"Who said it?" Matt demanded.

Chastity pulled away. "I'm not telling! If you said something to them, I'd be even more of a freak. I just want to go away."

"Running never solved anything," he stated.

"But it won't hurt like staying here. When we move, I can start over. I won't have to be Saint Hope's daughter. You have no idea how hard it is to have people always look at you with disappointment in their eyes. I can't be as good as her. I'm not perfect."

Matt's gaze found Rachel's, and she hoped he could now understand why she and Chastity needed to leave Johnstonville. Then he turned back to Chastity.

"Yes, I do. I truly do. The best way to fight that is to be the best *you* that you can be. Make 'em forget the comparisons." Then he stood. "You know where my office is. If you ever need to talk, I'll be there."

Then he left, leaving Rachel with a head full of questions.

RACHEL PAUSED AT the base of the porch steps Wednesday afternoon to do her post-run stretches. The exercise had done nothing to lessen her stress-induced headaches. She'd been trying since Monday's disastrous dinner to break through Chastity's brooding by picking her up from school and inviting her to join in on her runs.

No luck. Each time the teen had clammed up and refused to talk. She claimed it was because she needed to study for upcoming final exams which started Friday, but Rachel knew better. Matt had reluctantly given them room to work things out, but he'd texted Rachel daily for updates. She appreciated his support more than she could ever tell him.

The front door flew open. A red-faced Chastity stood in the opening. "You lied. You lied about everything!"

Taken aback, Rachel followed her inside and caught the door before Chastity could slam it. "What are you talking about? Chastity. Talk to me."

The girl pointed at the kitchen table. Rachel saw an envelope, some papers and her wallet. Her thoughts screeched to a horrified halt, her gaze returning to the envelope. It was the one from the lawyer, and its contents—including Chastity's original birth certificate—were scattered across the tabletop. Her stomach hit rock bottom.

"What were you doing in my purse?" Her voice was almost level.

"I left the paper Coach gave me to give you about tomorrow's career day in the car. I was looking for your keys so I could get it. Who is Noelle?"

Rachel inhaled deeply, fighting for calm and trying to find a way to dispense the truth that wouldn't destroy everything.

"She's me, isn't she?" Chastity demanded with an edge of hysteria in her voice. "I saw the birth certificate and the picture hidden in your wallet. It's the same baby picture Mom had in her wallet. You had a baby girl on my birthday and named her Noelle. She's me. Isn't she?"

Rachel's worst nightmare was coming true. "I can explain."

"You didn't want me! You gave me away!"

"Yes. Yes, I did want you. You have no idea how much. And I still do. But—"

"You lied about everything. How can I believe anything you say?"

"Chastity, sit down. Let me explain."

"I don't want to hear any more lies."

"Sit down and listen," Rachel ordered in the same way she would a difficult patient.

Chastity, unaccustomed to a harsh tone from Rachel, jerked a chair back from the table and flopped into it, folded her arms and averted her face.

Rachel slid into the chair beside her, mainly because her legs were shaking so badly she almost couldn't stand. Full disclosure was the only option if she wanted a chance of Chastity not hating her.

"I was only seventeen when I got pregnant."

Chastity jerked upright, condemnation on her face. "So you preach at me about using protection, but you didn't."

Mortification burned Rachel's face. "Actually, we did. That's how I know none of it's foolproof. I was too young to be a good mother. I was still in high school. I didn't have a job or any way to support myself or a baby. But I loved you from the moment I found out about you, and I was going to try."

"Is *he* my father?"

Rachel didn't have to ask who. "Yes. But Matt didn't know about you until Monday when I went to school to get your records. I never told him. So none of this is his fault. None of it. I made the mistakes. I'm the one who messed up. No one else."

Except Hope. But Rachel wouldn't destroy the child's memories.

"How did I end up with Mo—Hope?"

"Hope is—*was* your mother in every way that counted. She went with me to my last ultrasound appointment, and I think when she saw your sweet face on the screen she fell in love with you, because immediately afterward she offered to adopt you, so that I would know you were well cared for and that you'd never have to do without."

"Why didn't you want me? Did you know something was wrong with me?"

Rachel's eyes stung. She reached across the table and took Chastity's hand. When her daughter tried to pull away, Rachel held on tightly. "Look at me." She waited until Chastity belligerently complied. "There is absolutely nothing wrong with you, but, no, we didn't know about your dyslexia then. In fact, I didn't know until Matt told me. Neither you nor your mom ever mentioned it."

"Because she told me not to. I'm stupid."

"No, baby, you're not. Learning differently has nothing to do with intelligence. Did you know that Albert Einstein and Thomas Edison and a whole bunch of other famous, successful actors, inventors and musicians have dyslexia? You should look it up sometime. You're in good company."

"That's what Mom always said."

Thank you, Hope. "And she was right."

"But you gave me away."

"Because I loved you enough to know that you deserved a better mom than me. Hope—your mom—seemed perfect. She never lost her temper. She was patient and kind and smart and generous, and she had a good job. And I was…a screwup. A brat. I was always getting in trouble. I did dumb things to get my parents' attention until they got so tired of me they sent me here to live with your mom. That's why I came to Johnstonville. Because my parents were sick of me.

"Even then I kept messing up. And your mom kept bailing me out of trouble. Chastity, I wanted you to have a mother who could afford to give you the things you deserved, like a roof over your head and good medical care. And as much as I wanted that to be me, it wasn't.

"Giving you away was the hardest thing I've ever done in my whole life." Her throat closed up. She gulped at the knot until she thought she could speak again. "But I truly believed it was the best thing for you."

Tears streamed down Chastity's face. Her lips quivered. "You should have kept me. I'd have been a good kid."

"But I wouldn't have been a good mom." Rachel brushed back Chastity's hair. "I want you to understand. There was nothing wrong with you then. And there is nothing wrong with you now. It was me. I'm the one who wasn't good enough for you. Or Matt."

Chastity sniffed and swiped her face. "But your life is so much more exciting than stupid Johnstonville. You go places, you do things. Mom and I were stuck here."

"If I'd kept you we'd have most likely been living in poverty in government housing. I probably would never have finished high school. That means I wouldn't be a nurse. And all those cool things I do now…they wouldn't have happened. I have the opportunity to do those because your mom helped me get scholarships for school, and she raised you. But I lived for our vacations and our phone calls and emails. I loved being with you and hearing from you. Never ever doubt that."

"Do you want me now?"

"Yes. Yes, I do. You have no idea how much. I can't wait to move into our new house. But Chastity…" She took a deep breath and prayed for the first time in over a decade that she and Matt could work out this issue. "Matt wants to know you, too."

Chastity made a face. "Is that why he came to dinner?"

"Yes."

"Did Mom know he was my dad?"

Another tough question she didn't want to answer. "Yes."

"Is that why she wanted to marry him? So he'd be my dad for real?"

"I don't know for sure. But I suspect so. The Johnstons are a wonderful family. She probably wanted you to be a part of it."

"So Mom lied when she told everyone my dad's name was Adam, and he died in a fire."

Rachel should have known Chastity was too smart not to put the puzzle pieces together. "She only did it to protect you."

"So Mom wasn't perfect, either."

Rachel sighed. "No. Nobody is."

"You could have kept me if you'd wanted. We'd have been okay."

"That was a gamble I wasn't willing to take at your expense. I didn't want to fail you, so I did what I thought was best for you. I always will."

Chastity huffed a breath, then an excited light entered her eyes. "That makes Jess and me cousins. I can't wait to tell her."

Rachel winced. "You can't, Chastity."

"Why?"

"Remember how ugly that lady was about me? Remember, I upset a lot of people when I lived here before. They haven't forgotten or forgiven. Telling the truth about this can only hurt people, yourself included. I know you're excited to have cousins, but for now we need to let the story your mom told stand."

"So you're telling me it's okay to lie."

That wasn't the message she wanted to send. "No. Lying is wrong. And this is a perfect example that even lying for a very good reason will eventually catch up with you."

"That sucks. It really sucks. And it's not fair. Y'all lied, and I have to pay for it." Chastity flounced off to her bedroom.

Rachel dropped her head into her hands. Would Chastity ever understand the choices Rachel had made and forgive her?

Rachel needed Matt. More than ever. With his calm rational point of view, he would help her make this right.

THE SOUND OF Rachel's text tone stopped Matt mid-stride Thursday morning.

"Whoa, Buddy," he commanded his dog. The English setter stopped, sat and waited for further instructions. "Good boy."

Matt pulled his phone from his armband and read, Chastity knows. EVERYTHING.

He whistled in a breath, his heart thumping faster. Sensing Matt's disquiet, Buddy tilted his head, lifted a floppy ear and whimpered. "It's okay, boy."

He checked his watch. Chastity should have left for school by now, unless this discovery kept her home. Then he texted back, Coming over.

If Rachel didn't like it, tough. Detouring by her house meant getting to school later than he wanted, but he didn't have anything scheduled until helping with career day after lunch. This couldn't wait. "Let's go, Buddy."

Rachel was outside when he turned up her driveway. The strain on her face contradicted the gentle sway of the porch swing. Only then did he remember his knee brace. He'd been meaning to tell her about his aborted career. Looked like today would be the day.

Buddy rushed to meet her, planting his paws on the seat beside her. Rachel reached out to pet him with unsteady hands as she buried her fingers in Buddy's silky fur. Her face was pale except for the shadows beneath her eyes.

"Who's this? And what's that?" She pointed to his hardware.

"That's Buddy. One of my mom's rescues. He ended up at my house because I suspect she knew I needed him to help me rehabilitate from this. And *this* is a by-product of me blowing out my knee in my first NFL game."

Sympathy filled her eyes. "So you made it."

"Right. I was a one-play wonder. A large group of Johnstonville's citizens chartered a bus and bought tickets they couldn't afford to come see me play. They spent a hell of a lot of money to watch me crash and burn." He hesitated, then decided to reveal all. "I thought I saw you in the stands, and I got so nervous my dyslexic brain scrambled the play. First and last time on the field during pro-fessional game."

Sympathy softened her expression. "That's when you came back to Johnstonville? And why you think everyone's disappointed in you?"

"I did a few other things first, but I wanted to repay the town for supporting me, so, yes, I came home. Is Chastity here?"

"No. Pam already picked her up."

"Did you tell her?"

Still scratching his dog, she shook her head. "Last night while I was out for a run she found the file I'd given the lawyer. Her original birth certi-cate was part of it."

"You left it in plain view?"

"It was in my purse."

"She went through your purse?" That wasn't good.

"Not maliciously. She left the career day paper in my car and went looking for my keys to get it. I should have hidden the file somewhere, but I thought it was safer in my purse than anywhere else, until I could lock it back in the safe at my apartment. Then Chastity went through my wallet and found a picture of me and her taken the morning she was born. I was still in a hospital gown and wearing the hospital bracelet. I've always kept that picture with me in a hidden compartment. Chastity was wearing the going-home outfit that I'd bought her—the same one she was wearing in the picture from Hope's wallet. I'd already told her that was taken the day her mom took her home."

"Going through your wallet was an invasion of privacy."

"Not a fight I want to pick right now."

"Is she okay?"

He'd never seen Rachel look as defeated and afraid as she did now. "I don't know. She refuses to talk about it. She's upset because Hope and I lied and because she can't tell Jessica they're cousins."

Part of him was glad Chastity knew, glad he was closer to being able to claim her. But another part of him worried how she'd handle knowing her life had been a lie perpetrated by the people she'd loved and trusted the most, and how the citizens of Johnstonville would react.

"I'll talk to her."

"I don't know if that's a good idea." She shoved her hair back, then hugged her middle. "I don't know what to do. I can't lose her again. But I think she hates me."

The fear and pain in her voice got to him. He sank onto the seat beside her. "She's in shock. As you predicted, she's lost her mother all over again. Give her time. Then we'll talk to her. Together."

"I appreciate the offer, but this isn't your battle. I made sure she understood you didn't know about her till this week."

Rachel had put him before herself—again. It gave him hope. She'd matured so much from the days when he'd fallen for her, and the new qualities she brought to the table were even more attractive than before. Wheels turned, and a solution to all their problems appeared.

"You're adopting her, right? She'll be your daughter legally again soon?"

She nodded.

"We'll get married, then she'll legally be *our* daughter and Jess's cousin. Problem solved."

Rachel stared at him unblinking. Longing filled her eyes, then she ducked her head. "I can't marry you, Matt."

Her refusal winded him. "We're good together, Rachel."

Buddy whimpered and nudged the hands she clasped in her lap. "You don't understand. Have you never questioned why I had condoms with me that night in the barn? It's because I set out to seduce you. You were Johnstonville's golden boy, its brightest star, the unattainable guy no girl could catch. I set out to destroy everything special about you. You deserve someone who's kind and generous and worthy of the town's future mayor. That's not me."

Shocked, he took a moment to absorb the info. Then he realized if she were still that person she never would have told him the truth. "That was in the past. We'll make our marriage work."

She shook her head. "I can't marry you. You belong here and I can't stay. All the people I've wronged would never let me or Chastity forget my past. I won't risk them turning against my daughter or destroying your future."

And that's when he realized there might not be a way to win this time. He might lose Rachel and Chastity.

He needed his mom's or dad's advice. Maybe one of them would have a better perspective on how to work through the problem. But he couldn't ask them. Not yet. Until he and Rachel came to terms, he couldn't spread the news that he was a father. And he couldn't handle his family knowing Rachel had rejected him again.

CHAPTER SEVENTEEN

MARRY HIM.

Matt's suggestion whirled in Rachel's head like helicopter rotors as she pushed through the auditorium doors after speaking at career day.

It wasn't until Matt had proposed this morning that she realized how badly she'd wanted to say yes, to hell with the consequences. But she couldn't. Nothing had changed. Putting others first meant she still couldn't have him. And even if she wanted to be selfish, she loved him too much to ever be happy with the same kind of expedient marriage he'd discussed with her sister.

"Ms. Bishop," a young voice called out behind her.

Rachel turned and spotted a half-dozen girls hustling to catch up with her. She recognized some of them as the ones who'd shared the lunch table with Chastity the other day. "Yes?"

"We just wanted to thank you for coming today. Your job and your traveling sound so cool. Chastity is lucky to have an aunt who does all the neat stuff you do."

Did Chastity still think so? "I'm glad you enjoyed my talk. There were a lot of good speakers today."

"Yeah, but none who've been as many places as you. Will you keep traveling once Chastity's living with you?" the girl in front asked.

"Will you take her on your trips?" another added.

"Most of the places I volunteer are too dangerous."

"Bummer. Won't you miss it?"

"Parts of it, sure." Rachel caught a flash out of the corner of her eye of a red sweater. Chastity had been wearing red today. But the person turned the corner before Rachel could be sure. "But I'll find other ways to make a difference."

She debated trying to find her daughter but saw Pam exiting another door. "Good luck on exams," she told the girls and hustled after Pam.

"Pam," she called out, and Matt's sister turned.

"Hey, Rachel. Great presentation."

"Thanks. Yours, too. Listen, Chastity mentioned an end-of-year party at someone's farm. I don't know anything about the Joneses. Is it safe for her to attend?"

"The Joneses are a really nice family from our church. They've hosted this party every year for their older boys. Their oldest son played for Matt's championship team last year, and their second son is on this year's roster. Ella, their youngest, is in

Jessica and Chastity's class at school and church. She's a good kid. Jessica's going."

"Will it be well supervised?"

"Absolutely. You've nothing to worry about."

"Then I'll let Chastity go." She wasn't crazy about the idea, but it would give Chastity a chance to say goodbye to many of her friends.

"They'll have a great time. Want me to pick up Chastity on my way?"

"Thanks, it's nice of you to offer, but I owe *you*. Why don't you let me take Jessica?" She wanted to check the place out and meet the parents anyway.

"That'd be great. See you then!"

RACHEL PARKED IN front of a big red barn Friday evening and turned to Chastity. The teen had been giving off a weird vibe since discovering the truth of her birth on Wednesday, but tonight she was acting even stranger. There was a different kind of tension in the air.

Rachel stopped the car and opened her door.

"What are you doing?" Chastity sounded aghast.

"I'd like to meet the Joneses."

"And humiliate me in front of my friends?"

She closed the door. "Fine. You have your mom's phone, right? Call me whenever you're ready to come home."

"Yeah. Whatever." Chastity avoided meeting Rachel's gaze.

Rachel wished she understood Chastity's demeanor. It made her reluctant to let the girls out of the car. "Call anytime, whether it's five minutes from now or later."

"I said I would," Chastity snapped and bailed from the vehicle before Rachel could say anything else.

Jessica looked uncomfortable. "Thanks for the ride, Miss Bishop."

"You're welcome. Have fun." Rachel watched until both girls disappeared through the wide doors. She had a bad feeling about tonight that she couldn't explain. She dismissed the sentiment as new-parent anxiety and drove off, glancing in the rearview mirror several times. Maybe Chastity knew that tonight was a farewell. Or maybe she was getting nervous about the move.

Yesterday Rachel had hung a countdown calendar on the refrigerator to help with the transition. Tuesday was the last day of school, and on Wednesday she and Chastity would move into Rachel's apartment. They'd spend the next eight days exploring caregiver options for Rachel's working hours, shopping for the things they needed for the house and packing up Rachel's things. Then on the ninth day they'd close on the house. Three weeks later they'd return to Johnstonville, and while Chastity attended cheerleading camp, Rachel would oversee the moving process. That schedule was contingent on being able to convince Matt not to contest the move as he'd threatened.

Rachel worried all the way home, then she spotted Matt's truck in front of the house, and her stomach took its usual dive. She'd managed to dodge him at career day and wasn't yet ready to see him. The push-pull of wanting him and knowing she needed to make a clean break tugged her in opposite directions.

She climbed from the car and headed up the walk. He rose from the porch swing looking heart-stopping attractive in faded jeans and a pale blue polo that hinted at his muscular chest. "I'm taking you to dinner."

"I don't think that's a good idea, Matt."

"C'mon, Rachel. I've been smoking the ribs all day. The salad's made, and the potatoes are in the oven. It's a beautiful evening to sit on the patio and enjoy the sunset."

Alone? At his house? Could she trust herself?

Tucking her hair behind her ears, she debated the wisdom of confronting him tonight and telling him she and Chastity were moving in five days—with or without his approval. She might as well get the discussion behind her. And he'd already done a lot of prep work on the meal. "Okay."

"Ride with me."

"I promised Chastity I'd pick her up when she called."

"The party doesn't end until midnight. I'll have you back long before then."

Chastity hadn't seemed in a party mood, and if

Rachel couldn't convince Matt the move was the best for everyone, it could be an uncomfortable ride home. "The girls might want to leave early. I'll follow you."

They returned to their vehicles. He drove the route she ran daily, and less than a mile from Hope's house, he turned into the driveway of a two-story white brick New Orleans–style house she'd admired many times. She pulled in beside him.

Furniture groupings with thick cushions made both the first and second story porches inviting places to have coffee or read a book. A cluster of roses took up one corner of the immaculate green lawn, and a magnolia towered over the other. She inhaled the lemony scent of its blossoms as she exited her car.

"This doesn't look like a bachelor pad." It was the residence of someone with deep roots and traditions in Johnstonville. A future mayoral candidate.

"You can thank my mom for that. She's responsible for the flower beds. Gardening's her hobby. And she seemed to think the porch furniture was necessary, but I can't recall ever using it. The backyard's my terrain. Come in."

The beveled-glass-and-oak front door led into a center hall with wide-planked wood floors, a beautifully carved staircase and an eager, welcoming dog. Buddy's tail dusted the floor at ninety beats a minute as Matt greeted him. Then the dog turned his attention to Rachel. She scratched behind his ears.

"Come on back."

She followed Matt toward the back of the house. Through wide archways on either side she spotted a den with a masonry fireplace and a home office. The hall ended in a huge farmhouse kitchen that took up the entire rear of the structure. An abundance of cabinetry and a butcher-block work island with bar stools took up one end and a bright dining area with two walls of windows and a table for eight the other. The space would be ideal for big family dinners or entertaining. "Nice."

"Thanks. The floors and cabinets are original. I refinished them myself."

"You've invested a lot of time here."

He shrugged as he grabbed the salad from the fridge. "I like houses with character, and the renovations gave me something to do in the evenings during off-season. After dinner I'll give you the grand tour."

She couldn't trust herself anywhere near his bedroom. But she'd find a way to avoid that when the time came.

"Can I get you a beer, wine or tea?"

"Water?" She was nervous. There was a lot riding on their conversation tonight. She wouldn't mind a drink to take the edge off, but she needed her wits about her. And she might have to pick up the girls.

He filled a couple of glasses. "If you'll carry these, we'll set up outside."

He added a couple of ears of corn which he'd had soaking in the sink to a tray holding plates, utensils and a stack of napkins. He shouldered the door open and stepped down to a large brick patio with three different grills and a metal fire pit. The smell of smoking meat made her mouth water.

"I take it you like to cook?"

He followed her amused gaze. "Different tools for different jobs. Smoker, charcoal, gas," he explained, pointing to each. Then his lips curved as he indicated the fire pit. "Marshmallows. I remember how much you like s'mores."

That boyish grin reminded her of the campfires and sticky kisses they'd shared years ago. She picked up a tennis ball and threw it for the dog. Buddy sprinted after it.

"Now you've done it. He'll wear out your arm," he said as he lit the gas grill.

"Least I could do since you did all the cooking. I wish you hadn't gone to so much trouble. What if I'd had other plans?"

"Pam said you didn't."

She should have been smart enough to realize his sister had an ulterior motive when she'd called and asked earlier if Rachel had anything planned for her kid-free evening, but Rachel had believed Pam when she said she was only making sure the girls had a ride home.

She watched him lift the lid on the smoker and transfer the ribs onto a deep baking dish. Next he retrieved the pot and painted sauce across the meat. "My secret recipe."

"I'm impressed."

He winked, and her hormones went ballistic. "Tell me that after you've tasted it." He covered the pan with foil and set it in the center of the big wrought-iron table.

As predicted Buddy came racing back, panting happily. He dropped the ball at her feet, sat, wagged and waited. She hurled it again, and he was off.

Matt laid the corn on the gas grill. "You have to admit that after you've worked one of your long shifts, it'd be nice to come home to a cooked meal."

And then it hit her. Matt had his own sales pitch planned for this evening. He intended to convince her to stay, utilizing his cooking skills, his well-trained dog and his beautiful home. But she could not afford to picture herself and Chastity living here, no matter how much she wished for this. She had her daughter—something she'd always dreamed of. And that would have to be enough.

"I usually go out with my shift workers. We eat and recap."

"That'll change now that you have Chastity."

This was the opening she'd been waiting for, but she wouldn't risk an argument before dinner when he'd worked so hard on it. Better to wait until after. Maybe then he'd be in a better frame of mind.

"What made you get into coaching?"

An arched eyebrow noted her change of subject. "I love the game, and I wasn't ready to give it up."

"So, what did you do during the years between your injury and coming back here?"

"Eighteen months of surgeries and rehab. During that time I picked the brains of the offensive, defensive and strength coaches for the team, learning everything I could about how a team was run. When the doctors finally forced me to accept I wasn't going to play again, I went back to school and got a second degree in sports psychology. While there I lucked out and landed a job as a graduate assistant coach with my college's team. When the position here opened, I returned."

She doubted luck had anything to do with it. Matt's drive and determination to succeed had always been impressive. And that he'd accomplished everything with a learning disability was even more remarkable. "What was your first degree?"

"Business administration. I thought I'd be handling an NFL salary. I should have had a backup plan."

Feeling like a slacker letting him do all the work, she continued playing with Buddy until Matt said it was time to wash up and eat. She couldn't remember a date ever cooking for her. For the next few minutes they applied themselves to their dinners. She ate despite her anxiety over the upcoming post-meal conversation—her job had taught her to eat and sleep when she had the time.

When they finally pushed the plates aside, she blotted her mouth, scraped up her courage and tried to organize her thoughts. "That was delicious."

Matt leaned back in his chair. His serious expression made her stiffen. "There's a position available at a level-one trauma center forty-five minutes from here. It's a long commute, but you'd only be making it three times a week. They don't have a flight crew position available now, but as you know, turnover's high in your field. You'd have priority if an opening came up. I pulled a few strings and got you an interview next week."

Taken aback, she stared at him. "You shouldn't have done that, Matt. Chastity and I can't stay in Johnstonville."

His jaw went rigid. "I'm not letting you take her away from me, Rachel."

"You heard her. She doesn't want to stay here."

"I'll find out who's teasing her and deal with it."

She shook her head. "That would only make it worse, and it's only part of our problem."

"I gave you a solution to the rest. Marry me and we're all family. No questions asked."

Again, he didn't mention love. What would she

do if he did? And that's when she realized that as much as she treasured her job and her team, she would trade it all to spend the rest of her life with Matt. But only if he loved her. And he didn't. She was a means to an end. His proposal was merely a strategy to win the game. She opened her mouth to say as much but then decided against it. He'd probably say the words in order to achieve his goal, even if he didn't mean them. Matt had that kind of never-accept-defeat determination.

"Nothing you can say or do will turn me into mayor's wife material. You can't change my past or the fact that your so-called friends are already using it to hurt Chastity." He looked ready to argue, so she rushed on. "You can visit her anytime you like, staying as long as you want. But we won't stay here."

"How often do you think I'd be able to come down—especially during the season? And what about the rest of my family? Chastity has grandparents, aunts, uncles and cousins here."

"We'll try to get together for holidays, but—"

"Not good enough. You're not taking my daughter, Rachel. I'll get a lawyer and make damned sure of it."

She battled to hide her fear. "Fourteen years ago your threat might have worked. But I've lost Chastity once. I will fight you with everything I have to keep that from happening again."

Her phone vibrated in her back pocket. She

whipped it out. Matt rewarded her with a scowl. Then she saw the incoming number. "It's Chastity. Hello?"

"It's Jess, Miss Rachel. I think you'd better come. Chastity's…she's not…she's sick. I think."

She shot a worried glance at Matt. "She's sick how, Jess?"

"I—I don't know. I can't wake her up."

Heart in her throat, Rachel sprang to her feet. "Stay on the phone. I'm on my way. Are you okay?"

"Yes. I'm f-fine." But the words seemed hesitant.

Rachel raced toward her car with Matt right behind her. "Tell me what happened before Chastity got sick."

"I don't know. We got separated. Then I went looking for her, and I—" A sob cut off the word. "And she just wasn't…right. She was weird and wobbly. Guys were taking pictures and stuff. And then she passed out."

Dear God. A horrible list of possibilities streamed through Rachel's head. "Has she been assaulted?"

Fury joined the concern on Matt's face. He pointed at his truck. "You talk. I'll drive."

Rachel didn't argue. She grabbed her purse from her car and jumped in Matt's cab.

"I—I don't think so. She's just really limp, and her eyes don't look right. Oh! She's throwing up."

"Put the phone down. Turn her on her side.

Quickly. I'll wait." She heard the crackle of the phone being set down.

"What happened?" Matt demanded.

"I'm trying to figure that out. Chastity's nonresponsive and vomiting. Just drive. Fast. Please."

"'Kay, she's on her side," Jessica replied in a breathless, fear-laden tone.

"Good job. Jess, are her clothes messed up? I mean, is her shirt untucked or are the buttons of her jeans undone?"

"N-no."

"Good. That's good. Is she waking up?"

"Chastity. Chastity," the anxious cry carried through the phone. "No."

"Are there any adults around who can help you?"

"I—I don't see any. Should I go to the house—"

"No. Stay with her. We want to make sure she doesn't aspir—inhale her vomit. Okay?"

"'Kay."

"Is there anyone else with you that you could send to the house for help?"

"No. When I screamed at them about taking pictures, they all ran. Even the girls left. Miss Rachel, her lips are kind of blue."

Cyanotic. Rachel felt panic biting at her. But she had to stay calm. Losing it wouldn't help anyone. "But she's breathing, right? Put your hand in front of her mouth and see if you feel breath."

"Ummm…yes."

"Tell me where to find you."

"There's a path. Behind the barn. Ella's brothers and their friends had a bonfire in the clearing. Chastity was there."

Older boys were there? That introduced another set of worries. Rachel relayed the directions to Matt.

"Two minutes," he bit out.

"We'll be there in two minutes, Jess. Just hold on. You're doing great."

She heard a sniffle and then another, "'Kay."

Matt finally reached the driveway. He drove as fast as he dared. There were kids milling about. He passed the barn and took the path. Rachel spotted the girls, Chastity lying on her side and Jess kneeling beside her, propping her up. "Over there."

She opened her door and jumped out before the truck completely stopped. She hadn't gotten her daughter back only to lose her now.

SEEING THE MOTIONLESS teen knotted Matt's gut with fear. Rachel sprinted toward Chastity, scanning the area around them as she ran.

His daughter. He'd just found her. He couldn't lose her. His heart slammed against his ribs. Adrenaline pumped through his veins as he parked as close to them as possible—still twenty feet too far away because of the logs circling the bonfire—and climbed from the vehicle. He was used to leading. But he didn't know what to do. Rachel did.

Surrendering control to her was the wise thing. But it was hard. Damned hard.

Rachel reached the girls. Jess jumped to her feet. Rachel took a moment to put an arm around his niece and speak to her, but Matt couldn't hear the words, then she pointed at him. Jess ran for him, hurling herself against his chest like a good tackle. Automatically, he wrapped his arms around her, but he couldn't peel his gaze from Rachel on her knees assessing Chastity. Checking the pulse in her neck. Leaning an ear against her face to check for breathing. She knuckled the girl's chest and talked to her. But Chastity didn't respond.

"I'm scared, Uncle Matt."

"Me, too, Jess." No need to cover it up. He'd had players knocked out on the field before. It was always frightening. But he'd never felt this…helplessness. The urge to act swept through him again, but Rachel had sent Jessica to him for a reason. Was it because she didn't think Chastity would—

Severing the thought, he looked around. He needed to do something. *Had* to. "Should I call an ambulance?"

Rachel scanned the clearing again, and even the sky above her, then twisted to face him. "How close is the nearest hospital?"

"Twenty minutes."

"We'll take her. It'll be faster. Can you carry her to the car?"

"Yes," he answered instantly and without

thought. He scooped Chastity up. His knee protested her limp weight, but he refused to let it fail him now. He'd carried his sleeping nieces and nephews before, but this was different. Chastity was lifeless. He moved as quickly as he dared but chose his steps carefully.

"Jess, open the back door for him, please," Rachel shouted, then pulled out her phone.

"Who are you calling?" he demanded.

"The cops. This is a crime scene." She followed him to the truck. "My name is Rachel Bishop. I'm at the Joneses' farm on Whitaker Road. My thirteen-year-old was attending a party here and now has alcohol toxicity, possibly more. When she was found, she was surrounded by older boys taking pictures. The sheriff needs to get out here *now* and find out who in the hell is serving alcohol to minors and what other drugs might be on the premises. He needs to search for GHB, ketamine and Rohypnol. Tell him to confiscate the boys' phones."

Matt's anger spiked, giving him extra strength. He barely felt the last few strides.

"No. We're taking her to the hospital," Rachel continued. "There's no room for Life Flight to land and no time to wait for an ambulance. I'll give a statement later. She vomited in the clearing behind the barn beside a log if the sheriff wants a sample. Something red. A spiked punch, maybe."

Rachel paused again. "We don't have time. She's

hypothermic and cyanotic." Then she hung up and ran to the opposite side of the truck and climbed in to help buckle Chastity's seat belt.

"I'll sit with her. She needs to be upright."

He grabbed the blanket—the same one Rachel had wrapped herself in the day of the storm—and passed it to her.

"Thanks." As she covered Chastity, Matt noticed her hands shaking. Rachel wasn't nearly as calm as she'd been at the ball field. The fear blanching her face multiplied his.

"Do you have a bucket or something in case she vomits?" she asked.

"Forget the car."

Her face set in uncompromising lines. "I want evidence. Someone will pay for this."

Yes. They would. He heard sirens in the distance. Rachel wouldn't make any friends by having called the cops. But he didn't care. He wanted the guilty parties punished.

Matt grabbed his gym bag and tossed out the clothes. It was the best he could do. Then he climbed behind the wheel.

"Go. As fast as you can and still get us there in one piece," Rachel said.

He flipped on his flashers and hit the gas, keeping an eye on Rachel and Chastity in the rearview mirror as he drove. Rachel had both arms around their daughter, whose head lolled.

He glanced at his niece. She looked petrified.

"Jess, call your mom and tell her you're okay and you're with us. Then tell her what's going on."

"Yes, sir."

Jess made her call and kept it brief. "Mom will meet us at the hospital. Is Chastity…is she going to be okay?"

Rachel's mouth opened and closed. Her lips trembled. "I don't know. I hope so. If you hadn't called when you did—" Her voice broke. "She wouldn't stand a chance."

Rachel's eyes closed and her lips moved. He'd swear she was praying. Then she lifted her lids. "Jess, the police will probably want a statement from you later. They'll need you to name or describe the boys who were with her when you came up. Do you think you can do that?"

"Yes, ma'am." Jessica's voice shook.

"You did nothing wrong, Jess. Nothing. You did the right thing. You have nothing to fear. Thank you for calling."

Tonight wasn't going to help his case in persuading them to stay in Johnstonville or win him points in a joint-custody fight.

He couldn't lose them. But it looked very much like the clock was ticking down, and he didn't have a Hail Mary play up his sleeve to pull off a win before the buzzer.

Dear God, just let Chastity be okay. Then he'd figure out the rest.

CHAPTER EIGHTEEN

CHASTITY STILL HADN'T come around by the time Matt jerked the truck to a halt outside the ER entrance of the small community hospital. Rachel knew the longer she remained unresponsive, the worse the prognosis. She'd never been more afraid in her life.

Emergency room personnel met Matt with a gurney. Rachel held Chastity's hand and kept pace with them as they hustled toward a set of double doors. She delivered stats and the facts as she knew them. "Her clothes were intact, but she was surrounded by boys with camera phones. Please make sure she hasn't been r—"

She couldn't say the word. But one of the nurses nodded. "We'll check."

Someone stepped in front of Rachel. She tried to go around. "Excuse me."

The woman shifted to block her path. "Ma'am, we need you to give us some information."

"I gave them everything I had. Please, let me pass. I need to be with her." She'd heard those same words a hundred times. No, a thousand. But she'd never been the one saying them.

"They'll take good care of her. We'll let you see her as soon as possible. Now, please, let the doctors work. Come with me." She looked over Rachel's shoulder. "Sir, you'll have to move your vehicle away from the doors."

And then it hit Rachel square in the chest. She was one of those other people—the ones she left outside the treatment area. She'd always been one of the caregivers attending the patient. She hadn't given much thought to how the ones left behind felt.

On the verge of panic, she debated forcing her way past the lady. Then the doors closed. She saw the sensor on the wall. She couldn't go anywhere without an electronically coded ID badge or someone behind the counter to push the button.

Frantic, she turned to Matt. "Rachel, fill out the paperwork. I'll be right back."

Matt and Jess left.

"I need to be back there," she tried again. "I'm a MED EVAC/RN. I can help them."

"Are you employed by this hospital?"

"No, but—"

"Then you can't help. Not here. Someone will come and get you after your daughter is stable."

"But what if—" Her voice failed her. She tried again. "I don't want her to be alone."

"Ma'am, you're not going anywhere until we get her entered into the system." The woman had clearly lost patience. "For her sake, you need to give us as much information as possible."

The fight drained out of Rachel, leaving nothing but stomach-churning anxiety behind. The lawyer had told her to prove she was a good parent. She certainly hadn't been tonight. This was all her fault. She should never have let Chastity go to the party. Her gut had told her not to, but she'd been trying too hard to be Chastity's friend and not her parent. She would never make that mistake again...if given the chance.

Please, please, give me the chance.

The clerk's face softened. She touched Rachel's elbow. "This way."

Rachel collapsed into the chair indicated and tried to focus. She numbly replied to the questions, producing her insurance card and ID when asked. Thank goodness she'd added Chastity to her medical plan as soon as she'd become her guardian. The uninsured were supposed to get the same treatment as the insured. But sometimes that wasn't the case.

"Does Chastity have any allergies or medical conditions we should be aware of?"

Rachel opened her mouth but didn't have the answer. Besides dyslexia, what else had Hope hidden? "I don't know."

The woman gave her an odd look, then moved on to the next question. Rachel twisted in the chair and watched the doors where they'd taken her baby. Her mind raced through all the steps they should be taking. And all the things that could go wrong. Chastity had been unconscious too long. She was only taking six to seven breaths per minute, and those had been irregular. She'd been cyanotic and hypothermic, and anyone in that condition had a greater risk of dy—

No. She couldn't think about that.

Instead she mentally calculated how many drinks Chastity would have had to have in the two hours since Rachel had dropped her off to be in this condition. Had it been only alcohol? Or had drugs exacerbated her condition?

Firm hands squeezed her shoulders. She looked up. Matt. How long had he been behind her?

"Ms. Bishop?"

She jerked back to the present, her gaze swinging back to the hospital worker. "Yes."

"You and your husband can have a seat. Someone will come and get you when you can see Chastity."

Husband? Rachel's legs wobbled when she tried to stand. Matt grabbed her arm and helped her. Rachel didn't bother to correct the clerk. The situation was too complicated to explain.

Worry clouded Matt's eyes. Rachel wanted to reassure him Chastity would be okay. But what if she wasn't? Even if their daughter pulled through, there might be irreversible brain damage.

Had Chastity gotten drunk before? Hope had

never mentioned it. But her sister had neglected to disclose a lot of things. Chastity's best friend might know. "Is Jess still here?"

"Yes. She's with Pam." Matt led her toward chairs in the far corner.

Rachel looked back. "I can't see the doors from here."

"There are no closer chairs. They'll find us." He put his arm around her waist and urged her forward. She wanted to lean into him but didn't. His threat was too fresh in her mind. They both wanted the same thing. Custody of their daughter. But for that to happen for either of them, first Chastity had to come home.

Jess's face and eyes were wet and red. Rachel knew the ordeal had been traumatic, and she should leave the girl alone. But Jess or her mom might have answers that could help Chastity. "Have either of you ever known Chastity to drink before?"

"No," Jess stated instantly and with convincing certainty. "We stay away from kids who do that."

Rachel looked at Pam, who shook her head.

"What about drugs?"

"No." Again, said with conviction and an accompanying head shake from Pam.

"The boys you saw…did you know them?"

Jess glanced nervously at her mother, then shook her head. "I think they were Whit's college friends. I'm—I'm not sure. But I didn't recognize them from school. And they looked older than Joey."

"Was Whit with them?" Matt asked.

Jess hesitated, checked with her mom, then nodded.

Beside Rachel, Matt fisted his hands on his thighs.

"Matt," Pam cautioned, "let the police handle this."

Surprised that Pam thought her rule-following brother might do something he shouldn't, Rachel looked at him. His face was red, his jaw muscles bunched. He looked angrier than she'd ever seen him. Matt would not make a good opponent.

She covered his fist with her hand. "I'll call Officer Reed. I met with him to discuss Hope's wreck. He seems like a straight-up guy. Let him look into this."

"If he doesn't find out who's behind—"

"He will." She didn't know why she wanted to assure him.

Yes, she did. She wanted Matt around to be the father Chastity deserved. She didn't know how that would work, but she had to find a way.

MATT CHECKED THE waiting room's clock again. Midnight. He was ready to climb the walls. The hourly updates on Chastity were not enough. He needed to see his daughter. But no amount of pleading with the gatekeeper on his or Rachel's part had gotten them anywhere.

Ten minutes after Rachel's call, Officer Reed had arrived to take statements, handling Jess tenderly and getting a lot more out of her than Rachel had. But time had dragged since Reed left the hospital three hours ago.

Pam and Jess had left behind him, and Matt's parents arrived moments later. His father promised Rachel that the police chief was taking the situation seriously, even though the Joneses were a big name in Johnstonville.

Matt wanted to tell his parents that Chastity was their granddaughter. His dad would hammer harder on the case if he knew. But Matt kept his mouth shut. A crowded public waiting room wasn't the place to air the mayor's private business, and he wasn't sure how his mother would react to knowing she'd been deprived of her granddaughter all these years.

Rachel had said little. Each time the doors opened she bolted upright, then when no one came for them, sagged again. Her anxiety exacerbated his own—she knew more about Chastity's condition than he did.

He was scared. More scared than he'd been when it had been him lying in the ER, his knee destroyed. He'd known from the faces of the health care workers surrounding him that his prognosis wasn't good. He'd seen the same look on the faces of the staff taking Chastity back.

He shifted his attention to his parents. They looked tired. "Y'all should go home. We'll call you if there's any change."

His mother shook her head. "There is no way we're leaving until we know Chastity's all right. We love her like she's one of ours."

Rachel shot to her feet. "Excuse me."

She headed to the snack machines in the corner, but Matt noticed she didn't buy anything. She stood there with her shoulders hunched, hugging her waist, pretending to examine the contents and looking more alone than he'd ever seen her.

Alone. How many tough situations had she endured without backup? He'd always had his family. He considered himself a strong person, but what kind of fortitude did Rachel possess to face each adversity alone?

And then he got it. That's why she clung so tightly to her coworkers. Did they support her the way his family did him? The way Hope should have? When your flesh and blood turned their backs on you, what did it do to your ability to trust?

"Rachel might need change for the machines. Excuse me." He joined her, laying a hand on her rigid shoulder.

She startled, turned, glanced at him, then quickly averted her face but not before he saw the agony in every tense line. "Your parents…are wonderful. You have no idea how lucky you are to have them."

"Yes, I do." Tonight had made that abundantly clear. "I'm going to tell them about Chastity after this is over."

"Matt—"

"They'll keep it to themselves. But they deserve to know."

She hesitated, then nodded. "They'll hate me. But I can handle it. As long as they're kind to Chastity." She inhaled shakily. "I shouldn't have let her stay at the party. I had a bad feeling about the whole thing."

"Rachel, this isn't your fault. Teens experiment. I see it all the time. The Joneses are good people. They've been hosting their annual bash for years without incident. There was no reason to expect anything to go wrong tonight. Someone is responsible for this. But it isn't you."

"You don't understand because you've always been a rule follower. But I was her. I thought like her. I rebelled like her. Chastity is in the shape she's in because she's so much like me." Her eyes filled, but she blinked away the tears.

Her pain eviscerated him. He had no clue what to say to make this situation any less hellish than it was. Fourteen years ago he'd been able to help her. But tonight he didn't even begin to know how.

Then the double doors opened, and a woman in scrubs came out. "Mr. and Mrs. Bishop?"

Rachel hustled toward the lady. Gut in his throat, he went after her. "How is she?" Rachel asked immediately.

"She's a sick little girl. But improving. I'm Heidi. I'll take you to her."

More relieved than he thought possible, Matt shot his parents a thumbs-up before following the nurse. She led them through a maze of curtained cubicles, finally stopping and pulling back one. Chastity lay on the bed, her eyes closed. Her face around the breathing mask covering her nose and mouth was nearly as white as the pillowcase. An IV dripped liquids into her arm, and she had wires running from her chest. A urine bag hung on the side of the bed. Machines beeped and clicked all around her. His short-lived relief snarled into a knot of worry.

Rachel hurried to her side, kissed her forehead, then started checking every IV line and the settings on each machine.

"We're giving her fluids, electrolytes and supplemental oxygen," the nurse said. "We didn't find any indication of assault. Hear that, Dad? Stand down."

Matt processed what her statement implied. As Chastity's father, would he have sought vengeance? He wanted to believe he was better than that, but he'd experienced so many tumultuous emotions lately that he had no idea how he'd have reacted to a sexual assault.

Heidi turned back to Rachel. "I have a note here that says you're a MED EVAC/RN. So you know Chastity's not out of the woods yet. Luckily, we found no other drugs on board. That means we're not worried about liver damage, but we can't assess for brain damage until she wakes."

Matt's knee nearly buckled. "Brain damage? Is that a possibility?"

Rachel nodded. "It can result from the severe dehydration alcohol toxicity causes. Has she had any seizures?"

"No," Heidi answered.

"That's good. But you haven't been able to rouse her?"

"Not for conversation, but she's responding to stimuli and commands. The doctor will be with you soon." Heidi left.

Rachel dragged up a chair and took Chastity's hand. Matt wanted to do the same. But he hadn't earned that right yet.

"Chastity," Rachel called. "Chastity, wake up and talk to me." Over the next hour she repeated the command five times. On the fifth Chastity's lids fluttered open. Rachel's breath whooshed out. "Hey, kiddo."

Eyes so like Rachel's groggily looked around before zeroing in on Rachel. Chastity reached for the mask with her free hand. Rachel stopped her.

"No, you need to keep the oxygen on a little longer. How do you feel?"

Chastity grimaced. "Head hurts."

"That's to be expected. Do you remember what day it is?"

"Friday," the teen croaked after a moment.

"It was Friday when I dropped you off at the party. Do you remember the party?"

Chastity's eyes closed. Her chin dipped. She nodded and winced, a hand going to her temple.

"Do you remember what happened?"

A flush darkened her cheeks. "I drank punch, then... I don't remember."

Rachel glanced at Matt. The relief in her eyes was impossible to miss. "Memory intact. A good sign." Then she turned back to Chastity. "Why did you drink the punch, Chastity? You know alcohol's bad for you."

Tears seeped from Chastity's eyes. "Because I—I wanted to prove to those idiots that I'm not a Goody Two-shoes like Mom... And—" She sniffed and closed her eyes.

"And?" Rachel prompted.

"I heard you tell the girls at school that you'd have to give up traveling because of me. I'm going to mess up your life."

"No, baby. You won't. And what you heard me telling those girls was that I'd give up volunteering in dangerous areas. You are too important for me to risk that. That doesn't mean I'll give up traveling or helping people. It means I'll only choose places where you can go with me. We'll see the world together."

More tears streaked Chastity's cheeks. "You didn't want me before. You gave me away. You probably want to again. Especially after th-this."

"I wanted you then and I want you now, but I told you, I wanted better for you than I could have given you back then."

"I was a mistake."

Rachel brushed back her hair. "You might not have been planned, but you are the best thing that ever happened to me. I love you, Chastity."

Chastity's lips quivered. "You sure?"

"Absolutely. I'm so glad to have you back in my life. I'm sorry we had to lose your mother for it to happen, but life without you has been…hard." Rachel's voice broke over the last word.

Matt didn't doubt her sincerity. Any lingering doubts he'd had about her being selfish and taking the easy way out by allowing Hope to adopt Chastity vanished. Rachel had put Chastity's welfare first at great personal cost.

Her love for her daughter—*their* daughter— was unquestionable.

Chastity's hesitant gaze skidded to Matt. "I bet you wish I wasn't your kid now."

The pain in her eyes hit him like a head charge to the gut. How was it that these two females could turn him inside out? "The only thing I regret is that I missed out on the past thirteen years."

More tears streaked down her cheeks. "For real? Even though I'm dyslexic?"

"For real. And remember, I'm dyslexic, too. That makes us a pair."

"I'm sorry," Chastity whimpered, her gaze bouncing between Matt and Rachel. "I screwed up. I swear I won't again."

Rachel brushed Chastity's cheek. "Yes, you will, baby. And so will I. We're not perfect. We're going to make mistakes, Chastity. I suspect we'll make a lot of them while we try to figure out how to be a family. But what's important is that we learn from them and we stick together."

"Can we still move to our new house?"

Rachel looked at Matt. These two had a bond that he was not part of. He couldn't tear them apart, and if he tried he'd lose any chance of having a relationship with either of them. How could he force them to stay in Johnstonville when it wasn't in their best interest? But if he let them go, would Chastity ever be willing to visit and stay with him? Would he ever feel comfortable staying with her and Rachel? Or would he always be on the outside of their circle desperately wanting in? And what if Rachel married someone else? Could he bear to see the woman he loved loving another man?

It gutted him to realize he might never have a close relationship with his only child or the future with Rachel that he wanted. But it was time he emulated Rachel and put Chastity's needs first.

He nodded. Rachel held his gaze for a moment, then she turned to their daughter. "We'll go as soon as your exams are over."

Chastity smiled behind her mask. At that moment Matt had a taste of the agony Rachel must have suffered thirteen years ago when she'd placed their baby into Hope's arms.

Game over. The buzzer had sounded. He'd thrown up a Hail Mary, missed his intended receiver and lost the most important game of his life.

He dug in his pocket and pulled out his truck keys. "Here. I'll catch a ride home with my folks. I'll pick up the truck later. Just leave the keys under the front seat."

Rachel's eyes widened. "Matt, you don't have to—"

"Yeah, I do." He leaned forward and kissed Chastity on the forehead. "I'm glad you're okay. I'm even happier that you're my daughter."

With his dreams crushed again, he took one last look at Rachel. He loved her. And he'd lost her. Again. He left the cubicle, not wanting witnesses if he lost control.

He'd almost made it to the double doors when Rachel calling his name stopped him.

She grabbed his arm. "Thank you."

"I still want to see her, and we'll figure out

some kind of child support. Tell me what you need and—"

"All we need is for you to love her."

And then she left him, his pride and his heart in tatters. He knew his life was not over. But it sure as hell felt like it.

MATT'S FATHER SAT across the picnic table from him Sunday evening after his siblings and their tribes had gone home. He shoved a cold bottle of beer across the table.

"You look like you need this, son. What's going on?"

Matt had been dreading this conversation for four weeks, but his parents deserved to know they had another grandchild—even if they couldn't brag about her—before Chastity returned for cheerleading camp next weekend. He struggled to find the words.

"You have the most promising team since your return to Johnstonville High," his father continued. "Everybody's talking about the summer camp workouts, so it can't be your job."

His mother joined them, setting a chocolate cupcake she must have hidden from the hungry hordes in front of him. "I've never seen you so down. You barely even looked at the Fourth of July fireworks last night. Are you missing Rachel?"

His mom had always been perceptive.

"I made Rachel pregnant fourteen years ago. I

didn't know. She didn't tell me." He laid the bare fact before them. Both parents' mouths dropped open. "Chastity is my daughter."

His mother's fist hit the table, toppling the cupcake. "How dare she keep that from you? A man deserves to know when he's fathered a child."

She should know. She'd told his dad when Matt's pending arrival had surprised them both.

"Carol, just because Rachel made a different choice than you doesn't necessarily make it the wrong one. Adoption might have been the best thing for Chastity," his father, ever the diplomat, replied. "Hard to know without the facts."

"I could never have given up my baby."

"And I'm glad you didn't give me up, Mom, but it's more complicated than that. There's a good chance Hope kept my letters from Rachel, so she didn't know I wanted to marry her. Even if she had, Rachel didn't think she had anything to offer me or our child. She hadn't finished high school when she discovered her pregnancy. And she didn't want to keep me from following my NFL dream."

"A baby definitely would have made it difficult for you to always be on the road." Leave it to his father to stick with the facts while his mother stewed, emotions chasing across her face too fast for Matt to decipher. "How did Hope end up raising my granddaughter?"

Matt had a knot the size of his fist between his

shoulder blades. It had been there since he'd said goodbye to Rachel and Chastity in the hospital.

"Hope promised if Rachel relinquished Chastity to her instead of strangers she'd allow Rachel to be a part of Chastity's life."

"Hope lied," his mother snapped. "She lied to all of us and played on our sympathies with that fictional story of tragically losing her husband. And she cut Rachel off from her own baby. If Hope was here I'd tell her what I think about that." His mother's about-face surprised him.

"Why didn't Rachel tell us when she was here?" asked his father, again trying to defuse the emotions. Matt had never appreciated his father's peacemaking as much as he did now.

"She didn't want to sully Hope's reputation or jeopardize my future candidacy as mayor with news of me impregnating a seventeen-year-old and having a child out of wedlock."

His father whistled out a breath. "Valid points."

His mother's eyes narrowed on him. Matt knew that look. It meant he wasn't going to like what was coming. "You love her, don't you?"

A direct hit. Matt searched for a way to avoid answering.

"That's why you've lost weight and why you've been moping around all month."

Caught in the crosshairs, Matt shifted. "Yes."

"Then why didn't you ask her to marry you and stay here?"

"I did. She refused."

Anger sparked in his mother's eyes again. Matt held up a hand. "Besides worrying about sabotaging my future, she's afraid of what finding out that Hope was a liar and that Chastity is the daughter of 'Rachel the Rebel' would do to Chastity. People here aren't kind or forgiving. And Chastity's already caught some flack."

The starch seeped from his mom's shoulders. "Yes. I know. Memories are long in Johnstonville. Rachel and I had a couple of unpleasant encounters with people when she volunteered with me. She handled them well, but I could tell she was hurt. Does she love you?"

Matt focused on the untouched beer in his hand. The sweat rolling down the brown glass mirrored the trickle down his spine. "I don't think so."

"Have you asked her?"

"Mom, what difference does it make? My life is here, and she and Chastity are better off elsewhere."

"Do you want to be mayor, son?" his father asked.

"Generations of Johnstons—"

"Stop right there. Forget your ancestry and answer the question. Do you want to be mayor?"

Matt had never considered whether he wanted to fill his father's shoes. It was expected. "Not particularly, but—"

"There is no 'but.' The job is unpleasant if your

heart's not in it. The phone rings all hours of the day and night, and, frankly, people are crazy."

But his dad loved the job. "Even if I decided not to run for mayor, I can't move out of state. What about my job?"

"Last time I checked there were schools in Georgia."

"True, but I owe the people of Johnstonville for standing by me when I…when I let them down."

"You haven't let anyone down, son. Except maybe yourself."

"What about the NFL? That was your dream. And then it was mine."

"I traded a few years of potential glory for decades of being a man who makes a real difference in his family, his church and his community. Do you think I'm sorry I chose you over that?"

"Aren't you?"

His father reached across the table and covered Matt's hand. "No, son. I'm where I'm supposed to be. I was blessed to work beside my daddy on the farm till the day he died, and I wouldn't trade one second of that for a dozen years playing pro ball."

Matt's throat clogged. "You don't farm now."

"Why should I when I can lease the land for enough to pay our bills and not battle weather, insects and market fluctuations or get dirty?"

Matt's mother laid a hand over his other one. "I've never known you to give up on something that mattered to you. If Rachel and Chastity matter to you, then maybe you need to rethink a few things."

Matt frowned. "To be with them I'd have to move away."

"That's what it sounds like," his mother stated.

"Son, all we want is for you to be happy," his father said. "Follow your heart whether it leads you around the corner or across state lines."

His mother nodded.

Dumbfounded, Matt stared at the most inspirational coaches he'd ever had. This was not the way he'd expected the afternoon to go. He had some reevaluating to do. And then he had to decide if he was brave enough to take the field and throw up one more Hail Mary pass.

RACHEL TOOK ONE last look at Hope's empty house, then stepped out onto the porch to lock the door for the last time. Tires crunched in the driveway. She spun around, then her stomach dropped with disappointment when she recognized Carol Johnston's van rather than Matt's truck pulling in.

She hadn't seen or heard from him since that night in the hospital. Had he told his parents about Chastity? If so, did they hate her? But that didn't look like anger on Carol's face as she made her way up the walk.

Rachel blotted her damp hands on her pants legs. "I'd invite you in, but the movers just left with the last of the furniture."

Carol nodded toward the for-sale sign. "So it's done. This one's sold, and you and my granddaughter have a new home."

She knew. Rachel's knees wobbled. "Yes. The agent's surprised we got an offer so fast."

She ached to ask about Matt. She'd driven by his house numerous times, but his truck hadn't been there. "I'm sorry for keeping Chastity from you."

"Don't be. I had the joy of her company without the worry and responsibility of knowing she was my granddaughter."

Rachel blinked in surprise.

"But now that I know, I want to be a part of her life." Carol sat on the top step and patted the bricks beside her. "Have a seat. I want to tell you a story."

Rachel sat. What else could she do?

"Once upon a time an eighteen-year-old cheerleader fell head over heels in love with the captain of the football team. She was prom queen. He was her king. She had grand plans of going to college, and so did he. He had so many scholarship offers he couldn't make up his mind where to go. There was even talk of him being drafted into the NFL straight out of high school. And then she turned up pregnant."

Rachel gasped. Matt had told her his parents were high school sweethearts. He'd never mentioned an unplanned pregnancy.

"Her parents and his were furious. Abortion wasn't an option. And adoption...she couldn't do it. She had to forget about college and nursing school. He had to forget about football. They got married because they had to. Her daddy would have shot her lover if he'd refused. It wasn't the happiest of unions at the start."

Carol stared off into space for a moment, then met Rachel's gaze, her blue eyes filled with sadness. "For a long time I resented Bill, and when I looked at Matt's sweet baby face, I resented him, too. They'd trapped me and killed my dreams of getting out of Johnstonville. I was miserable and didn't care if anybody knew it, but Bill never said one unkind word or showed in any way that I'd ruined his plans.

"Then I got pregnant again. And again. Before I knew it, I had three children under five and I was overwhelmed. Then the day came for me to take Matt to school for the first time, and instead of being relieved to have one out of my hair, I couldn't bear to let him go. I cried my eyes out. Bill had to come and drive us home.

"That day I realized how lucky I'd been to spend every day watching my children grow up. Seeing their first smiles, their first steps and hearing their first words. I'd been too busy feeling sorry for myself to realize how fortunate I was, and that supposed pregnancy curse had actually been a blessing. Some would say, my calling. I was a damned good mother."

Rachel's eyes stung. "I'm sure you were and still are."

Carol reached out and took her hand. "I'm not telling you this for sympathy. I'm telling you because sometimes we're so caught up in the what-could-have-beens that we don't see the blessings right in front of us. I don't think you've seen yours yet."

Confused, Rachel tried to figure out what Carol was saying. "You don't hate me for depriving you of your grandchild? Or Hope for lying to you?"

"I won't lie. I did when Matt first told me. That lasted about two minutes. Then I realized you'd done two things that I didn't have the strength to do. First, you gave my son a chance to pursue his dreams, whereas I'd taken Bill's. And second, you gave a childless woman the opportunity to experience the kind of love only a mother knows. That tells me you're a very special person, and a generous one.

"This is all part of His plan, Rachel. You needed to learn the value of loving and losing, and to build a life for yourself so that when your second chance came, you'd be eager, willing and able to care for your child. The choices you made turned you into the strong woman you are now—a woman Chastity can respect, admire and emulate."

"I—I never thought of it that way."

"I know we can't advertise Chastity's paternity, but I consider myself lucky to have you and her as part of my family. You can call us anytime for anything, and the Johnstons will be there for you. And you will always be welcome in our home."

Speechless, Rachel sat stiffly as Carol hugged her and rose. "I won't keep you any longer. I know you're eager to pick up Chastity from camp. This week without the girls has been tough on all of us. And thank you for letting her go even after… well, you know. I think she and Jessica needed this time together."

Then Matt's mother returned to her car and left.

Flabbergasted, Rachel stared after her. She'd always dreamed of having Matt's family in her corner. Now she had it.

But she didn't have Matt.

CHAPTER NINETEEN

MATT DIDN'T RECOGNIZE the Jeep parked in the driveway of the address Jess had texted him. Had Rachel already replaced him? He debated rolling past the house. But he'd driven eight hours to see Rachel and Chastity. And he'd already made changes at home that couldn't be undone. If he didn't take the field and say his piece today, then he'd forfeit the game and have no one but himself to blame.

He followed the sidewalk to the front of the house. Sunflowers towered over his head, bordering a vegetable garden that would meet even his mother's high standards. He reached the front porch and rang the bell. A young woman opened the door. Did he have the wrong address?

"Can I help you?"

"I'm looking for Rachel Bishop."

"Hey, Coach! What are you doing here?" Chastity said from behind the stranger.

His daughter. She looked better than she had when he'd last seen her in the hospital, and the color in her cheeks looked natural, rather than cosmetically applied. She looked so much like Rachel he couldn't believe he hadn't seen the resemblance before.

"I came to talk to Ra—your mom."

"She's not home from work yet." She flipped a hand to indicate the young woman. "This is Kelly. She's my babysitter-slash-tutor. She's studying to be a special education teacher at Georgia State, and she's helping me with the dyslexia. Matt has it, too. I got it from him. He's my dad."

Sacked by the comment, Matt tried to regain his footing. Pride and happiness vied for supremacy inside him. "You look good. Taller."

"Thanks. I've grown an inch, and I've been working out with Rachel every day so I'll be ready for cheerleading tryouts. Oh, and I still call her Rachel because Mom was…well, Mom. And Rachel is so much more than just a mom. She's my friend, too."

He was glad they were getting along. But would there be room for him?

Kelly stepped back. "We're about to have lunch. You're welcome to join us if you like tacos."

"Thanks." He had the worst case of pregame jitters in history and wasn't sure if he could eat. But his future depended on what happened next, and the game clock was ticking down.

"Are you spending the night?" Chastity asked.

"I, ah… I didn't tell Rachel I was coming."

"Cool. A surprise. Well, your room's ready if

you need it. C'mon in." Chastity reached for his hand and curled her fingers around his. The simple, trusting gesture filled him with an emotion he couldn't identify.

She all but dragged him inside. "We still need to buy some furniture and stuff, but with me being at camp all last week, we haven't had time to shop, and the movers only delivered the stuff from Johnstonville a few days ago. I want everything perfect before Jess visits next week."

He hadn't known Jess was coming, but he'd been out of town and hadn't spoken to his siblings since he'd had the life-changing discussion with his parents two and a half weeks ago.

"Looks good." The house had the character of an older home with hardwood floors and nine-foot ceilings, but it also had the open concept of a newer one. Chastity led him to a spacious eat-in kitchen. It and the adjacent den overlooked a fenced yard and a patio larger than his.

She caught him looking outside. "You can't see it from here, but there's an outside stone fireplace that backs up to the one inside the house. Pretty cool, huh? We're going to have an outdoor kitchen as soon as we buy a grill and a table. And we're getting a dog. But I had to get through camp first."

The table was set for three, but Chastity added another place setting. The significance of that hit him. "Are you expecting a guest? I don't want to intrude."

"Rachel will be home any minute," Chastity said. "She worked last night."

Matt's nerves torqued up another notch. The two-minute warning. It was win-or-lose time.

THE HOUSE WAS PERFECT, Rachel thought as she drove past the front yard. She had her daughter under her roof and a job and coworkers she loved. Kelly had been an amazing find to care for Chastity. So why did it feel as if something were missing?

Then she turned the corner and spotted a truck in her driveway. Matt's truck. The car lurched when she braked too hard. Any tiredness she'd felt after pulling a busy twenty-four hour shift vanished. She hadn't heard from Matt since he'd left her at the hospital over six weeks ago. Why was he here now?

She parked behind Kelly's Jeep and grabbed her overnight bag. Her palms were damp, and her hands shook as she let herself into the house. She heard the deep rumble of Matt's voice. Her stomach did a loop-de-loop that would make the Six Flags roller coaster proud.

She crossed through the den, her heart racing faster. Then she spotted him at the kitchen table, and her feet stopped. His make-her-forget-her-own-name blue eyes swung her way, and her lungs ceased functioning. A dull roar filled her ears, and dizziness swamped her.

The smile on his face fell. He rose. "Hello, Rachel."

She dragged a breath through her tight chest. "Matt."

"Chastity, let's go look at the puppies on the SPCA website," Kelly suggested.

Chastity shot her a look, then nodded. "Yeah. We'll be upstairs if you need us."

Then the girls were gone, and Rachel and Matt were alone. Silence stretched between them. "I've missed you, Rachel."

She gulped. She'd missed him, too. But what good would admitting that do? "I wasn't expecting you. But you're welcome. Anytime. I told you that."

"I hope you still feel that way when you hear what I have to say."

He had come to contest Chastity's custody. Panic knocked her back a step. "Wh-what do you mean?"

"I've resigned my position at Johnstonville High."

Shocked and relieved, she asked, "Why?"

"I tried to continue business as usual after you left. Summer football camp started. I usually love scoping out my new team, but something wasn't right. With me. Football has been my first love for as far back as I can remember. Then that Christmas you unseated it. Then after you left, I went back to my old habits and buried myself in the sport. For a while it was great. Satisfying. Then you returned. And football wasn't enough anymore."

His hands fisted, then relaxed by his sides once, twice and a third time. She realized Matt, usually the epitome of calm, was nervous.

"But what about being mayor? What about your family and Johnstonville?"

"None of that matters if you don't have the right person—people—to share it with." He took a deep breath, then exhaled. "I need you in my life, Rachel. Chastity, too. But especially you."

Shaken by the words she'd only dreamed of hearing, Rachel numbly backed toward the sofa and collapsed onto it. Matt followed and sat beside her.

"I've taken a job as a defensive line coach at the University of Georgia."

A balloon of hope swelled inside her. She tried to suppress it. "That's just down the road. And it's a promotion, isn't it?"

He nodded. "It is. But that's not why I took it." He captured her hand, his palm warm against hers. "I want to see if we can make this—us—work. I love you, Rachel."

Happiness, excitement and a tangle of other emotions expanded inside her. Love welled up, clogging her throat.

"I fell in love with a spunky rebel fourteen years ago. But I'm even more in love with the strong, giving woman you've become. If you don't feel the same, I'll accept that. But if you do—" He looked at her hand, then stroked the pad of his finger along her left ring finger. The simple touch was electrifying. "If you do, I want to do this right. The way we should have the first time around. I want to date you. Marry you. Be your partner, your lover, your friend. We can take it slow and—"

"No." The word exploded from her tight chest. She saw the dismay quickly followed by pain on his face, gulped and tried again. "No. I mean I don't want to take it slow. We've already waited fourteen years too long. I love you, Matt. I love that you excite me like no one ever has, and yet you're the calm port in a storm. I know I can lean on you, that I can trust you. I love that you care about your family. And I want to wake up beside you, raise our daughter with you and build a future with you— one that makes up for all the years we missed."

Matt cupped her face tenderly. "You won't regret it."

Then he kissed her. She felt the love in his touch, tasted the passion on his tongue, and her heart swelled with love and hope.

A squeak from the other room jolted them apart. Rachel saw Chastity with her hand covering her mouth but her eyes wide-open and excited.

"Please, tell me you were smart enough to say yes?" the teen asked.

Rachel laughed. "Yes."

Chastity's shriek of happiness nearly deafened

her. Chastity jumped, displaying some of the moves she'd learned in cheerleading camp. "I am so glad. You've been miserable since we left Johnstonville, and Jess says Matt has been, too. You guys need to be together to be happy."

Then she raced forward and threw her arms around both of them. "We are going to be the most amazing family ever!"

Yes, Rachel thought. They were. They'd loved and lost each other, and because of that, they would never take a day together for granted.

* * * * *

LARGER-PRINT BOOKS!

GET 2 FREE LARGER-PRINT NOVELS PLUS
2 FREE GIFTS!

HARLEQUIN®

Romance

From the Heart, For the Heart

YES! Please send me 2 FREE LARGER-PRINT Harlequin® Romance novels and my 2 FREE gifts (gifts are worth about $10). After receiving them, if I don't wish to receive any more books, I can return the shipping statement marked "cancel." If I don't cancel, I will receive 4 brand-new novels every month and be billed just $5.09 per book in the U.S. or $5.49 per book in Canada. That's a savings of at least 15% off the cover price! It's quite a bargain! Shipping and handling is just 50¢ per book in the U.S. and 75¢ per book in Canada.* I understand that accepting the 2 free books and gifts places me under no obligation to buy anything. I can always return a shipment and cancel at any time. Even if I never buy another book, the two free books and gifts are mine to keep forever.

119/319 HDN GHWC

Name	(PLEASE PRINT)

Address	Apt. #

City	State/Prov.	Zip/Postal Code

Signature (if under 18, a parent or guardian must sign)

Mail to the **Reader Service:**
IN U.S.A.: P.O. Box 1867, Buffalo, NY 14240-1867
IN CANADA: P.O. Box 609, Fort Erie, Ontario L2A 5X3

Want to try two free books from another line?
Call 1-800-873-8635 or visit www.ReaderService.com.

* Terms and prices subject to change without notice. Prices do not include applicable taxes. Sales tax applicable in N.Y. Canadian residents will be charged applicable taxes. Offer not valid in Quebec. This offer is limited to one order per household. Not valid for current subscribers to Harlequin Romance Larger-Print books. All orders subject to credit approval. Credit or debit balances in a customer's account(s) may be offset by any other outstanding balance owed by or to the customer. Please allow 4 to 6 weeks for delivery. Offer available while quantities last.

Your Privacy—The Reader Service is committed to protecting your privacy. Our Privacy Policy is available online at www.ReaderService.com or upon request from the Reader Service.

We make a portion of our mailing list available to reputable third parties that offer products we believe may interest you. If you prefer that we not exchange your name with third parties, or if you wish to clarify or modify your communication preferences, please visit us at www.ReaderService.com/consumerchoice or write to us at Reader Service Preference Service, P.O. Box 9062, Buffalo, NY 14240-9062. Include your complete name and address.

LARGER-PRINT BOOKS!

HARLEQUIN

Presents®

PASSION
GUARANTEED
SEDUCTION

GET 2 FREE LARGER-PRINT
NOVELS PLUS 2 FREE GIFTS!

YES! Please send me 2 FREE LARGER-PRINT Harlequin Presents® novels and my 2 FREE gifts (gifts are worth about $10). After receiving them, if I don't wish to receive any more books, I can return the shipping statement marked "cancel." If I don't cancel, I will receive 6 brand-new novels every month and be billed just $5.30 per book in the U.S. or $5.74 per book in Canada. That's a saving of at least 12% off the cover price! It's quite a bargain! Shipping and handling is just 50¢ per book in the U.S. and 75¢ per book in Canada.* I understand that accepting the 2 free books and gifts places me under no obligation to buy anything. I can always return a shipment and cancel at any time. Even if I never buy another book, the two free books and gifts are mine to keep forever.

176/376 HDN GHVY

Name	(PLEASE PRINT)
Address	Apt. #
City	State/Prov.	Zip/Postal Code

Signature (if under 18, a parent or guardian must sign)

Mail to the **Reader Service**:
IN U.S.A.: P.O. Box 1867, Buffalo, NY 14240-1867
IN CANADA: P.O. Box 609, Fort Erie, Ontario L2A 5X3

**Are you a subscriber to Harlequin Presents® books
and want to receive the larger-print edition?
Call 1-800-873-8635 today or visit us at www.ReaderService.com.**

* Terms and prices subject to change without notice. Prices do not include applicable taxes. Sales tax applicable in N.Y. Canadian residents will be charged applicable taxes. Offer not valid in Quebec. This offer is limited to one order per household. Not valid for current subscribers to Harlequin Presents Larger-Print books. All orders subject to credit approval. Credit or debit balances in a customer's account(s) may be offset by any other outstanding balance owed by or to the customer. Please allow 4 to 6 weeks for delivery. Offer available while quantities last.

Your Privacy—The Reader Service is committed to protecting your privacy. Our Privacy Policy is available online at www.ReaderService.com or upon request from the Reader Service.

We make a portion of our mailing list available to reputable third parties that offer products we believe may interest you. If you prefer that we not exchange your name with third parties, or if you wish to clarify or modify your communication preferences, please visit us at www.ReaderService.com/consumerschoice or write to us at Reader Service Preference Service, P.O. Box 9062, Buffalo, NY 14240-9062. Include your complete name and address.

HPLP15

READERSERVICE.COM

Manage your account online!

- Review your order history
- Manage your payments
- Update your address

> ### We've designed the Reader Service website just for you.

Enjoy all the features!

- Discover new series available to you, and read excerpts from any series.
- Respond to mailings and special monthly offers.
- Connect with favorite authors at the blog.
- Browse the Bonus Bucks catalog and online-only exculsives.
- Share your feedback.

Visit us at:
ReaderService.com